Praise for Mark Kurlansky

"Mark Kurlansky's fiction provides the same pleasures we have come to expect from his nonfiction. It's beautifully written, observant, and acutely intelligent." —Francine Prose

"Brilliant.... Journalistic skills might be part of a writer's survival kit, but they infrequently prove to be the foundation for literary success, as they have here.... Kurlansky has a wonderful ear for the syntax and rhythm of the vernacular.... For all the seriousness of Kurlansky's cultural entanglements, it is nevertheless a delight to experience his sophisticated sense of play and, at times, his outright wicked sense of humor." —*The New York Times Book Review*

"For those of us who love both stories and food, this book is a delectable feast. Mark Kurlansky's sixteen-part novel is like a long, wonderful meal with friends. It is nurturing, succulent, and most of all, a lot of fun."
—Edwidge Danticat, author of *Brother, I'm Dying* and *Claire of the Sea Light*

"Kurlansky powerfully demonstrates the defining role food plays in history and culture."
—*The Atlanta Journal-Constitution*

"Kurlansky continues to prove himself remarkably adept at taking a most unlikely candidate and telling its tale with epic grandeur." —*Los Angeles Times Book Review*

"Kurlansky has a keen eye for odd facts and natural detail."
The Wall Street Journal

ALSO BY MARK KURLANSKY

*Ready for a Brand New Beat: How "Dancing in the Street"
Became the Anthem for a Changing America*

*The Eastern Stars: How Baseball Changed
the Dominican Town of San Pedro de Macorís*

*The Food of a Younger Land: A Portrait of American Food—
Before the National Highway System, Before Chain Restaurants,
and Before Frozen Food, When the Nation's Food Was Seasonal,
Regional, and Traditional—From the Lost WPA Files*

*The Last Fish Tale: The Fate of the Atlantic and Survival in Gloucester,
America's Oldest Fishing Port and Most Original Town*

The Big Oyster: History on the Half Shell

Nonviolence: The History of a Dangerous Idea

1968: The Year That Rocked the World

Salt: A World History

The Basque History of the World

Cod: A Biography of the Fish That Changed the World

A Chosen Few: The Resurrection of European Jewry

A Continent of Islands: Searching for the Caribbean Destiny

ANTHOLOGY

*Choice Cuts: A Savory Selection of Food Writing
from Around the World and Throughout History*

FICTION

Edible Stories: A Novel in Sixteen Parts

Boogaloo on 2nd Avenue: A Novel of Pastry, Guilt, and Music

The White Man in the Tree and Other Stories

FOR CHILDREN

The Cod's Tale

The Girl Who Swam to Euskadi

The Story of Salt

TRANSLATION

The Belly of Paris (Émile Zola)

City
Beasts

Fourteen Stories
of Uninvited Wildlife

Mark Kurlansky

RIVERHEAD BOOKS

New York

2015

RIVERHEAD BOOKS
Published by the Penguin Group
Penguin Group (USA) LLC
375 Hudson Street, New York, New York 10014

USA • Canada • UK • Ireland • Australia • New Zealand • India • South Africa • China

penguin.com
A Penguin Random House Company

"The Leopard of Ti Morne Joli" was originally published in *Haiti Noir*, Akashic Books, 2011.

Excerpt from "On Eternity" by Bei Dao, Eliot Weinberger, from *The Rose of Time*, copyright © 2010 by Zhao Zhenkai, translation copyright © 2010 by Eliot Weinberger. Reprinted by permission of New Directions Publishing Corp.

ISBN: 978-1-59448-587-9

An application to register this book for cataloging has been submitted to the Library of Congress

First edition: February 2015

PRINTED IN THE UNITED STATES OF AMERICA
1 3 5 7 9 10 8 6 4 2

Book design by Laura K. Corless
Interior illustrations by Mark Kurlansky

With love to Marian and Talia
and the worlds we share

and to Leslie Lee,
a good writer and friend
and one of the last romantics

In time he understood that nature was not something outside the human world. The reverse is true. Nature is the real world, and humanity exists on islands within it.

—E. O. Wilson, *Anthill*, 2010

CONTENTS

ODD BIRDS IN NEW YORK _____ 1

DOMINICAN REPUBLIC: Twice Bitten in San Pedro _____ 27

MIAMI: The Alligator Teeth of an Unknown God _____ 57

THE GLOUCESTER WHALE COD _____ 75

HAVANA: A Murder of Crows _____ 101

GLOUCESTER: The Science of Happiness in
North Shore Frogs _____ 129

IDAHO LOCAVORES: A Trilogy of the Sawtooth Wolf _____ 141
  PART ONE: Hunger on the Big Wood River___143
  PART TWO: Sheepish in Sun Valley___151
  PART THREE: Night in Stanley___173

NEW YORK NITPICKERS _____ 187

HAITI: The Leopard of Ti Morne Joli _____ 203

COYOTE_____227

    PART ONE: Stalking in New York___229

    PART TWO: Mexico City: In the Capital___249

SAN SEBASTIÁN: Begoña and the Bear_____261

ODD BIRDS IN NEW YORK

Some 6,000 years ago the people in Mesopotamia created the first written language. At first it was simple line drawings. They developed about 2,000 characters, all pictures of objects. After about 2,000 years the written language, now known as cuneiform, had developed into wedge-shaped symbols, dashes put together in different configurations. Each of these geometric characters represented an idea or often just a sound. Mesopotamian society revered the elite few who could write and read these texts, which were written on clay tablets. If these scribes were revered, birds were sacred animals because their feet left messages in clay that resembled cuneiform but were another language, one even the scribes could not read. Perhaps the messages were intended only for other birds.

▼ ▼ ▼

ar up in the northern regions of New York City, in a
place known as the Bronx, in what was called a zoo,
was a huge birdcage made of metal, wrought and
twisted and crafted to perfection. In the cage lived some of
the most beautiful birds in the world, including a bright
green quetzal from Guatemala. The quetzal didn't know
that he was originally from Guatemala, just like he didn't
know that he now lived in the Bronx. Nor did he understand
the idea of a zoo. But he may have suspected that he was
beautiful.

For most of his life he had lived in this tall cage with laurel branches to perch on and all the avocado he could eat.
There were also other birds from different places or maybe
the same place. He didn't really know. This quetzal had
been in the Bronx for so long that he no longer remembered
the green highlands of his birth, and he was not unhappy
where he was.

He was a quiet bird who kept to himself, often spending
hours on a branch without moving until everyone forgot he
was there. But he had a friendly look, his close-cropped
fuzzy green plumes setting off his little round head. Hairless monkeys, some with hair on the tops of their heads,
came to the cage to see the birds and they always liked the
quetzal when they could spot him. He tried not to be spotted and they never harmed him.

Late at night there were screams of faraway monkeys—loud, shrill notes held for long seconds. But it was in the distance and not very troubling. The quetzal had a vague notion that nights were much noisier in his native land. He liked the quiet night in the Bronx. But now he was hearing an odd creak. He heard it again. He looked up at the bolted metal struts of the cage, the only sky he could remember, and suddenly the cage began to fall in. Birds screeched and squawked and chirped the news: the aviary was collapsing.

Metal was crashing to the ground louder than monkey screams, and feathers seemed to be everywhere. The quetzal had only one thought—he had to get in the air where it was safe. So he spread his green wings and showed the golden tips and unfurled his two-foot tail that was almost twice the length of his glowing green body.

It is difficult not to notice a quetzal in flight, which is why they prefer not to move too much. They fly with a long, undulating green feather tail, and the fine scarlet under feathers of the body show from below. The ancient peoples of Central America, the Mayans and the Aztecs, believed the quetzal was a god. They called it a winged snake. Even today its official name is the Resplendent Quetzal.

But now everyone was too busy to notice the resplendentness of the quetzal's flight. Some of the birds went to the bottom of the cage, where there were huts and branches to hide under, and others took refuge in the nearby trees. But the Resplendent Quetzal took off for the Guatemalan highlands that were buried in his memory.

One of the birds in the chaos below was a scarlet ibis from the Caribbean island of Trinidad, where he was born in a dark, briny marsh known as the Caroni Swamp. From his very long beak to his even longer legs, he was a bright red, and the bright plumage at his head gave him a showy look, not completely inspiring trust. But despite the gaudiness, he was a startling beauty.

The scarlet ibis did not know what Trinidad was, but he did remember that he came from the Caroni Swamp. He would go there now except that he had no idea where it was. He remembered fishing for shrimp in black water with his long beak and the way his whole family, even cousins, would all settle into the same tree and enjoy the peace of sunset. Now there was no red light of sunset, only blackness and a bright round silver moon bigger than the eye of a giant.

He looked up and saw in the silver-bright light what the ancient Mayans had seen, the beauty of the red-and-green winged snake. The scarlet ibis himself was a god in the Caroni Swamp and the descendant of an ancient ibis that the Egyptians considered to be the moon god Thoth, who had invented language. He took three huge steps and folded his long thin legs under his red body and, spreading his enormous scarlet wings, took to the air, climbing over the Bronx until he was right next to the quetzal.

The two gods, the Winged Serpent and Thoth, felt good flying over the Bronx. The scarlet ibis felt that he was really flying for the first time in years, stretching his neck and his wings, feeling strong. He would not come down until he found the family tree in the Caroni Swamp. The winged snake could come with him if he wanted to.

But while he searched for the Caribbean swamp, the quetzal was in the highlands, dreaming. Flying and dreaming was what he was meant to do. Misty memories crept back, of a place where the little avocados were not scattered on the ground but grew on trees and the laurel was thick above the mountains and the clouds brushed the treetops above a red-and-black-soiled earth. These memories visited while he snaked through the air with his long tail.

The two flew into the night drunk, on their little sips of freedom.

For a time they were gods and they needed only this feeling of flight. But where were they going and how to get there? Each wondered why the other was joining him. Were these the quetzal's highlands? Where was the ibis's swamp? Alone in the sky feels good for only a short time. They needed family. They needed other birds. So then they became companions because that was what they needed. Where were all the other birds? The ibis could not remember ever being this alone.

The quetzal had only one relative in North America, a cousin in Arizona called the coppery-tailed trogon, who was also green and red and white. He, too, was said to be very beautiful, but he was a trogon, not a quetzal, and the quetzal didn't know about him or Arizona. He knew only how to find the broken cage in the Bronx and he was considering returning.

The scarlet ibis, like most of New York, had relatives in Florida. The Florida relatives were pink flamingos, but to a scarlet ibis a pink flamingo is very pale, with bad eating habits. Instead of the pointed bill with which the ibis delicately picked through food, flamingos had a scoop for digging up mud, which they then sucked through strainers in their bills. He also had closer relatives on Long Island and in New Jersey, known as the glossy ibis, not as brightly colored and more common, but not known to him. He did not know where to find any birds and he, too, was considering heading back to the Bronx.

In truth, the scarlet ibis and the quetzal had been living a very easy life in the aviary, being fed gourmet meals and doing very little flying. Now they were getting tired and looked for a place to land. In the dark the expanse below shimmered like a forgotten moonlit sea somewhere that the ibis had once flown over.

But as the night sky turned purple and yellow on the edge of morning, they saw that this was something very different. They saw squares and boxes. They did not know that this was real estate, or how much it was worth in a seller's market, that it was honeycombed with monkeys even tunneling under the ground. They didn't even know that there were straight wide paths for machines that made monkeys move faster, only the machines moved too slowly because there were too many of them, or that there were panels selling things or posting warnings from Homeland Security. They knew none of this. All they knew was that this did not look like a good place for birds or for gods.

Ramona Pensky, who loved birds, was never going to give up her Fifth Avenue apartment. Where else in Manhattan could she wake up to birdsong? She went to court to keep her apartment facing the park. Once her lawyer revealed that her husband had *used* the World Trade Center attack, pretended to be caught downtown when he was two blocks away at Lydia Paulsen's apartment, shacking up while others were dying—the lawyer was brilliant—the apartment was awarded to her even though she could barely afford it. Every morning she listened to the birds, put on her embroidered Barneys slippers, strolled to the window, and gazed into the park anxiously on the toes of her slender feet. She was a small, delicate woman, and it would be easy to say that she resembled a bird, though most birds were smaller and had rounder bodies than did she. She wondered why from her apartment overlooking the park, no matter how hard she looked, she could not see the birds but only heard them. Very small birds, she supposed.

The ibis and the quetzal spotted a spacious green rectangle. There were trees and lakes. The quetzal hoped the wooded hills might be his highlands and the scarlet ibis circled a marshy area to see if it was the Caroni Swamp. But his family tree wasn't there, and though it was not yet dawn, all the ibises seemed to have already left.

The quetzal slowly descended onto a tree branch, letting his long tail float into position like a parachute gracefully landing. A very large crow, maybe a raven, was staring at the quetzal in a way that made him uncomfortable, so he moved to a higher branch. The raven had only been thinking that it might be fun to pull on that tail.

The scarlet ibis landed his bright red plumage in an even higher branch, a swath of color looking too large to be a fruit but very ripe. They sat in silence in the tree as the morning light began to butter the green grass below. They were both thinking the same thing. They were hungry. This meant something entirely different for each of them. The quetzal was looking up, as quetzals do, and the ibis was looking down, as is their habit. What crustaceans were in the waters? What fruits were on the trees?

Instead they saw birds in the grass. They had brown coats and rust-colored breasts, not bad-looking birds, the two in the tree thought, but not nearly so beautiful that they should be strutting and sticking their chests out. They had that eagerness characteristic of smaller birds.

From their tree perches the two watched to see what food the rust-breasted birds were finding. The quetzal hoped they were looking for avocados, though they were not looking in the trees. The scarlet ibis hoped they were looking for shrimp, but they were not looking in the canals or at the water's edge. Then they realized.

The birds were eating worms. The quetzal and the scarlet ibis had seen birds eat bugs. In the Bronx they had seen the vermilion flycatcher—very quick. But you didn't need to be quick to catch worms. The rust-breasted birds were very good at finding them, pulling them from the ground, holding the slithery things in their beaks and then swallowing them.

The ibis spread his scarlet wings and gently drifted to the ground. The quetzal followed. The scarlet ibis drilled the ground with his long beak and pulled out a worm. It was slippery and slithered off his beak. Hungry as he was, he did not really want to eat it. Suddenly they heard a group of voices like an ancient bird choir.

They looked up and saw that they were surrounded by angry little brown birds with rust chests. The brown birds did not want these two eating *their* worms. These brown rust-chested birds were robins and they seemed very proud of that. Their beaks turned almost red with pride—or was it anger?

It was clear that this was not the Caroni Swamp or the highlands and they did not belong there and these American birds, the robins, did. The robins were the first birds of spring and they were entitled to the worms. Every place has its rules and those rules usually favor the local birds, which is why most birds prefer not to travel. They would see if the pigeons could help. Pigeons always know how to find food.

Dr. Ifigenio Sanchez stared at the sky. He shouldn't complain. He lost only two birds. Why those two? Why the ibis and the quetzal? Did they have stronger urges toward freedom than other birds? Stronger memories of home? Where would they go? They were not species that would adapt well to New York or the Northeast. Would they know to fly south? Dr. Sanchez suspected that they wouldn't go far. It was an unusually warm spring, so they might not get sick. But would they find food? How determined were they to feel freedom? And how long would that last? He alerted the city, the Audubon Society, and several New York bird-watcher groups. Now he could only wait.

The scarlet ibis and the quetzal had run into pigeons before and nothing good had ever come of it. In the Bronx they didn't even allow pigeons inside. But it was a bird they knew—knew a little, though they didn't understand them. Dr. Sanchez always called them rock doves. They were unimaginative hunters and they had good and durable marriages, neither being particularly admired traits in the bird world. But pigeons, even without hunting, were fat and always had food. That was because they knew how to get food from the monkeys, a useful skill.

And so the scarlet ibis and the quetzal put down the robins' worms and went looking for the pigeons. Neither had ever personally met a pigeon, but they had often seen them outside the aviary. They were not difficult to find. Pigeons, the opposite of quetzals, were always found around the hairless monkeys, and the ibis called them boat birds because they always came into the swamp in boats. It took only a one-minute flight to locate a path that the monkey/ boat birds used, and as the ibis and quetzal came in closer they could see it was crowded with fat, gray pigeons. They lowered themselves to the ground with great reluctance because the ibis did not like to expose himself to boat birds out of their boats and the quetzal didn't mind hairless monkeys outside the cage, but not in the open like this.

No sooner did the scarlet ibis have this thought while drifting down to the pavement than one of the boatless ones shouted to the other, "Look! It's one of those birds we saw in Florida!"

They thought he was a flamingo, but the scarlet ibis didn't catch the slight. Both the pigeons, who were really rock doves, and the monkeys, who were really humans, were staring at them. The pigeons immediately gathered around them—some skinny and worried, some fat with oily rolls on their necks. One of the fattest pigeons, a round, gray, tough-looking bird with a fat neck with the purple and green colors that oil makes in a rain puddle, thrust out his greasy rainbow chest as though to say "Welcome to pigeon park."

Was this place just for pigeons? the quetzal wondered, and while he was wondering the fat pigeon cocked his blue-gray tail feathers up and defecated on the ground, which seemed to answer the quetzal's question.

Quetzals have never thought well of indiscriminate defecation. A quetzal will eat fruit to fill up on the seeds and then choose carefully selected spots to drop them so that the fruit seeds will grow. But a pigeon, it seems, will relieve himself anywhere for no particular reason. In fact, the fat pigeon did it again.

There were rules. The robins got the first worms. The pigeons pooped where they liked. And how could they fit in with the rules here?

Eight people had already phoned Dr. Sanchez with sightings and he had a crew in a van heading out of the North Bronx for Central Park to grab those birds before they got sick. He wasn't sure how accurate the sightings were. One said they saw a parrot. One said she saw two ibises—one scarlet and one green. One said he saw a quetzal swimming in the boat basin, which was something a quetzal wouldn't do. Of course, Dr. Sanchez thought, there was always the possibility that they would stay in the park and learn how to adapt their lifestyle. He really couldn't say if quetzals or ibises were good adapters. But it seemed likely to him that they would not survive in New York.

On the other hand, hawks, eagles, all kinds of exotic species have ended up in the park, and often, if they were tree dwellers, they ended up nesting high in the eaves of the older buildings along Central Park West and Fifth Avenue. He grabbed his binoculars.

The pigeons, when they were not fed by monkeys, got food through special arrangement with the sparrows. Sparrows do not have a good reputation. They are known for spending all of their time around the monkeys, begging for favors. But this is also true of these rock doves.

The quetzal watched a sparrow hop up to a large monkey eating a sandwich that she had taken out of a black bag. The quetzal had to admit that the sparrow was a fine-looking bird, brown-colored, plain and simple, which is how birds like their women. Dressing up and being vain, to birds, is very masculine. Feminine charm resided in its quiet, unpretentious appearance. The woman the sparrow hopped over to was overly adorned, but that was the way with monkey women.

Hop. Hop. Hop. *Oh, look at me.* Hop, hop. She had to hop around the monkey woman for three minutes before the woman noticed, but finally the woman started breaking off pieces of bread and throwing them at the sparrow. The sparrow bravely stood there, hopping to avoid these dangerous bready missiles being hurled in her direction. Hop. Hop. Hop.

Finally the fat pigeon snapped his wings, lifting himself in the air, and went over to where the sparrow was hopping and picked up most of the bread for himself and ate it.

"Oh, poor little sparrow," said the monkey woman. "What about you?" She threw even more bread and the sparrow ate a few pieces, though other pigeons came over and ate most of them. The fat pigeon looked even fatter when he got back to the quetzal.

The scarlet ibis picked out a boatless one in a green plaid suit adorned with gold chains. It was unusual to find a male monkey who dressed with such masculine pride. Hop. Hop. Hop. Went the little sparrow irresistibly. The monkey held out his sandwich, the entire sandwich, but the sparrow kept hopping, waiting for crumbs.

This was too much for the scarlet ibis, who leapt over a little wooden fence, took to the air, swept down and plucked the entire sandwich in the tip of his long beak, and flew off while a chorus of angry pigeons and sparrows complained.

But it was a salami sandwich and an ibis would no more eat salami than eat a worm, so he tossed it to the other birds. He had to find some shrimp soon or his color would fade and he would start looking like a girl!

None of this suited the quetzal. He lived alone and plucked food where he found it and didn't beg and didn't eat with other birds. But . . .

There was a monkey man dressed in dull, dark colors, as though he were trying to look like a woman. Hop, hop, hop went the sparrow.

Suddenly the quetzal saw green. The man had an avocado sandwich. The quetzal did not need a strategy, he knew what to do. He unfurled his two-foot-long tail feather and leapt in the air. The human was so startled by this rare sight he did not notice all the avocado fall out of his sandwich to the ground, where it was quickly consumed by the pigeons. When the quetzal landed, the sparrows were finishing the last of the bread, the avocado was all eaten.

Birds don't cry. They have no tears.

Ramona Pensky could see the whole thing from her window. She saw that Arab or whatever he was, tall and thin, an Ichabod Crane with a spyglass, pacing around in front of her building, looking in the windows, up on the roof. Why? What was he up to? She wasn't going to let this happen to her again. She had been victim to one attack already. In her mind, her husband's dalliances on the day of the World Trade Center attack made her a victim. Her lawyer had argued this and the idea had become fixed in her mind.

Signs had been posted all over the city saying "If you see something, say something," and they gave a phone number that she had written down. Buses had signs on them boasting of the number of New Yorkers who had called. Two months ago in a snowstorm, out of desperation because she could not find a taxi, she took a subway and an announcement came over the loudspeaker asking her to report "any suspicious activity." The announcement had been striking because the recording was clear and she could understand every word, unlike the useful announcements such as the one about the local train going express that would have saved her an unnecessary journey to the Bronx, had she been able to decipher it.

The piece of paper with the phone number was right where she'd left it on the breakfront.

She decided on a coy approach. "Don't you think it's strange that an Arab has been casing out my building with a spyglass?"

"A spyglass?"

"A spyglass," she confirmed.

"Yes, that is strange."

"I thought so, too."

"What does it look like?"

"Tall, thin, big nose, black curly hair. An Arab."

"No. The spyglass."

"The spyglass?"

"You mean one of those things pirates use?"

"You think it is a pirate? Like from Somalia? They're kidnappers, aren't they?"

The quetzal was drunk. The ibis was feeling a little wobbly, but the quetzal was resplendently smashed. He fell out of a tree. In a situation like this it would have been a perfectly human thing to just go get drunk, but these birds were not human and that is not what an ibis normally does and it was certainly not the way of the quetzal. But it was becoming clear to them that they were not going to be able to survive on shrimp or on avocados. It was equally clear that this area was rich in food. Let the robins have their worms and the pigeons and sparrows their bread crumbs. Berries grew in the bushes, and small fruits and nuts hung from the trees. But much of this food had survived the winter and had slightly dried and fermented, and this seemed to be having a pronounced effect on their navigation systems. But they were not alone. They saw a titmouse staggering and a number of finches waddling awkwardly on branches. A brown creeper was so drunk he was feeding on a tree from the bottom up, whereas there is an unspoken code among birds that you always feed from the top down. And there was no excuse for the unsteady flickers.

Ramona Pensky wanted to see one of those signs that showed how many people had reported suspicious activities. She wished she had written the number down so that she could now see if the number had gone up. Had it gone up by one?

The police had been convinced that Dr. Ifigenio Sanchez was an Arab until he showed them his driver's license and they noticed that he had a Spanish last name. They assumed that he did not speak English and began speaking very slowly. "Green card."

"What?"

This was not going to be easy. They tried again slowly. "Where . . . is . . . your . . . gr-e-e-n card? *Dónde está?*"

"I don't have a green card."

The two policemen nodded knowingly at each other.

"I'm a U.S. citizen. I work for the Bronx Zoo."

But they were no longer listening, because in their minds now, he did not speak English. They just repeated in slowly unfolding syllables, "DO-min-I-CAN-no."

"I'm from Costa Rica, but I am a naturalized citizen."

Dr. Sanchez explained about his position at the zoo, his citizenship, where he kept a passport to prove it, who could be called to speak for him. The two plump men faced him with their hands on thick black belts that seemed to have the entire contents of a hardware store hanging from them.

There is a point in a conversation when one side is alone because the other side has stopped listening. The two faces simply go blank, the light goes out, and no further transmissions will be received.

Dr. Sanchez recognized that this was the situation he now found himself in and so he stopped talking. He knew that he could reason with them at the police station, but by the time he got the police to listen, the quetzal could be dead. There were hawks to worry about—Cooper's, sharp-shinned, even some red-tailed.

Lolly Messerheim had dressed in her bird-watching khakis with all the big pockets. Actually it had big everything, because she had gotten the whole outfit at Filene's for only $25, but it was a size or two too large, which made her look smaller than she really was, which she didn't mind because, as the chart in her bathroom clearly showed, she had too much weight for her height. She had pens, pencils, a sketchbook, field guides, a camera, long lenses, and her notebook, in which she checked off her sightings. She had gotten up early to catch the visiting warblers that had come in the night before and glutted themselves on the celebrated bugs of Manhattan before continuing on to the warbler orgies of the northern grounds—a happy time for warblers and for Lolly Messerheim, who had already checked off several new species in her book. She had spotted a little black-and-white eastern phoebe on a bush, wagging its tail, about to pounce on a fly. Egotistical little birds, they are easy to identify because they tell you their name.

"Fee-bee, fee-bee."

In excitement and not without humor, Lolly chimed back, "Lo-lee, lo-lee," but then she found a yellow-rumped warbler with that little spot of color, a little greenish worm-eating warbler who didn't care about the bugs, and a little chubby yellow pine warbler. Or it might have been a palm warbler. It took off before she could see if it had that touch of red on the head. But she got some photos and she would look later before marking her book. She even saw a prairie warbler, which weren't usually in the park this early in the spring. She supposed this was because it was so unusually warm, which led her to reflections on the impact of climate change on bird cycles. Something to think about.

The warblers were waking up and leaving, off to have mad sex in Canada. Who could blame them? More would come in tonight.

Then Lolly saw the kind of sight that leaves no New Yorker indifferent.

There was an open table at the restaurant by the boat basin. It was out on a wooden deck over the water. People wait for hours for such a table, but there it was with no line on this first warm, sunny day of spring. Like a warbler headed north for a rendezvous, she tucked in her tail and darted straight for the table, not waiting to be seated. She flung her camera, binoculars, and notebook on the table to leave no doubt about possession. New Yorkers, like birds in egg-laying season, are very clear on issues of territory.

She ordered shrimp and a bottle of California chardonnay. It felt good to sip the wine even though it was much too oaky, tasted a bit like sucking on a tree. But Californians didn't want you to miss the oak. She examined her photos. She could see the corner of a rust-colored cap on that one warbler. She opened her book and checked off palm warbler. Such fast little creatures, she was pleased to have gotten the shot. And even more pleased to check it in her notebook, the first palm warbler she had ever sighted. She sipped the chardonnay and felt the warm sun. If she had been a warbler, she would have wagged her tail.

Not far away, a slightly inebriated scarlet ibis was creating a sensation splashing in the water. There were a few small crustaceans he could eat, but his coordination was off from the fermented fruit and he wasn't landing quite right. The commotion of all the monkeys frightened the quetzal and he remained in the upper branches of the tallest trees. But the scarlet ibis was not worried because now the people were back in their boats where they belonged.

And then from high up, the quetzal spied something. The monkeys, the ones not in the boats, were sitting around eating—unbelievably—shrimp and avocados. Now the ibis saw it, too. Stealing food from monkeys was a dangerous proposition, but this could not be passed up.

Still tipsy and full of excitement, the scarlet ibis swept across tables, knocking over glasses, causing screams of panic. Thoth run amok. But he was getting his shrimp.

The quetzal, watching from the heights, had not gotten so alcohol foolish that he was about to go near these flailing monkeys. Still, several plates had been knocked to the deck and large chunks of chartreuse-and-yellow avocado were lying there, unobserved.

Harold Rab was an attorney, a trial lawyer, a big one. He was six feet, five inches tall and was dressed entirely in white, which made him look even larger in the sunlight. He was discussing his case in the headphones of his cellphone in such a loud voice, explaining what he needed and where, that everyone could hear what a big case it was. In fact, management had been thinking of asking him to turn off his phone or leave.

But when the ibis swooped in clumsily for his shrimp, the big red bird became tangled in the headphones and, panicking, took off quickly, carrying the headphones with him, the cellphone dangling below like a ball and chain. The ibis shook it off and it sank into the boat basin, temporarily delaying the case's defense strategy.

"Son of a bitch," shouted Harold Rab in a throaty roar that made Lolly look in his direction. He was now standing with his tennis racket in a batter's stance as a beautiful green bird . . . *Oh my God,* Lolly thought, *it's a quetzal . . .*

She had never seen a quetzal. She had once spent ten days in Guatemala trying to find one, but she never did. Now this large, angry man with the tennis racket seemed about to kill one. She had no time to think. She grabbed the bottle of chardonnay, ran over to the man, reached up and slammed the bottle as hard as she could on the man's head.

It was not what she had expected. The bottle did not break the way it always does in the movies. Instead it bounced off his head with a sickening thud, like a wooden club hitting rubber. Was the wine too oaky? Would a bottle of sauvignon blanc have worked better? Just a passing thought that she quickly dismissed.

Bolling, Homeland Security."

Asshole, thought Captain Frank Flicker. *He called me. Why does he always have to make me feel like I called him?* "So what did you find, Carter?" Frank was not sure how this sounded, because he could never remember if Carter was Bolling's first or last name.

"Will figure it out," said Bolling. He was just a voice on the phone, but Frank knew what to expect: a hard man with a clean-shaven square jaw and a bald head—the type any bird would have recognized as without feathers.

"I think it's figured out."

"There's cults and schisms of cults. And they all need watching."

"But the zoo vouched for this guy."

"How'd he spell that? Was it N-I-T-H, -nithologist? Or N-A-T-H, -nathologist?"

"I don't know the spelling, Carter. But I talked to the zoo. They said they did have someone by that name. They said they did. I asked if he called himself a -nithologist or -nathologist and they said he was. They said they had eight of them. I asked if there were more operating in the Bronx and they said 'Maybe.' That's all I got."

"Interesting."

Carter claimed that everything was interesting. It made it appear as though he knew something others couldn't see. Frank thought he had learned this trick from watching Basil Rathbone in old Sherlock Holmes movies. But this was only a guess. "You know what I think, Boll—er—Carter?" There was a pause because, of course, Carter or whatever his name was didn't want to know what Frank thought. But he would tell him anyway. "I think our guy Sanchez is just an odd bird. I've been ten years in this precinct. Once the weather warms up for spring, every odd bird in the city turns up here. You should have seen who we just busted for assault and battery. Assault and battery! This hundred-pound woman who pounded this big guy over the head with a wine bottle. She said his tennis racket was hurting the birdies."

"Just hold him. I want to question him."

"Don't have anything to hold him on."

"So you refuse to cooperate?"

"Just hurry up."

"I'm on my way."

"I'm telling you, Carter. Just one of these odd birds."

"We'll see."

Night came to Central Park. New warblers would be coming like a fresh crop of tourists checking in. The small and misnamed screech owl—no bird would call him that—cooed a soft and breathy vibrato before silently flapping his white wings in a stealth hunting mission. Night heron with their white shirts and black suits, like potbellied attorneys, flew to the boat basin in search of fish. It was past time for the ibis to find his tree for the night. But he had no one to nest with. He leapt into the air, stretched his broad wings, and headed north. Freedom felt good, but not if it meant feeling hungry, afraid, or alone. To escape all that would also be freedom, and he was soon back in the Bronx. It was dark now, but he could still see from the air that the aviary had been fixed.

And the quetzal? He flew to the safety of the highest treetop, but then a little lower he saw a laurel, his favorite tree. He was learning how to find food here and which fruits to avoid because they made him feel funny, and how to stay away from the monkeys. Everyone wants freedom, but every bird has its own idea of what it is.

Dr. Ifigenio Sanchez was relieved when he returned and discovered that the ibis had returned. The quetzal was going to be more difficult. Quetzals knew how to hide.

Lolly Messerheim could see that she had chosen the wrong wine and the wrong person to hit over the head. But she was home now and she took out her notebook and triumphantly placed a check mark next to the words "resplendent quetzal" and then noted the date and "boat basin, Central Park."

DOMINICAN REPUBLIC

Twice Bitten in San Pedro

The tarantula is named after the province of Taranto in the southern Italian region of Apulia. There it is believed that a bite from this spider leads to a seizure of hysterical dancing known as tarantism. Early references to the condition go back to 1100 BCE. The tarantella was banned by the Roman senate in 186 BCE, but people secretly continued tarantism because it not only saved people from the poisonous spider bite, it seemed to cure depression. It is still danced today in Taranto. No one dies of the bites and dancers seem to feel happier after performing the tarantella. Scientists have conducted studies on a theory that the dance somehow stimulates the endocrine system.

The first time Baldito Gil got bitten he was riding in a black Mitsubishi Montero. But he would get bitten again and the second bite would be very different.

Change does not come often, but when it does it is an unstoppable force. In San Pedro a few old things might stay, mostly mosquitoes, the old joke went. But the old ways were dying and they were being replaced by baseball.

No one minded. Who wouldn't rather work in baseball than sugar? Sugar was fit only for Haitians. So when the Dos Hermanos refinery sold off a large plot of land to the ex-shortstop Dante Galvinez, no one minded. Most of that land had not been under cultivation for years. It was just rotting like fruit on the ground. It was thought to be dead land. Even the braver birds, the big black *cao-cao* and the leggy white *galsas,* stayed off of that land. If you passed along the dirt roads near it, there was a weird hissing sound that hurt your ears and sounded like it was from another world. Frants Belsaint, who claimed to have "special knowledge" because his father was a Haitian, warned Dante about the land. Of course, Frants had warned about most things. He was usually proven right, but no one was impressed. Predicting disaster in San Pedro was a safe bet.

"The *galsas* don't land there. That is a very big *fukú.*"

Dante thought that this was probably true, but at the price the refinery was asking for their dead land it was more of a gift than a *fukú*. Besides, he didn't believe in curses in baseball, only poor training and bad strategies.

At any time, Dante tried to have twenty boys to develop. They paid him nothing because they had nothing, and then he got a third of their signing bonus, sometimes more, depending on how poor and desperate the family was. He had bought the land and built dugouts and two diamonds and high fences so kids in the neighborhood wouldn't steal his balls every time there was a home run or a meaty foul. Originally he was going to rent it to a Major League team for a camp. The Minnesota Twins, where he had played shortstop for three years—what a cold, white place that was— were looking for a place to rent. But then he decided that there was more money in being a *buscón*. A lot of people looked down on them because they took money from kids, but *buscones* saved those kids and some became Major Leaguers.

D ante had been a good shortstop and he thought he had the makings of a good businessman, but what he really took pride in was that he was a great scout. He signed eight players to the Mets and later signed twelve to the Blue Jays. In all, he brought three all-stars and a Gold Glove to the majors. But he collected his salary and watched the *buscones* make the real money, a piece of the signing bonuses. He could be a great *buscón* because he was a great scout. He could just look at a fourteen-year-old. The way he was built, the way he bent over, the way he ran or threw something, and he could see what kind of ballplayer he would be. He saw a boy running and knew if he was going to be able to steal bases. He taught him how to hit and he grew into the American League top base stealer for three years. He saw a thirteen-year-old dancing in the street. His big feet and hands told him he would be tall. His dancing was rhythmic and graceful and he was left-handed. He became a star relief pitcher for the Boston Red Sox.

Everyone could look at the kids in Consuelo or Quisqueya out in sugar country where baseball began and find some ballplayers. But Dante could find them anywhere. One day he was walking into town on the bridge over the Higuamo, with Elvio, his young assistant, who was convinced of Dante's dazzling abilities the way a good assistant should be. As Dante looked toward the mouth of the river at the small rowboats fishing in the mangrove swamp, a kid on one boat caught his attention. Like all the kids—like Dante himself before baseball saved him—he was only bones, a brown-skinned skeleton. But this kid had shoulders like the crossbeam on a ship. Dante watched him throw out nets. He had power in those shoulders and Dante saw the kid haul in the nets with a rhythmic steadiness.

"Look at that," Dante said to Elvio. "What do you see?"

Elvio stared at the boats and the mangrove. "Fishermen?"

"Anyone special?"

Elvio picked out one who he deemed about thirteen or fourteen because he knew that was the age that they needed to find.

"And what do you see when you look at him?" asked Dante. Elvio looked and looked, but he had no answer.

"You know what I see?" asked Dante. "I see a center fielder."

Elvio looked at Dante with appropriate awe. A center fielder. Not right or left, not infield. A center fielder.

"I wonder how he'll hit," said Dante to himself. And then added, for Elvio, "We're going to Punto de Pescadores. Do you realize this is about the only neighborhood in San Pedro that hasn't produced a Major Leaguer? All they do down there is fish. We'll see."

*B*ueno," Omero said repeatedly, with no discernible emotion.

"*Claro,*" was Josias's equally flat response.

They sat on a long bench, just a plank and a few sawed-down thick poles in front of their small pink house that for all its bright paint looked completely dark inside. So did the bright blue house next to them. All the brightly painted houses along the water looked dark. Their long, slim boats that had been dragged up just high enough to be out of high tide rested in a line in the dirt in front of the houses.

They all sat shoulder to shoulder, staring at the murky

lagoon—Baldito's father, Omero, and his grandfather, Josias, sat at one end with netting in their laps flowing down their legs and piled on the ground. They had fast-moving tools in their hands that looked like extra fingers. Their hands looked like wood that had dried in a field in the sun. But the fingers moved with the speed of insect legs.

Their faces were like masks that revealed nothing. Their skin was weathered leather. Omero's leather was broiled a dark brown, making his almost hazel eyes shockingly light so that he seemed to see more than other people. Josias's skin was the red chalky color of dried clay. The fishermen said he was Taíno and descended from the first fishermen in San Pedro and that was why he knew everything—where the fish were going, when they were coming back, what the weather would be.

"So he is already fourteen?" asked Dante.

"*Bueno.*"

"*Claro.*"

These men looked tough—tough as cane cutters or anyone else in this tough town. Dante thought the conversation was going surprisingly well. He understood that fishermen did not say a lot of words. It was the magic of baseball. It seduced everyone. He continued growing bolder. "Fourteen is late."

"*Bueno.*"

"*Claro.*"

Rosalia was stewing fish in the kitchen, releasing an

aroma that reminded Omero and Josias that they had dinner to look forward to as soon as they were through with these smiling men.

"But we will train hard every day. I will provide the equipment. Everything. Then when he is sixteen and a half. The exact day. When is his birthday?"

"August twenty-first," said Omero.

"Apogee tide," added Josias. The implication, lost on Dante and Elvio, was that February 29 was a day to be fishing.

"So Septem... Octo... Nov... Dec... Jan... Feb. The last of February."

"That will be a leap year," Josias pointed out. "You can use the extra day. That's a very good day." Of course, he meant an extra day for fishing.

"Yes!" said Dante, trying to sound enthusiastic so that his growing frustration didn't show. "On that day I will show him to scouts. I will have showed him before, but that day they can bid. I will bring over everyone interested and it will be like an auction."

"Bueno," said Omero.

"Slavery," said Josias.

"What? No, just trying to get the best price."

"Claro," said Josias, as though correcting his own mistake. Dante stared into Josias's eyes that did not move. It was impossible to see what he was thinking.

"Then I take a thirty percent commission." He usually

tried for a third but he wanted this to go smoothly and he
had other ways of making money on this.

"Bueno."

"So we have a deal?"

"No," he heard one of them say softly, and the two started
carefully folding their net on the ground. All the while they
were both saying in a soft, inoffensive voice, "No. No. No."
Dante had the feeling that when they were through with the
net they would both leave. He had to remind himself that
they lived there.

Finally Elvio, who couldn't keep his silence anymore,
said, "Why not?"

Omero turned and fixed his pale eyes on Elvio, which
scared him because this was the first time in this limited
conversation in which Omero had looked at anyone. "Baldito
is the anchor. Do you know what that means?"

"No," said Elvio nervously. Omero explained that the Gil
family fished well because he had three sons with whom to
fish. The three boys would let out a net holding the ends
while Omero operated the oars, slapping the water and
making a commotion to frighten the fish and drive them
into the net. After a few hours Omero would haul it in with
the help of his sons. Even when he was still small, Omero's
youngest son, Baldito, was "the anchor," the one who played
the central role in pulling on board the heavy net full of
fish. His arms, too long for his small body, held surprising
strength, and that was needed because the net was filled

out like a balloon with fifty or sixty pounds of silver, white, and colored little fish writhing, squirming, breathing their last.

"Take one of the other boys," said Omero. "I need Baldito."

"The others are already too old," Dante explained, not bothering to add that he saw nothing to develop in them.

Omero shrugged, and he and Josias started to vanish into the darkness of the pink house.

"You don't want your son to be a Major League Baseball star?" Dante called out in desperation.

Omero's light eyes shined out from the darkness of the doorway. "How much money will there be if you get him signed?"

Finally, Dante thought, *he is going to talk business.* "The signing bonus could be anything from fifty thousand dollars to maybe over a hundred thousand." Dante was already thinking he would be worth three hundred thousand but he would let the scout keep some of it and he would keep $100,000 for himself, and then take thirty percent of what was left and the family would never know. It was easy. Done all the time.

"We want fifty thousand dollars," said Omero.

"Sure, maybe more."

"If I am going to lose my anchor for two years I want fifty thousand dollars guaranteed. You can take thirty percent of everything over that."

Why argue? thought Dante. He was going to get a lot on this. Let the fucking fishermen have their $50,000.

———

When Baldito's father told him that he had to train to be a baseball player, Baldito was confused. He had never thought of being a baseball player. People in sugar mills became baseball players. He was a fisherman. Adding to his confusion, Josias said to him, "Just watch out for that field they've got."

"What do you mean? Watch out for what?"

"Ask Frants," Josias whispered. At just that moment Omero came up and hugged him. "This is from God, absolutely from God."

Josias nodded in agreement.

"Why?" asked Baldito.

"We were finished," said Omero.

"Finished?" said Baldito. "The catches are down, but the fish will come back. They always do."

"No, they won't," said Josias. No one argued with Josias about fish.

"It's the cement," said Omero. A Mexican cement factory had been built on the river. The town was very happy about this because it created hundreds of jobs and they were much better jobs than those at the sugar mills, which operated only part of the year. But the cement factory dumped something in the river that was killing the fish. "If we can get fifty thousand dollars," said Omero, "we can buy a big boat that can go to sea with a big engine and enough money for gasoline and we can catch the big fish at sea. So you have just saved us."

"If I can get signed," said Baldito.

"You can get signed," said Josias, and so it was true because he was Taíno and knew things even though he knew nothing about baseball.

B aldito did talk to Frants.

"The field is cursed, boy. That's all there is to it. Dante Galvinez is a fine, honest man. But he was swindled. He bought cursed land. I know. It was my father who put the curse on the Dos Hermanos. He got his right arm caught in a crusher. They didn't do anything for him. He lied in a cot in the batey for ten days, crying in agony. Finally someone came and cut his arm off. Dos Hermanos told him that there was no work for a one-armed man. When he asked for his back pay they said that it was spent on his operation. Operation? There wasn't any operation. They just chopped off his dead arm. Dos Hermanos didn't understand this, but my father was from the Artibonite and he knew a lot of things. He had a lot of power and he told Dos Hermanos that he was cursing them. He said, 'Your sugar will become worthless and your land will be haunted with the screams of the sugar workers you have mistreated.'

"It all became true. The sugar is worth nothing now and those back fields are full of groans and screams. That's why they stopped planting there. No one would work it with that terrible noise. Even the *galsas* and the *cuervos* that aren't afraid of anything stay away. Now it's a baseball field, but you can still hear it. You'll see. It's not a whisper. It's a scream."

Baldito didn't know what to think of this story, but it was at this time that Dante took him for a ride in his black Mitsubishi Montero with the smoked windows so no one could see who was inside. Everyone knew it was a Major League Baseball player because they were the only ones who had Mitsubishi Monteros. This large luxurious sport-utility vehicle with air-conditioning and stereo sound to play bachatas and comfortable leather seats was the first car Baldito had ever ridden in. He understood that someday he would have one, too. Dante drove him past the enormous houses of Sammy Sosa, Alfredo Griffin, George Bell. All the Major Leaguers. Most of them didn't live in these houses anymore because they lost them in divorces, but they built other ones in other towns. This, too, was in his future. He, too, would have many wives and many houses. He had to succeed because the family was counting on him, but something else happened in the Mitsubishi Montero. He got bitten by the baseball bug. This was just the first bug bite.

At the time Baldito Gil reported for training Dante Galvinez had seventeen prospects and Baldito was clearly the most promising. "This kid is money," said Dante to Elvio, who smiled greedily. He made Elvio say several times that he was a genius for spotting him. Elvio didn't mind repeating it because he thought it was true.

As a batter Baldito had what scouts called "pop." When his bat made contact with a ball the ball leapt into flight. He seemed to be one of those rare people who could see the pitch as it left the pitcher's hand and know where it would go. Dante brought in Romeo Santos, a pitcher he had played with in the majors. Santos drove up in his Montero, wearing blue jeans and a yellow cashmere sweater with a thin gold chain around his neck and looking lean and fit. The sweater impressed people because only a man who is constantly air-conditioned wears sweaters in San Pedro. Most people did not even have the electricity, even if they could buy an air conditioner.

Romeo looked at Baldito as though he were a coat he was thinking of buying. "A nice-looking boy," he said, and walked to the mound. Santos was known as a "tricky" pitcher. His pitches were full of movement—sliders, sinkers, curveballs. He had his own pitches with names he invented, like the "killer ball," a kind of cutter that looked like an easy outside pitch to a right-handed hitter but then darted to the right at the last moment so that it looked like it was headed right for the batter. Given his reputation for hitting batters, most stepped aside, but the pitch did not hit the batter and was a strike. His "crazy ball" headed for the center of the zone but at the last minute dropped so quickly it bounced off the plate. Most umpires would have called it a ball except that hitters could not resist swinging at it, and they always missed.

Crazy Ball had become his nickname. Everybody said that he was crazy. He still had his arm and could have still been in the majors but no one wanted him because he was too crazy. When he was with the Dodgers he announced before a game against the Giants in Candlestick Park that he was going to hit one of them with a pitch but it would be a surprise when he would do it. The umpire warned that he would be thrown out of the game if he hit any batters. On his first pitch of the game he fired a fastball into the Giants' dugout and was suspended from baseball for fifty games. The Dodgers dropped him after that and no one else wanted him. He sometimes played in the Dominican League for the local Estrellas, but even they did not welcome him anymore.

He could still pitch even without many warm-up throws, and he showed Baldito every pitch he had. Baldito hit every one of them. He knocked the "crazy ball" into a palm tree beyond the center-field wall. Everyone on the field applauded, and Santos, who had beads of sweat showing on his forehead and would have to either remove his sweater or return to air-conditioning, walked to home plate and said, "Son, go tell your father that you have beaten the greatest pitcher in baseball," and he got into his Montero and drove off, sending up a cloud of yellow dust behind him.

Baldito told his parents exactly that. He was going to save his family, buy the boat, and drive a Montero.

There was more good news for Dante. Baldito was a

switch-hitter and could bat equally from either side of the plate. He was so ambidextrous he did not know whether he was right-handed or left-handed. Dante taught him to bat both but to throw right-handed "just like Mickey Mantle," he would say to scouts. And like Mantle, he would play center field. Dante thought he might sell him to the New York Yankees. He was going to bring far more money than the Gil family imagined, and as long as Dante could keep it quiet, a lot of that extra money would be his. Baldito ran like a hundred-yard sprinter and he was a natural base stealer. Dante had been right about his arm. He could fire a ball from the deep outfield in seconds to any base. And they were accurate throws. "You know, Elvio," Dante whispered to his assistant. "We may have our hands on a five-tool player." Elvio laughed with glee.

Everyone wanted a five-tool player—someone who mastered all the varied skills of baseball. His weakest skill was his hands. He was fairly good at catching flies and fast enough to get to them from anywhere, but he was surprisingly clumsy at fielding grounders. So that was what Dante worked on.

In truth, Baldito was not comfortable in the outfield. Frants had been right. It was a spooky place and made strange loud hissing noises. Baldito could hear the screams of the cane workers. The field became particularly loud when they practiced ground balls.

One afternoon when the boys stood in a circle around Dante and Elvio, which was how practice ended, Dante

said, "Anything troubling any of you, come to us. Any problem on the field or off. Come talk to us. We want to take care
of you."

Baldito chose Elvio, who was closer to his age. "There is
some weird spooky noise in the outfield."

Elvio seemed concerned. "What kind of noise?"

"A hissing or buzzing. But loud. More like a hoarse
scream. Like someone trying to scream without being too
loud."

"Like someone screaming a whisper."

"Exactly. What do you think it is?"

"I don't know, but we will take care of it."

Baldito felt relieved. It had been hard to perform in the
outfield with that sound. He should have said something
sooner.

The next day after practice Dante and Elvio offered him
a ride home. There was something purposeful about the
invitation. He sat in the front next to Dante, and Elvio, in
the backseat, was leaning forward. Baldito felt good riding
through San Pedro, sealed off so that no one could see him,
comfortable in the air-conditioning while he looked out
and watched people sweat.

"Baldito," said Dante. "What do you think of Romeo
Santos?"

"He's a great pitcher."

"He is that," Dante agreed. "Who knows, maybe even as
great as he says he is." He and Elvio chuckled. Baldito was
becoming uncomfortable.

"You know," said Dante, "they threw him out of the majors. Just threw him out because they thought he was crazy."

"That's right," Elvio confirmed. "He just said too many crazy things."

"Yes," said Dante. "You say crazy things and it gets to the majors and you're out."

Baldito understood. How would he face his father and his brothers and his grandfather if all their hopes were gone because he had listened to some crazy story from Frants Belsaint?

Baldito worked hard and he became a more and more polished ballplayer. By the time he was sixteen the scouts were talking about him all over the Dominican Republic. If he was as good as they said, they would bid high to get him. Some said it might go to a million dollars. But that was if he really was that good.

He really was that good at everything but fielding grounders. In fact, he was making spectacular long-distance catches so that he would not have to pick the ball off the ground. Every time a grounder came into center field there was that noise and he couldn't concentrate.

On February 4, Dante brought the Yankees scout to watch him. He called Baldito over to meet this small black man with the sun at his back. As he got closer he could see that he was an aged and amiable *moreno,* as dark-skinned people were called.

"I've heard great things about you, Baldito."

Dante had taught Baldito that a little confidence was good, so Baldito simply said, "I think I'm ready, sir."

The scout smiled. He had said the right thing. "Well, let's see what you can do."

They had arranged a game with another program from Consuelo. Baldito thought that it would be played in Consuelo, but it turned out to be a game in the haunted home field. Consuelo had some prospects they were showing, too, including the starting pitcher. He had a 92-mile-per-hour fastball, but it did not have much motion and the only other pitch he had was a changeup. He threw nothing but fastballs until he had a two strike count. Then came the changeup— the same pitch at 75 miles per hour. Baldito deliberately worked the count until he got the changeup. His first at-bat he hit it for a triple. Then, to everyone's amazement, he stole home. Dante did not encourage dangerous plays like stealing home, but it was a right-handed pitcher with a slow motion and a slight turn so that his back was to the third-base line and Baldito knew he could make it. Elvio ran up to him and said, "Dante says to just play your game. No showing off." Baldito swallowed the rebuke.

For the first four innings the outfield was quiet. Every hit that came to center field was high in the air, and Baldito, with his great speed, was able to make the catch. Then he could show off his throwing arm and fire the ball into the infield for a double play.

But then Dante put in a new pitcher, Feliz George, a tough fifteen-year-old who came from the sugar fields and would not go back. Feliz threw everything low so the batter could not get underneath the ball to lift it into the air. There were always a lot of hits off of Feliz, but they were always grounders and most of them were easy outs.

Fortunately they had a good shortstop, so the grounders were not getting out to center field. But in the sixth inning a grounder took an odd hop, which was not unusual in this irregular field, and got by the shortstop and bounced to the left of Baldito. He ran in with his glove at the ready, as he was trained. The scream was so loud that it occurred to him that maybe he really was crazy. And then he saw something too horrible to be real. Next to the ball was a huge black-and-orange spider almost eight inches wide, and its thick body and legs were completely covered with hair.

This monster was screaming at him. So were a lot of people. "Baldito, the ball! Throw the ball!" With a sick feeling in his belly, he reached his glove down to grab the ball and the monster—this couldn't be real—reared back like an attacking bear or a frightened horse and spit at him. It was a cloud of mist or spit and it stung his left forearm but he reached in his glove, grabbed the ball, and fired it with his accustomed speed and strength to first base.

Unfortunately by then the runner had made it to second base, and after Baldito threw to first the runner sprinted on to third. So what should have been a routine out at first turned into a triple.

Baldito raised his feet with his spiked shoes high and stomped the ground over and over, but the spider had retreated to the safety of his silken nest under the grass. When the game was over Dante said to him, "You blew the play. Happens all the time. Not such a big thing. But that temper tantrum—stamping your feet out there. Don't ever let anybody see that again. I think that ruined it for the Yankees." Then he slapped Baldito's back. "It's all right. There's others interested."

A red itchy rash started to heat up his left forearm. He could not talk to the people in baseball about it so he showed his rash to Frants, who shook his head sadly.

"It was a huge hairy spider," Baldito told him, and Frants nodded with comprehension.

"A tarantula."

"Is it serious?" Baldito asked.

"Depends."

"But it can't kill you, right?"

"Not directly."

Everything was a riddle with Frants, and Baldito was losing patience. "What does that mean? 'Not directly.' So it kills you indirectly?"

"Some say it makes you crazy. And that can kill you."

"Crazy how?"

Frants made a gesture like washing his hands. "Who can

say? There is all kinds of crazy. Some say all the crazy people in the world are people who got bitten."

Baldito thought it was possible that Frants had been bitten. Is that what was going to happen to him? Would he end up like Frants, dispensing wisdom that made no sense? Baldito decided his last hope was to talk to Conky Rojas, who ran a clinic from his little green-and-red-trimmed wooden house near the Porvenir Sugar Mill. Conky was not crazy. When a baseball player in San Pedro, or anywhere in the Dominican Republic, had an injury they went to Conky. Conky could cure most anything. There was always a line along the banana bushes outside, but Baldito didn't mind because, standing in that line, he felt like a real ballplayer. Three of the men in the line that afternoon were Major Leaguers nursing their injuries back home during the off-season.

When Baldito finally got inside, Conky, a small, bony African-looking man with fingers that were unnaturally long for his small frame, looked at the rash. "Have you been near spiders?"

Baldito would have to tell him. He whispered, "Yes, huge, hairy spiders."

"Tarantulas. Lucky he didn't bite you."

"He didn't?"

"No. That would be much more serious. He just sprayed you. Rub these leaves." He looked in a cabinet and took out a roll of green leaves and handed them to him. "Just keep rubbing it with these leaves and try not to scratch and it will go away."

"And what happens if it does bite me?"

"Oh, if it bites you . . . just stay away from them."

"But suppose it does."

"Well, it won't kill you."

"What will it do?"

"Well . . . Well, they say a bite from a tarantula makes you crazy."

"Crazy?"

"Just stay away from them."

"And there is nothing you can do?"

"Oh, I think there is. If you ever get bitten, the one you want to talk to is Romeo Santos."

"Rome—?"

"Yes."

"But he's already crazy."

Conky Rojas closed his eyes and nodded knowingly.

Baldito knew that day would come, and it did with Red Sox, Houston, and Tampa Bay scouts present. The ball rolled into the outfield and Baldito ran in for it and when he got there the tarantula was sitting on it as though he'd claimed it. Baldito reached down with his glove and scooped up the tarantula and the baseball. When he reached for the ball he could feel the tarantula bite his hand. As soon as he had the ball in his right hand he threw the spider down as hard as he could and quickly snapped a throw to first base, aimed perfectly at the first baseman's glove, and he made the out.

"Hey," said the Tampa Bay scout to Houston. "Who said this kid can't field."

Baldito looked in the grass where he had slammed the tarantula down and he found two hairy twigs, broken-off joints of the creature's legs. But it could move well without them and it was gone. It would be back, though, more angry than ever. He looked at his hand and there was a red welt just above his thumb. Was he going to become crazy? Didn't crazy people think they were normal? How did you know if you were crazy?

These questions raced through his mind as he walked into town. He had to see Romeo, but it was well known that Romeo spent all night in the clubs along the Malecón and did not get up until about four in the afternoon. Baldito wandered through town, testing his craziness. Every minute until he did something about it the spider venom was making its way to his mind. Would he get crazier with time? So now was he only a little crazy? He stopped at the stand near Porvenir where a friend sold cane. He bought a stick and peeled off the end and started chewing and sucking in the sweetness. This was normal, right? He talked to his friend for a while about baseball. The friend wanted to know how his training was going and how much money he thought he could get for signing. And that seemed to go well. He didn't have an impulse to say anything strange. He didn't say, "I think they will offer fifty million dollars."

Baldito had a friend, Paquito, who sold oranges by the Tetelo Vargas Stadium. "Hey, Paquito, do me a favor. Ask me a question."

"Any question?"

"Yes, any question, and see if my answer makes sense."

"Are you crazy?"

"Why do you say that?" answered Baldito with an urgency that frightened Paquito.

"I was joking, man. Just joking."

Paquito was smiling, Baldito thought. He was trying to calm him down. Talking to him the way you talk to a crazy man.

"Okay," said Paquito. "Who is the all-time greatest baseball player?"

"Tetelo Vargas!"

Paquito smiled when he heard the local hero's name and they bumped knuckles of their right fists together. "You're not crazy, man."

Baldito wandered on past the little shopping mall Sammy Sosa had built with the statue of Sammy that looked nothing like him. When he got to Romeo's apartment building it was exactly four, though Baldito was not certain because he had no watch. Several Major Leaguers lived in the building and their black Monteros were lined up inside the gate. Romeo answered his door in a plush velvety wine-colored bathrobe and dark sunglasses that hid his eyes. Baldito could feel the cold air rushing out of the apartment like he was standing in the doorway of the walk-in on the dock where they froze the fish.

Baldito told him that he had been bitten by a tarantula and Conky Rojas had told him to talk to him.

With the sunglasses on Baldito could not tell what Romeo's reaction was, but he yawned, showing excellent white teeth, and scratched his head and asked Baldito to come back in about an hour.

When Baldito returned, Romeo still had his sunglasses on but was wearing a lavender cashmere sweater and blue jeans. Baldito thought that Romeo's living room was the coldest place he had ever been in his life. Maybe the freezer on the dock was this cold, but he would go in there for only a minute.

Romeo dramatically stuck a long, thin finger straight up, as though demanding silence. "What should I offer you . . ." After a long pause he smiled and said, "Papaya juice."

He walked over to a large glass bowl of papayas in the dark, cold room. He held several, squeezed and caressed and sniffed them and chose the one he wanted and disappeared into the next room, from where Baldito could hear the clanging of equipment. "I just got a new papaya juicer," Romeo shouted.

After several minutes in which Baldito was shivering alone in the dark, Romeo reentered, holding out a large glass with a baby-flesh-pink liquid. Baldito started to take the glass and jumped backward.

"Don't drop it." Romeo laughed. On his lavender cashmere arm was a tarantula making its way toward the drink. Another one was crawling up the side of his head, making its way to the top of his thick black hair. "Meet Rico and Pepito," said Romeo. "They're pets."

"Pets?" Baldito was considering the possibility that he had lost his mind and none of this was real. "Do they ever bite you?"

"We have our little disagreements. Especially Rico. He has a bad temper."

"What happens when they bite you?" Baldito asked, but he knew the answer.

Romeo smiled. "You go crazy."

"Isn't there anything you can do?" *Why am I asking?* thought Baldito. It was already too late. *Besides, everyone knows that Romeo is crazy.*

Romeo went to a cabinet and started playing a merengue very loudly. It was Tempo Dominicano's "Confusiones." He began swaying his hips, moving his feet to the music, smiling with his eyes closed, Rico and Pepito clinging to him. "Come on, Baldito. No time to waste. When were you bitten?"

Baldito began moving to the music. It felt good. He was smiling, too. He had never danced very much, and in fact had preferred sad bachata about broken hearts to the fast-paced merengue. But it would not have surprised anyone that he danced well. He could feel how good he was. How his body expressed the music. How the rhythm carried him. By the time they got to Benny Sadel's "Yo Soy Así," he seemed to be in a trance. After several hours of dancing, Romeo drove them to a club on the Malecón.

Baldito noticed that Romeo also danced very well and the most beautiful women wanted to dance with him, their dark satin skin taking on a moist sheen as the night wore on. It was one of the things you got for being a Major Leaguer, Baldito thought, like a Mitsubishi Montero.

But soon it was noticed that young Baldito was also an incredibly good dancer, in fact getting better with each merengue, and so young women wanted to dance with him, too. But really he was dancing with himself, feeling nothing but an upbeat rhythm—without stop until daybreak.

Fortunately Dante had brought no scouts that day because Baldito did not get a single hit, missed a number of fly balls he should have chased after. He went home and slept and the next day he was playing well again. The tarantula was back with its missing legs, angrily hissing at him, and a week later it bit him again.

Baldito knew what to do. He felt good when he was dancing. Better than when he played baseball. As long as there was merengue he did not have to worry about anything. Of course, dancing merengue would not get his family their boat or him his Montero.

His family was worried. They all went to sleep at sunset

and woke up when it was still dark to go fishing, so on nights when Baldito was dancing they never saw him.

He was no longer playing as well as he used to, and the scouts could see that he was not the hot prospect that they'd heard he was. But Dante accepted his disappointments, he had many, and on February 29 he signed him to the Cubs for $300,000, a respectable bonus that he reported to the Gils as $200,000, from which their share was $140,000, which was more money than they had ever imagined possessing. Dante made $160,000. Elvio had to admit that Dante was a genius.

The fishermen threw a party for Baldito by the water in Punta de Pescadores, and Dante and Elvio came. Rosalia was going to make her special fish and dumplings, but they had no electricity in the house that week so she cooked the fish with roots and coconut in a big pot outside on an open fire as in the old days. Baldito played merengue on a player with powerful speakers—his first purchase with his signing bonus, playing Gran Manzana's "Cuando Llegara" over and over and dancing to it with his eyes closed as the brass notes bounced over the quiet water and the fishermen sipped little glasses of sweet and strong guavaberry.

The Gils bought their boat and a big enough engine to go to sea and brought back to market long *carite* with angry faces, and roundheaded dorado that died with foolish grins, and sleek marlin, long and shiny silver and blue, looking like they dressed for the occasion, and smaller oval bonito only two feet long but bringing high prices. These big sea fish were the ones that brought money. Two or three of them could bring in more money than an entire boatload of *cabriles*.

Life was good again. Baldito was sent to the Cubs training camp in Boca Chica, where there was a lot of very good food and no tarantulas in the outfield. But there was also no merengue. He missed that.

MIAMI

The Alligator Teeth of an Unknown God

A mise meshune oyf im.

May a strange and ugly thing come his way.

—Old Yiddish curse

▼ ▼ ▼

Finally Yoni had nailed this son of a bitch. The rabbi scratched his beard rabbinically and Yoni couldn't help but smile. The rabbi who knew everything was caught. Yoni was two points ahead and Herschel was stuck with one last tile and he couldn't use it.

It was a *K*, and that was five points, and if he couldn't use it Herschel would lose five points. Yoni smiled. Why didn't the rabbi give up? He had him. There was no open spot for the letter *K*. But Herschel smiled. He even laughed. He slapped the tile on the board the way the Cubans did when they played dominoes.

What had he done? He had used the word "harmony," Yoni's word, and placed the *K* next to the *A*.

"Ka?" said Yoni. "What's a ka? There's no such word."

"Look it up," said Herschel.

The big, thick book was sitting on the table in front of Yoni. He quickly stroked the pages with his index finger and there it was.

Ka: an unknown god.

"You can't outsmart the rebbe," said Rifka, the bulbous macaroon monster that was his wife, popping another Israeli chocolate-covered macaroon in her mouth. She had chocolate on her fingers and a little on her ample jiggly white cheek. Yoni looked at his wife with disgust, the round, round body, maybe over the three-hundred-pound mark by now, that wig that looked like the dead straw of a plant that wildly went to seed and died, the dull, dark hair under it looking even worse. With pain Yoni reflected, as he often did, on the absurd fact that this was the only woman to whom he had ever made love—a popular euphemism— whom he had ever touched.

"Anyone want the last macaroon?" she asked cheerfully as she ate it. They imported the macaroons by the case for her and she pointed out that it was a good thing that she ate so many because that made it possible for her to get a whole-sale price.

Her bloated flesh held in its tight white and blotchy pink skin like a foam-rubber pillow shoved in a too-small pillowcase—or at least he imagined it would feel like that. He hadn't touched her in almost ten years and a hundred pounds. It was an arranged marriage, and the night after the wedding when they were alone for the first time was the worst night of either of their lives. They tried a few more times, but not many, and then they made up medical myths about why they didn't have any children.

"Macaroons are gone. Let's go," she said. He wasn't sure if she was trying to be funny. She never was very funny. He never knew why his parents picked her for him. You weren't supposed to ask. He had mentioned the possibility of a divorce once and all her white flesh turned red. She was furious and would not even discuss the possibility. So was she happy? Yoni didn't know. Maybe as long as she had enough macaroons she was happy. He had talked to Herschel once about a divorce and he said that it would be extremely difficult if she would not cooperate.

They went home after the Scrabble game, parked the car in the driveway, went into the house. Rifka went to the cabinet where they were kept and took out a flat box of macaroons. Yoni watched the way the fat on the back of her upper arms jiggled like ripples in soup being stirred.

"Want some?" she asked, but didn't wait for an answer, sinking into the couch, jamming two in her mouth with her left hand while her right was waving the remote control as though conducting a symphony.

Yoni watched and thought, *This is my life.*

Then, almost as though in sympathy, he heard an odd deep, soft grunt from outside. Was it an owl? There were ravens that settled into the treetops at sunset and screeched, and there was a parrot with a scream so loud and grating that Yoni had tried to chase it away by throwing rocks. Once, he even hit it and it shouted indignantly while it recovered its balance. But it wasn't hurt and it didn't leave.

He took a flashlight and wandered into the backyard. It was supposed to be a backyard, but his home had been arranged by the same people who'd arranged his marriage and it turned out that the backyard where his future children were to play was really more of a swamp. You put your foot in it and a puddle formed. Children could never play there. But there were no children. Rabbi Herschel always says, "God finds unexpected solutions."

Through the tropical night sounds of insects he could hear Rifka's television program; it was about chefs who hated one another's food. Why did she care? It was all *traif* that she couldn't eat. His shoes made sucking noises as he made his way through the "yard." Then he almost stepped on it.

He jerked back quickly and froze, not daring to move. It was only a long series of bumps and ridges in the glow of the flashlight. And an eye that was looking at him. It was an alligator. He estimated that it was twelve feet long—about twice his height—but it might be bigger. It had wriggled in the gaseous mud and created a pool for itself and only the top half was exposed.

Suppose he ran? How fast are alligators? Probably faster than he was in this muck. He looked at his feet and saw that they were sinking into the ground. But for some reason Yoni didn't want to run. He was not afraid. He was oddly certain that this alligator had not come to harm him. Rabbi Herschel always says, "God always comes in the form that is needed."

This was a god. It was Ka—an unknown god. The alligator seemed to smile at the thought.

Yoni stood in the yard, his black shoes sunk to his socks in mud, his white tzitzit blowing in the breeze, the sacred fringes that were to remind him every day of what he longed to forget at least one day. Like every day of his life, he was wearing black pants, white shirt, black hat.

He was carrying a bag of raw chickens. He took one out and lobbed it toward the alligator, imagining that the creature would rise up with his enormous jaws and swallow it. Instead he remained motionless and halfway submerged. The chicken made a slapping noise as it landed on his head, right between his eyes. It didn't make him angry. The chicken rolled down to the mud next to him. He curled his neck and got his large mouth around it and swallowed. Wasn't that interesting.

The next one Yoni landed in front of the alligator, which splashed him. Again, no particular reaction. But then the beast moved forward, putting the chicken in his mouth, and swallowed it whole. Yoni fed him a dozen chickens—glatt kosher, specially ordered. Tomorrow he could get a shipment of kosher steaks.

All the while he was feeding the alligator, Yoni kept asking why it was here in his yard. He understood that the alligators were leaving the Everglades because of a lack of water. He had a client who owned some sugar fields and the opposing counsel had claimed that his client was sucking water out of the Everglades for his fields and this would drive the alligators out of the swamp. Yoni had, of course, argued that this wasn't true, but even if it was, why had the alligator come to him? There must be a reason—"a purpose," as Rabbi Herschel would say—why this alligator came to Yoni Friedman at this particular time.

Religious people hate alligators because they so clearly descended from dinosaurs. This meant that dinosaurs had existed and there was evolution, Darwin was right, and the Book of Genesis was a fairy tale that children should outgrow or—as Yoni liked to say in silence to himself but never uttered out loud because it could bring bad luck—"the Book of Genesis is bullshit."

Had the alligator come to Yoni Friedman's house just to tell him that his life was a lie? He already knew that. There must have been something more—more of a purpose. He noticed that the alligator did not chew his food. He grabbed it with his teeth and then swallowed it whole. To be eaten by an alligator—say, for Rifka to be eaten, for example—would not be the painful experience that you might imagine.

To replace the kosher meat he was feeding the alligator he would buy unkosher chickens or steaks at the Publix supermarket on Miami Beach. Though there were some orthodox in that neighborhood, it was far from South Miami and he was not known there. Once, on leaving the store, a black man carrying a trash bag of empty cans and smelling slightly overripe in torn and stained khaki clothing said to him, "How's the *kashrut* going, man?" *Kashrut*—the Jewish dietary laws—was not a word you expected to hear from homeless black people, but still, there was nothing to worry about. Besides, maybe after six months of *traif* he would tell Rifka and she would divorce him. Probably not, though.

Feeding her to an alligator might be a far more reasonable solution.

Rifka liked the *traif*. Of course, she didn't know it was *traif*. He told her that he found that if he removed the kosher meat from those thick plastic bags and wrapped it in aluminum foil it would taste better. She agreed. Both the chicken and the steak were much more flavorful this way.

The alligator had some reservations. Sometimes he would grunt and moan after steak and Yoni realized it had too much fat and he had to trim it off.

But this was not the *traif* that interested Yoni Friedman. It was something else entirely, and her name was Acacia Bras. Acacia was a young Cuban attorney whose client was involved in a case with his firm. It was an unusual event for him because he had few dealings with people who were not Jewish. Mostly he helped Israelis invest in Miami. In the thirty seven years he had been on this planet he had seldom had contact with non-Jews. Even the waiters at the restaurants he patronized were Jewish. But he had a client from Tel Aviv who was trying to buy some property in Hialeah who had a conflict with the seller, who had Acacia for a lawyer. Normally Yoni was known for his fast settlements, but he was in no hurry to settle this one. In fact, it dragged on for months and might never have been settled were it not for the issue of overbilling his client.

Acacia stared at him in a way that was inappropriate for a woman. And Yoni returned the favor. He was enthralled with every detail of her—the wrinkles on her knuckles, the bumps on her knees. He dreamed of seeing the rest of her, but he could not even imagine what that would be like. He had never seen a naked woman.

What drew her to Yoni, what fascinated her about him, was the depths from which he desired her. No one had ever wanted her so badly. He never said so. He would never talk about such things, but Acacia could feel him wanting her, caressing her wildly with his eyes. This man would give up his friends, his religion, his god, even his wife to have her. She was a little surprised at how exciting she found this.

"Haven't you ever wondered what *traif* tastes like?" Acacia asked him.

Of course he always had. "Is pork really good?"

Acacia took his right hand in both of hers. "Two important Cuban words for you: *media noche.*"

He liked the sound of it. He also liked the touch of her hands. He was never touched by women. *"Media Noche. What is it?"*

"Que sabroso, mi amor."

Why is it, Yoni asked himself, *that everything Cuban women say is so sexy?* Just "The food is delicious," and you are in love. "What is it?"

"A sandwich." She laid one hand on top of the other as though making the sandwich. "A slice of pork." She paused to see his reaction. "A slice of ham." Still no response. "Some melted cheese and pickles."

"Oh my God," he said with a little-boy smile. "Triple *traif.*"

"That's right. Want to get one?" Her smile seemed almost like a wink.

He nodded eagerly. "Where do we go?"

"Calle Ocho—but you can't go like that."

This was a huge triumph for Acacia. She was going to rescue this man. Not only was he going to eat forbidden food, but he was going to change his way of dressing. He trimmed his beard from the long scraggily one he had always worn to fashionably close-cropped. He bought blue jeans and a blue checked cotton shirt and brown loafers, the first brown shoes he had ever worn. He got them all on sale at Burdines. Fifty percent off on the shirt. He did wear his *kippot*, but not a hat. And he flipped it in the backseat when he picked up Acacia.

They went to a large, brightly lit restaurant with Cuban music and ordered the two sandwiches. Yoni wondered if he would gag or vomit on the pork. But he didn't. He liked it. He didn't love it. It didn't taste extraordinarily different from anything he had ever tasted—kind of a cross between chicken and veal. But there were so many other foods to explore. Yoni decided that he "loved Cuban food."

In South Miami, Rifka was getting back from a meeting about organizing the baking for the break-the-fast for a holiday fast the following week. It always took a lot more planning to break a fast than to fast. Rifka was always in charge of the desserts. But when she got home and got out of the car she noticed a strange smell. It was not an unpleasant smell but a bit heavy, musty, maybe meaty.

She had no idea, but it was Ka, the unknown god in the backyard. He was feeling good, feeling that he had found the right spot to set up his hole. He decided to make an official announcement that this was his hole and so he used the gland in his throat to emit the correct odor.

Carrying the leftover macaroons from her meeting, Rifka followed her excellent nose to the backyard, where the heel of her right shoe became caught in the mud and Rifka fell face-forward, landing on her enormous belly, partly submerged, actually much like an alligator.

The macaroons tumbled out and rolled down to within an inch of the alligator, and a few of them he barely had to move to eat.

Yoni Friedman had entered a fantasy world, a kind of dream in which everything that had been his life up until now, including his wife, didn't exist anymore. He was not certain what Acacia thought about this. He could tell by the slight way she moved to music that she was a great dancer. What would it be like to dance with a Cuban woman? He had never danced with a woman. In his world, men danced only with men, holding hands in a circle, always moving counterclockwise. Why counterclockwise? He couldn't say. He always avoided dancing, but this would be very different.

As they made their way out of the restaurant to a song Acacia called a bolero, sung by someone she called Benny something, his name almost sounding Jewish, Yoni saw something that shocked him. At first he thought he must be wrong, but he wasn't.

In a quiet corner booth sat a Cuban woman sharing a lobster with a thin, dark, clean-shaven man. Yoni hoped to someday have the nerve to eat a lobster. There was something familiar but out of place about the man. Did he know him? It was Rabbi Herschel without a beard. He looked up at Yoni with fear in his eyes. But of course Yoni had the same fears, so neither man said anything. Herschel was wearing the exact same clothes as he was wearing—the same blue jeans and blue checked shirt. He must have found the Burdines sale, too. Yoni noted with pleasure that Herschel's Cuban woman was not as attractive as his. But Herschel had completely shaved off his beard. How was he going to explain that?

Yoni looked forward to the prospect of chaos.

He turned to Acacia and proposed a lobster dinner.

"That would be really nice, Yoni. But where is this going?"

"What do you mean?"

"I mean, you're married. Are you sure you don't have children?"

"I'm sure," he said, and then almost added "thank God," an old habit that he never liked. He took her hand tenderly, a new gesture he had learned from her, and said, "Don't worry. Ka will arrange everything."

"Who is Ka?"

Yoni smiled. "An unknown god."

Acacia slowly shook her head and thought, *This man and his gods.* She knew about such men, believers. Her father saw Yoruba gods everywhere—in the trunks of trees, on the tops of palms. He had dolls with whom he shared his smuggled cigars and a shot of every bottle of rum was spilled on the ground as an offering. So if Yoni put his faith in a god called Ka, Acacia could understand.

When Yoni got home he heard Rifka shouting from the "backyard." The alligator had found her. Had he attacked? Was she in his huge toothy grip, being dragged into the swampy muck? Was there blood? A struggle? He wished he had come home just a little later. But then he realized that she wasn't screaming. She was laughing.

He had heard his wife screaming many times but was much less familiar with the sound of her laughter. He went out and found her in the mud, too fat to get up. But the alligator looked as passive as ever. And then he realized—she was feeding him macaroons.

"Look," she shouted gleefully. "He likes them." She was tossing macaroons like a coach at practice, the chocolate-covered confections bouncing off the alligator's dinosaur armor. He would occasionally eat one.

It seemed to Yoni that the alligator was tolerating this because Yoni regularly fed him meat. But what would happen if he didn't feed him meat anymore? He might just leave, but he had a nice hole full of water, and according to the case as presented by the opposing side, alligators were leaving the Everglades because of a lack of water. If she kept feeding him macaroons and nothing else he would look for something bigger to eat. He realized that there was a moral issue here. Though he could not recall any specific commentary on the subject, it would be immoral to feed your wife to an alligator. He should warn her. There was no risk that she would stop. He could not remember one instance of her heeding his advice. In fact, the more he persisted, the more determined she was to do the exact opposite.

"Rifka," he warned. "You should be careful. This is a dangerous wild animal."

"What dangerous?" she said. "He eats macaroons. He's a landsman."

Yoni had tried his best. But just to make sure, he told her again, "Rifka, what you are doing is very dangerous." Now she was certain to ignore him. He started to walk away.

"Wait a minute." Rifka suddenly shot a distrustful glare at her husband.

"What?"

"What's with your beard? You look like modern ortho-dox," she said with a sneer.

"Maybe." He shrugged.

"They're not Jewish," she opined. "I mean, sure, they're Jewish, but it's not real Jewish practice."

"But suppose they eat macaroons?" he wanted to say but didn't.

Yoni was a lawyer and he understood that it was important right now that no one see him out with another woman. So he went to pray at the morning minyan, something he hadn't done in more than a year. He wanted to hear what was being said about Herschel's clean-shaven chin.

But when he got there Rabbi Herschel was already dovening, muttering and bobbing his head, and he had the same long, scraggily beard he always wore.

Could he grow it overnight? Perhaps from some hormone treatment. No, Yoni realized, it must be fake! Rabbi Herschel had a fake beard. And that meant that Rabbi Herschel was a big fake!

This thought made Yoni very happy. Maybe there were others with fake beards and Cuban girlfriends. He looked around the shul at the bearded enraptured men, wrapped in prayer shawls, mumbling their Hebrew prayers. Yoni looked for telltale signs of fake beards. Perhaps Manny Kaufman over there, who shouted rather than mumbled his prayers so that no one could tell he was faking. Yoni dreamed of what special moment, perhaps during the high holidays, he would reach over and expose Herschel with a tug on the beard. Or, maybe even more enjoyable, have a long, candid conversation with the rabbi about what a fraud it was. The whole thing was fake. His marriage was fake.

But none of this would ever happen because he and the rabbi had struck an unspoken bargain of silence. Each would be silent as long as the other was silent. *Religions were built on such bargains,* Yoni thought.

Still, he avoided Acacia. At first he reduced the food he gave the alligator so he would be hungry. He did not want to completely stop feeding him because he was afraid the alligator would leave. But he had no results. When he came home each afternoon he would hear Rifka down there, giggling and tossing macaroons. He would shout in a loud voice, "You have to stop this, Rifka. It's dangerous." In so shouting he established his alibi and at the same time guaranteed that Rifka would not stop. Every day he reduced the amount of chicken he fed the alligator until finally he fed him nothing at all.

But she was still out there every afternoon, giggling and tossing macaroons. Could an alligator live on macaroons? Finally he came home to a silent, empty house. He cautiously walked out into the "backyard." The yard at first looked like it had been covered with litter as though blown in from somewhere. Then he realized it was macaroons strewn around the yard and two empty boxes with their plastic dividers. The alligator was there, making a deep, soft moan. There was a round muddy spot where Rifka usually stood and a long muddy trough down to the alligator hole.

It was all clear. The alligator had grabbed her, dragged her to his hole, held her under the water until she was drowned, and then eaten her whole. There were probably not even any screams. Yoni could see that there was no blood—a merciful end—except for the poor alligator. How could he swallow all of her at once? He was moaning softly. He had eaten too much fat.

Acacia was not sure how she felt about Yoni now that he was not married, not religious, bareheaded, just a guy, this lawyer she was going out with. She would have to decide, which never occurred to Yoni, because he had never been in a relationship that involved choice.

This story cries out for some moral lesson—something about God and man, about religious hypocrisy or keeping and breaking covenants or about the sanctity of marriage, not to mention human life. But this is not the Talmud. It is not an allegory. It is a story and this is just what happened. If there is any lesson to be learned, it is never feed macaroons to an alligator.

THE GLOUCESTER WHALE COD

There are very many aquatic animals that are even larger than land animals. The obvious reason for this is the rich nature of water.

—Pliny the Elder, *Natural History*

▼ ▼ ▼

The macaroni doesn't lie," hissed Bonagia in her raspy voice. Angela nodded in agreement, though she never really saw how macaroni could lie.

"I see *ngustia*," Bonagia cautioned in Sicilian dialect. She saw worries ahead.

Angela had inherited Bonagia from her mother, who also asserted that macaroni always told the truth. Once a week, more on holy weeks, Bonagia would roll into their house and toss dried macaroni on the kitchen table. Bonagia seemed to roll, not walk, since there was never a visible leg movement. She was four feet tall, possibly that wide, though it was not certain, since she was always covered in floral prints to her ankles that revealed only a general roundness.

The macaroni tinkled like wind chimes on the green-spotted Formica table, and then Bonagia would poke at it and say, "I see *ngustia*, big *problema*. I see trouble."

Angela's mother believed Bonagia had predicted her husband's death. But Angela's mother was married to a fisherman and there is always *ngustia* and *prublema* in a fisherman's life. If he isn't lost at sea he will lose his mortgage, have bad catches, need boat repairs he can't pay for, lose nets, receive a new round of regulations further restricting his days, his miles, or his catch, and if none of that destroys him, the oil prices will go up or a force-9 gale will blow for the next three days. Any of those things and Bonagia would nod and say, "The macaroni doesn't lie." But Angela, also married to a fisherman, didn't need macaroni to see where life was headed.

Angela let her come over out of respect to her mother. While they sat, staring at dried pasta and drinking red wine, Beverly Boston was next door, staring into her computer and sipping a martini. Angela could see her through the window and noticed with a small degree of pleasure that some unpleasant age thing was developing under Beverly's chin. The light from the screen revealed it.

Angela had married Salvy Tatoli, and in any other town, Beverly Boston and Salvy Tatoli probably wouldn't have known each other. But this was Gloucester and they were next-door neighbors on Smith Cove, an inlet in the lee of the wind on the east side of Gloucester Harbor. It was named for Captain John Smith, who in the early seventeenth century, charting the Massachusetts coastline, had recommended the spot for anchoring. That was why the Tatolis happened to settle there more than three hundred years later.

Salvy's grandfather came over in 1927 on a salt bark from Trapani, Sicily. Although more a sailor than a fisherman, he saw the tremendous cod catches in Gloucester and he settled there and bought an eastern side trawler, a schooner with its masts sawed off and an inboard engine. He bought a house on Smith Cove, really more of a shack until he married and they fixed it up. The view was beautiful, but the smell kept real estate prices down. The splayed and salted codfish laid out to dry in the nearby fish flakes of the Gorton-Pew company made the neighborhood too redolent for anyone but fishermen. His wife, Salvy's grandmother, complained about it, but she, too, got used to it. The Tatolis could see the white building with the tower across the harbor, where a company was learning how to freeze fish. In time there were no more flakes for fish drying and this cleared the air in the neighborhood for people like Beverly Boston.

Beverly was not as different from Salvy as she appeared. Her family, the Bastanics, had arrived twenty years later than the Tatolis and opened a hardware store downtown. They sent their daughter Beverly to college in Boston and she came back a different girl. She wore fashionable clothes and shoes with dangerously high heels that made her long legs look perfect.

"Beverly sure has great legs," Salvy once commented to his father while they were sorting the cod and haddock from a net off Georges Bank. His father said nothing and his grandfather laughed and Salvy knew not to bring her up again. But it was true that she had very nice legs.

Beverly's parents thought she had become too fancy at college, and to tease her about it, they started calling her Beverly Boston. But she didn't mind. She liked the name, in part because when you got on the highway to leave town the sign said: "Beverly Boston," two of the upcoming towns, so the name was about leaving.

But then she came back and bought a house on Smith Cove. Nobody was surprised. They always come back. No one ever escapes Gloucester. Kids go off to college and settle somewhere else. But they always come back. If Gloucester is all you know, every place else seems a little phony. Beverly still wore great shoes—shoes unlike anything the broken streets of Gloucester had ever seen—long, sleek, handcrafted shoes by Garolini, Paul Mayer, and Stuart Weitzman—her three favorites. Salvy never cared about the shoes but was glad to have her long legs next door even though she seemed to have brought a husband with her.

He was a quiet man who wore herringbone sport jackets and was said to be a professor in Boston. No one knew him in Gloucester. Some said he was a history professor, others science. Some said he was a poet. He may have been a genius or he may have been a fool, but the important thing was that he wasn't Gloucester. Salvy's cousin described him as a "gewgaw she brought back from college." Salvy agreed even without knowing what a gewgaw was.

Salvy had not gotten married for years and a lot of people had thought it was because he was thinking about Beverly Boston and her long legs. Finally he married Angela, a Sicilian girl, like he was supposed to.

Angela had heard the rumors about Salvy and Beverly. It didn't worry her. Angela, with her thick black hair and burning black eyes, was, according to many, the most striking woman in Gloucester. Her mother had been beautiful, too, but Angela always thought it was wasted beauty because her husband had died and she spent her life around only women, Sicilian widows and the wives of fishermen and her. It was not the life Angela wanted, but of course her mother hadn't chosen it, either.

Angela always secretly thought that fishing would soon die out, they would be forced out of Gloucester, and it would be taken over by the Beverly Bostons. That would be their escape route.

The next year, just like Angela would have predicted if anyone had asked her, Beverly ran for mayor. Many people run for mayor, especially in years when there was no incumbent. Incumbents usually won because it was believed that anyone who had been mayor and still wanted the job deserved it. The pay for being mayor was so low that it represented a considerable loss to anyone who already had a job. The leading contenders that year were a Sicilian ex-fisherman and an Irish ex-fisherman. Fishing was going so badly now that fishermen were willing to come in and be mayor.

Beverly Boston said that fishing was over and that Gloucester should be a tourist attraction. This was enough to make half the town hate her. But the fishermen vote was split between the Sicilian and the Irishman. Beverly Boston got all the people who didn't think the mayor should be a fisherman. Secretly, she also got Angela's vote. Her escape plan. Just as secretly, she also got Salvy's vote. The legs. Angela and Salvy told each other and everyone else that they voted for the Sicilian.

The Tatolis had sold their eastern side trawler and bought a steel-hulled bottom dragger with a net that ran off the big spool on the stern. Those days when Salvy first went to sea with his father and his grandfather and they hauled in tremendous catches of huge fish and laughed and made money and Salvy stood on the bow as his father brought her into Gloucester harbor to the downtown dock where the lumpers lined up to unload the great catch on the deck, the gulls following them in screeching a salute and Salvy feeling proud because all the land people could see him and his family triumphantly back from sea—those were the days Salvy remembered as the best of his life.

Now it was just him and his cousin, who was married to Angela's childhood friend Mena. Like Angela, Mena secretly wished the fishing would end and her husband would move into the real estate business like a number of fishermen they knew.

The catch was barely enough. They weren't allowed to catch all they could, and instead of lumpers the officials from New England Fishery Management were waiting at the dock to inspect their small catch. How could you feel proud now? But he continued so that his son, Domingo, born on their best Sunday, would someday know the joy of working at sea with his father. He was still too young, although Salvy had already taught him knots. Domingo had a lobster pot that he baited and dropped and hauled from their dock in Smith Cove, and he proudly supplied the family with two or three clicking, shiny, dark monsters every week. Soon Salvy would take him to sea.

Salvy was born to fish. He claimed he could hear fish swimming below the surface of the water. Sometimes he would prove it with a heavy lead jig shaped like a cod with a razor-sharp triple hook coming out of the mouth. He would stand on the dock with his head slightly cocked to one side and instruct Domingo to listen hard. Domingo listened as hard as he could. He heard the ripple of the harbor lap the reedy shore and sound like a small dog at a water bowl. And he heard the rumble almost like peaceful snoring, of inboard engines moving into the harbor and the slap of their wakes on the hulls of moored boats. But that was all. Salvy would shout, "There," and toss the lead jig into the water, holding on to the line with both open hands. When he hit the bottom he would give a sharp yank or two and the line would straighten at a low angle and Salvy would reel it up on nothing but his bare thumbs—a striper or blue or flounder or sometimes a cod.

Angela could see how this thrilled Domingo and wished it wouldn't and hoped that soon they would be away from fishing, though she could not imagine what else her husband could do.

Salvy still loved sliding out of the harbor under an early purple sky, past Eastern Point off the port and then seeing the twin lighthouses and the black shadow of land vanish off the stern. The first apricot rays of light dabbed the gray and forceful ocean as they motored out to sea where they could pretend to be wild and free even if New England Fishery Management was using electronics to watch their every move. Fuel cost too much and their days at sea were limited, so they were not going far, but still they were going to sea and there was no other life. His cousin Anthony had gone to college just like Beverly Boston and he had come back to fish.

Bonagia lived up the hill at the fort facing the harbor and she always saw when Salvy had gone to sea and would gather her macaroni and go to Angela. "*Ngustia, prublema,* not good," she said, and shook her head.

"Why do you let her in?" said Mena.

"It's for my mother."

Angela did not suffer the same kind of torment that had been her mother's life because Angela had a phone that could call Salvy at sea. After Bonagia left with her macaroni—sometimes she would leave it and instruct Angela to cook it for dinner for *bona furtuna,* but Angela, much as she hated throwing away food, always dumped it in the garbage the minute she left—Angela always called Salvy at sea just to make sure. Sometimes he didn't answer but he would call later. This morning he couldn't answer because they were hauling up the net, birds shouting, dumping fish on the morning-lit deck. Then Salvy heard Anthony shout, "Whale! Goddamn whale!"

Salvy could only hope he was wrong. There were whales out there—big ones—humpbacks and finbacks. Getting one in your net was the worst trouble—trouble for the net and trouble with the fisheries and the government.

But when Salvy looked on the deck at the sparkling, shivering tangle of dying fish, he saw it. It was a whale cod.

"Whale cod" was the term the Boston market used for codfish that were more than six feet. Years ago they were not unusual, just one of the size classifications. But the market had stopped listing the category because none ever came in anymore. No one had seen a whale cod in a long time. This one had avoided everyone's nets for thirty or forty years. She had been around in his grandfather's day, before the good days ended with a flying steel door that hit his grandfather as the net ran out and knocked him overboard, never to be seen again.

Unless this cod had seen him. The cod had been around before that winter when his father was chopping ice off the windward side and slipped in the rigging and instantly froze to death in the sea, his body never found, either. Maybe this fish had swum by both their bodies. She could hear the rumble of the draggers, and whenever she did she ran far and fast and so had escaped all those nets and after forty years of surviving, one day she hadn't listened and glided right into Salvy's net, just the same way as his grandfather after a thousand trawls one day forgot to stay out of the path of the out-running door.

The more Salvy thought about this big fish on his deck, the more tragic it seemed. This fish was owed some respect.

"Maybe we ought to dump it over. Look, it's still alive," he said to his cousin.

They often dumped fish over, both dead and alive, if their quota was used up or the price wasn't good. But right now they had a new cod quota and the price had been good. Anthony phoned the Gloucester auction and asked what cod prices were like. They were high.

"What about for whale cod? We've got one."

"Come on. No such thing," answered Manny di Santos, a veteran in the fish business for whom whale cod was just a legend from the past.

"But suppose we do have one. Is it a good price?"

"It would be a lot of pounds."

"Yeah, but I'm not using them up if it's not good."

"It would be a real rarity, probably a good price. Big steaks."

So Anthony assured Salvy that it was a good price and they shouldn't dump it. Salvy thought a minute in silence. "Let's keep it alive."

"What for?"

"I don't want it to die. It's a survivor."

They pumped seawater into their deck tank and the two of them wrestled to get the huge slippery giant into the tank.

By the time they came to the dock Salvy had made up his mind. The inspectors already knew. A crowd had gathered to see the whale cod. The *Gloucester Times* was there with a photographer and their star reporter, who had broken the story about the couple that was eaten by their dogs because they didn't feed them.

"I'm not bringing it to market," said Salvy.

"What?" said Manny di Santos.

"I don't think you can do that," said the inspector.

"Why not? Fishermen dump fish and don't bring them to market all the time."

"What are you going to do with it?"

The fishermen at the dock were getting noticeably angry. "Got to stop this foolishness, Salvy," said Flynn, one of the leaders in the Fishermen's Association. "We are in the business of bringing fish to market. Not adopting pets."

But Salvy wouldn't turn it in. He took it to Smith Cove and built a net pen and dumped the well-fashioned netting in the cove in front of his house, moored to the dock. Mayor Beverly Boston watched. She was pleased.

Later Salvy constructed a pen from knotted monofilament held up by Styrofoam buoys. Domingo, with his skilled little fingers, helped him. Tommy Laughlin, an old-time Newfie, showed Salvy how to make it based on the cod traps they used up in Newfoundland. But this was much bigger, almost like a fish apartment, with several large net rooms like his grandfather had talked about building to trap giant bluefin tuna in Sicily. Salvy lowered herring into one of the net rooms to feed the cod. The cod thought she had journeyed her whole life to find this safe place full of food.

"It's magnificent," Salvy declared.

"That it is, boy," said Tommy in his Newfie lilt. "But don't keep her here long or you will have the whole world hating you."

"Why would they hate me?"

"Because you are going against all the rules. We hunt down animals and we kill them so people can eat them. Don't try to turn us into game wardens running zoos."

Several other fishermen stopped by to deliver similar messages, though sometimes not as politely. One even used an old Sicilian gesture that was meant as a threat. That was his grandfather's language, not his, and Salvy wasn't afraid. But he could see how angry they all were.

Not everyone was angry. The mayor braved the little gravel path between their houses in her black suede Garolinis with the rhinestones along the back to tell him what a great idea she thought it was and how happy she was to see "a fisherman who understood the future." A shudder went through Salvy's sinewy body, but he smiled politely and said nothing. He was starting to understand why the other fishermen were angry.

The party boat, the cruise ship from Provincetown, the Harbor Adventures Club—all the shoddy attempts at tourism that he and his fellow fishermen had opposed—were interested in his whale cod. There had been a dozen more bad ideas like these that the fishermen and the community had been able to stop. Now everyone in Smith Cove, including the mayor, hated the party boat because it went by their homes with loud music and bright lights, stopped at Smith Cove to point out the home of "the fisherman Salvy Tatoli" and to say that there in the dark water Salvy kept a live six-foot codfish. Some said it was an eight-foot codfish. None of them had actually seen it. They turned their spotlights on the water as though the light could penetrate the murky greenish gray and light the codfish. The passengers strained to look over the side. The cod could see these bright moons above and knew to avoid them.

Salvy didn't need lights. He would stand on the dock and he could hear the whale cod swimming. He had always opposed tourism and now he was becoming a tourist attraction. He thought of taking the fish over to the display auction, where buyers would see the now famous animal and bid good prices for it. Fisheries warned him that he had to report to them before taking it to market. As Anthony pointed out, it would not be a bad thing to use up his cod quota at a high price without spending a lot of fuel on a big trawl.

But he could not kill it. He could not explain why, but this fish had to live, it deserved to live.

Finally the Harbor Adventures Club went too far. This was a group that took tourists on scuba diving tours of the harbor. The fishermen had tried to stop them, saying it was a menace to navigation and violated the city zoning ordinance that declared that the harbor could only be used for "marine industrial activity." But after a seven-hour City Council debate, it passed by one vote. Many City Council issues these days were decided by one vote. Three on the council believed in the future of fishing and three didn't. That left one who kept switching and two who could never decide, so these were the three everybody worked on.

When Harbor Adventures started bringing divers to Smith Cove to look through his mesh, Salvy made his mistake. He petitioned the City Council to stop Harbor Adventures. As soon as he did that the Fishermen's Association and their allies in town, all the people Salvy always supported, petitioned the City Council to ban the keeping of penned-up fish in Gloucester Harbor. This, after all, was not a marine industrial activity, either. Now everything was in the hands of the City Council, which was not what anyone wanted.

Paolo Fagacchi, a fisherman and close friend of Salvy's father, ran into Salvy at the Big Shop, a chain supermarket they had both opposed, where they now did their shopping. Paolo said sadly, "Salvy, why have you turned against us?"

"It's not true."

Paolo stared at him with eyes the color of sliced black olives buried deep in valleys of crinkling brown flesh furrowed and grizzled from years of staring at the sea and said, "Isn't it, Salvy? Hmh? Then take your catch to market."

Salvy almost did just that the same evening—but he couldn't.

Bonagia stopped by and spilled the macaroni on the table. She sucked in a gasp of air and put her fingers on her mouth, her wide eyes showing shock. She whispered, "You must kill the big fish. It is a curse. Kill it as soon as you can. *Mala furtuna*. It's a *malanova*, a curse. Kill it."

The City Council met every other Tuesday evening and argued late into the night. Salvy's petition was held off and the one against him was scheduled first since if it passed, the issue of the Harbor Adventures divers would no longer be relevant.

City Council meetings and their public hearings were televised live and Salvy stayed home to watch. He would periodically go to the kitchen to get a beer from the refrigerator but also to look out the kitchen window because he noticed something strange. The mayor was home. She didn't go to the council meetings. Like him, she watched them on television. She sat in a comfortable stuffed leather chair and kicked off her satinized beige leather Stuart Weitzmans. She had by her side an enormous deep glass containing what seemed to be a martini. She also kept grabbing a nearby cellphone.

Angela caught her husband looking out the window and simply shook her head disapprovingly. She was used to it.

On television the chairwoman, Elaine Petrocino, an old East Gloucester friend of the mayor's, was asking for public comment. She would allow three minutes. Then she looked down at her desk, maybe her cellphone, and said two minutes. Salvy was almost certain he had seen Beverly texting.

Flynn from the Fishermen's Association walked up to the microphone wearing his brown sport jacket and possibly the widest tie ever made with a picture of a swordfish leaping on it. Despite his rough appearance he had an Irish eloquence when he spoke that always caught people by surprise.

"Thank you, Madame President and council members," he began. "For nearly four hundred years, four hundred years, men from this town have been going to sea, chasing and capturing and bringing to market the fish that has fed America . . ." He went on about the men of Gloucester harvesting the sea. Everyone knew the speech. He ended, "So that Gloucester remains a fishing port forever where men harvest the riches of the North Atlantic and not a kind of African plain where tourists take safaris to see the animals or some kind of a northern Bronx Zoo." This last point was powerful, because one thing everyone could always agree on in Gloucester was that they did not want to be New York—a city of shallowness and vanity, where people spent their money foolishly and rooted for the New York Yankees.

It was only a matter of time until someone brought up the fishermen's monument on the boulevard and the five thousand Gloucestermen lost at sea, not failing to point out that two of them were Salvy's father and grandfather. Salvy went into the kitchen for another beer. Meanwhile, Beverly, on her second martini, was becoming more Gloucester than most people would have ever suspected. When a council-man proposed rereading the measure calling for marine industrial activity only in the harbor she sent Elaine the message "Shut this asshole up!" and since the chairwoman pointed out in a reply that she had to let him speak, Beverly replied, "Give the son of a bitch a rebuttal!"

But even at the meeting the tone was getting tougher. One fisherman warned that if the council approved this, he would go to the state attorney general. An animal-rights activist called Salvy "a perverted torturer of helpless fish."

Before Beverly finished her second martini she managed to write and send a statement for Frank Gianchialli to read. Frank was the councilman that kept switching positions, and Beverly often helped him. He began Beverly's speech, "Salvy Tatoli is a permeate in his . . ."

"Excuse me," said the chairwoman. "He is a what?"

Frank looked down at his text in confused silence, but in the meantime, Beverly, who had quick though not always accurate fingers, had texted the chairwoman, "I made a fucking typo. Let it go!!"

Frank continued. "Even by the high standards of cour-age of his profession, Salvy is a fisherman of rare bravery. He has the courage to recognize what we all know but are afraid to say. Commercial fishing is over. Gloucester has to do something else."

Salvy reached for his remote and muttered "Shit" as he clicked off the television.

The knock on the door came sooner than he thought. Fishermen do not like to stay up late. It was five fishermen, all Sicilians. They had been drinking and their brown eyes were all large, droopy, and red like hounds'. They were all older men of his father's generation and were led by Paolo, who greeted him in the old Sicilian dialect. "Salvy," said Paolo. "Don't go against your own."

"I'm not going against anyone."

"I hope not. I say I hope not because we work in a very dangerous profession. Accidents happen all the time. That's why we have to stick together." And then all five weather-beaten red-eyed men left.

"Can you believe that?" Salvy said to his wife.

"They're an older generation. Born over there," Angela calmly explained. "But in a way they're right. You can't go against your people. You have to put up with them because they are all we have." She flashed an angry gesture out the window. "You think Beverly Boston is your friend?"

"So now those guys are my friends?"

"They're your people," Angela answered with such angry black eyes that he couldn't speak.

And then there was a smack at the front door, something between a slap and a kiss. Angela and Salvy looked at each other, motionless, and then ran to the front door. There on the stoop was a thoroughly dead ten-inch flounder. It was one of those winter flounder from Georges Bank. They had a good quota right now, but the price still wasn't high enough because oil had become so expensive and Georges

Bank was a long way to go. Salvy even knew whose fish it was because he was the only one fishing Georges Bank for winter flounder at the time. He was one of the five who had just visited.

Salvy and Angela may have been new country, but they knew what it meant when a Sicilian left a dead fish on your doorstep. Salvy went down into the basement and returned with a double-barreled shotgun. He slipped a cartridge into each barrel and went outside and climbed aboard his boat. He waited for someone to try to disturb his fish or his boat. A raven settled his big wings into the mayor's tree and stared at Salvy with a hard topaz eye and let out a squawk that echoed across the smooth harbor water. Salvy raised his shotgun to show the bird and the raven did not squawk again, just stared.

Salvy listened for sounds in the water or against the hull. Would a diver come or would someone quietly paddle up? Would they go for the hull or just for the fish? The cove was silent except for a gentle lapping of the tide and an occasional sucking sound as the hull shifted her position. He could hear schools of baitfish hurrying below and lobsters crawling on the bottom. He said he could, anyway. He watched and listened all night. Just before daybreak, Anthony came.

He did not have to say a word to his cousin. They carefully examined the boat to be certain that there weren't any "accidents" about to happen. As the engine putt-putted out of the harbor, Anthony said, "When we come in, let's take the fish to market. I mean, who needs this? Right?"

Salvy didn't answer him, but he knew that he could not stay up every night. Fog pirouetted across the water's surface and soon erased every trace of the land behind them. The sea heaved in great gray bulges with lacy white foam edges. That rolled the boat easily, a comfortable rocking feeling.

Suddenly an oddly large wave hit them broadside. No one did it. No one was to blame, except that Salvy might have seen the rogue wave if he was not asleep in the pilot-house. Suddenly the steel boat went up and around sideways and crashed down, deck-first. Neither Salvy nor Anthony had a chance to get out of the freezing water. It was no one's fault, really.

The Fishermen's Association was there first, assuring her that they would look after her and Domingo, that there should be no worries. She smiled and nodded appropriately, even though she was not certain how her husband had died. She was not sure that he had not been killed. When someone dies at sea you do not know anything for certain. You cannot even be sure that they are dead because there is no body. All the people who rush over to help you with the mourning seem like they are pushing you. They want you to bury him, but you can't. Sicilian wives and widows came over in bunches with colorful broad platters of pasta and mountains of cakes and bowls of fruit as though anxious to get the party started and Angela knew that now she, too, would be with the women the way her mother had been and live a life she had never wanted and there would be no escape.

The Portuguese priest from town and the Sicilian one from Boston both came. Beverly Boston came to tell Angela what a fine man her husband was and the two fishermen who wanted to be mayor, the Sicilian *and* the Irish one, came.

Everyone came. She was trapped. There was a protocol. They all knew what to do when a fisherman didn't come back. Each had a role to play. Even the state senator, a small man in a dark suit, came, irritating everyone with his attempts to speak Italian and not Sicilian. A tall blond man from an old Gloucester family who wanted to run for Congress made the same mistake. *"Mi dispiace, signora,"* he said in an accent that could have been Albanian and a language that Angela did not even speak. Lots of politicians made that mistake. It was funny if you were in the right mood.

Bonagia came up to her and whispered, "I tried to tell you. Fish on the doorstep is a very bad sign, *me amuri.*"

Angela stared at her. How had she known about the dead fish? They hadn't told anyone. Angela said as little as possible. She could see how angry Mena was. Mena thought Salvy had gotten her husband killed for that damned fish. She stood there with Angela, talking to the priests, but their friendship would not ever be the same.

What could Angela say? It might have been true. She

didn't know. Angela knew nothing about her husband's death. Only that he didn't come back. So she just smiled. She smiled at Bonagia, who she didn't trust, and at the red-eyed fishermen who may have killed them and at the mayor, who her husband had liked too much. Whatever was said, she allowed them to take her hand and she smiled softly. This is what she had to do—what she was supposed to do. Salvy never understood how you had to act. She loved that about him.

"It's disgraceful," said Venera, another fisherman's widow who sold cannoli and looked like she ate most of them. "Her husband just dead and all she does is smile."

Nunziata, a stern, tough-looking woman who was Salvy's most forceful opponent on the City Council, just shrugged. "People are complicated."

Angela smiled at them all and listened to their sympathy and support. It was as though they were having a contest, all saying the same lines and seeing who could sound the most sincere. But Angela knew what she had to do. She knew the red-eyed fishermen with their sincere faces and mounds of orange-greased pasta and colorful frosted cakes were going to go get the whale cod. They wouldn't ask her. They would just take it and sell it at the auction and give her the money and act as though this was charity.

Angela got Domingo to help her and with a boat hook they opened the trapdoor with the Styrofoam floats and could only hope that the whale cod had the sense to leave. It seemed as though letting the fish live was as close as Salvy came to having a last request.

Paolo hauled the big fish trap onto his dragger with its big-spooled clanky noise, but there was nothing in it except a few small baitfish, two lobsters, and a crab. For months after, men were jigging Smith Cove and then the rest of the harbor—dropping a lead-weighted hook with herring on it and bouncing it in jerky movements off the bottom. They pulled up some striper but no whale cod. The legend lived, and some fishermen searched the harbor for it for years. It was known that somewhere under Gloucester Harbor was a whale cod. Someday someone would get it.

After Bonagia left—she stopped by almost every day now—Angela threw out the dried macaroni and thought of how her life had been written long ago and there was nothing she could have done to change it. To the snare-drum sound of the dried pasta hitting the trash she smiled ironically and thought, *The macaroni really doesn't lie.*

She looked out the window and saw Domingo staring out at the harbor and she thought she knew what he was thinking. The only enduring dream in his short life, so soon crushed like a fisherman's dream, had been to go to sea with his father. Already he was talking about taking his lobster to market to earn money for the family. And in the evening he stood on the dock with his head cocked to one side to try to hear the whale cod swimming. Angela knew Domingo wouldn't escape, either.

The whale cod was not getting fed anymore, and when Angela opened the trap, the cod deserted her net home, just in time, as it turned out. She wandered the harbor looking for food. Sometimes she would see dancing jigs on the bottom, but she was not going to be deceived by that. She found some good mackerel by the harbor opening and then went out to sea to swim and hunt as she had for decades. Finally someone had escaped.

HAVANA

A Murder of Crows

Life is not merely commerce or government but something more: a commerce with the forces of nature and the government of oneself.

—José Martí

S egundo stuck the knife in the soft part of the throat right under Miguelito's silly bucktoothed face and ripped downward until the organs spilled out on the table. No one but Segundo called it a Miguelito. It was called a *pesperro*, a big, ugly, pinkish fish with yellow fins that was caught off the rocks at the bottom of Havana Harbor. Segundo looked at the triangular head with nasty thin teeth protruding from its upper lip. Did this fish not look exactly like Segundo's dear childhood friend Miguelito?

Miguelito had been the lightest-skinned kid in the neighborhood and also the funniest-looking and so everyone learned at an early age that whiteness was not worth the price. It was if you were a Fidel or a Che, but those were special people, and in Segundo's downtown neighborhood white people just ended up looking like Miguelito.

Everyone used to laugh at Miguelito, make fun of the way he looked. Silvio called him *castorucho*, ugly little beaver. It was, of course, painful for Miguelito, but even as a child he was an optimist. Most kids were then. He would pretend they were saying Castro and not *castor* and that they were recognizing something heroic in him. This was an obvious fantasy because all of the heroes of the Revolution were beautiful, wonderful-looking, nothing like him.

The best moments of his childhood were when Conchita

Carmelo, the ample light-skinned chanteuse everyone called La Mulata instead of her real name that sounded so fake, would wink and smile at him as she passed by. He would let her pass to get the best view, because although people bought her records and spoke of her great voice it was clear that her greatest talent was that three-beat swing of her ass when she sang a cha-cha-cha.

Miguelito resolved to be a better revolutionary than anyone else in the neighborhood and become *un hombre peso*, a man to be respected. He joined all the youth programs and was active with the neighborhood committees when he was only a teenager. They were encouraged to look for suspicious activity, and if they saw something, to report it. Miguelito noticed things that others might miss. What were those boxes Juan Garcia stacked in his bedroom? Why did Eva and Otoña giggle and laugh and then become oddly silent when he walked into the room? You did not want Miguelito to listen to your conversation. It did gain him the respect he was seeking. No one made fun of Miguelito. Only his family talked to him and the rumor was that they were a little afraid of him, too.

At the age of sixteen Miguelito finally hit the kind of prize he had been seeking. He caught someone who really was working with the Yumas, really was with the CIA, and by turning him in prevented a plot that involved the sabotaging of three factories.

Unfortunately the man Miguelito turned in was his uncle. Everyone in the neighborhood knew him. They even liked him, Aurelio, a happy, heavy man who smoked cigars and laughed in clouds of yellowish smoke. Now when they went to the Parque Central to eat *pastelitos* of sweet guava paste and argue with the kids who thought the Industriales were the greatest baseball team in the world, Segundo would look up the Prado, the long tree-lined boulevard, at the old stone Morro Castle, where they kept Aurelio, probably no longer fat, without cigars, and maybe not laughing. But he had tried to destroy them.

Segundo went to the park with the other kids and sometimes ate a *pastelito*, and would talk to the vendor about how to make a good *pastelito* and what was the best guava paste. He didn't want to argue about baseball because he did not like the Industriales, preferring the Metropolitanos or even Pinar del Río—in truth anyone but the Industriales. A lot of the kids felt that way because the Industriales won too much. But to Segundo, it was an argument not worth making because Miguelito was a big Industriales fan and that made the argument dangerous. Who knew where it would lead. Segundo wanted to make the Revolution work for him.

In fact, it was working for a lot of the neighborhood. Segundo's family got a large downtown house with ornate belle epoque doorways and black-and-white-tiled floors. The electricity was fed in the windows on wires he and his sister had to be careful not to touch, but it was a good home.

Segundo became an engineer. Many of the kids in the neighborhood became engineers. Segundo worked in a factory that assembled Czechoslovakian helicopters. This was a good job, but for Segundo this was still not his chance—the big chance the Revolution would one day offer him.

On the block was a respected *babalawo*, Adé Jaen, important enough that he had even been to Nigeria, sent by the government. Adé was old enough to remember his grandfather, who was born a slave and had three horizontal scars on his cheek that meant he had come from the Yoruba people. Adé knew many things. When Segundo told his mother, who was, as they say, "cut" and a follower of Adé's, that he believed the Revolution had something special for him, she said, "Go to Adé and see what is your destiny," and she gave him three pesos. He gave the money to Adé, who sat on the floor and rolled a number of cola nuts and muttered in Yoruba and confirmed that the Revolution did have a special destiny for him, though he didn't say what it was.

Not everyone in Segundo's family was a good revolutionary. But most every family had a bad uncle. He had cousins who had left and now lived in Miami. Fidel said they had all become worms, *gusanos*. But they visited Cuba a few times and Segundo could see that they had not become worms, they had just become Yumas, and Yumas were slightly odd people.

The cousins were Segundo's father's father's brother's wife, his aunt Medea, and their son Arsenio. Medea's husband never came because he had vowed to never set foot on Cuba again until the dictator was overthrown. Perhaps he couldn't come because he had vowed this a few too many times. But it was clear that Medea reveled in being back in

Cuba, wanted to walk the streets and go to all her old places and talk about how they weren't the same anymore. Arsenio insisted that Cuba was dangerous and didn't want to go outside. But both of them were very sympathetic toward Segundo and his family, who they were convinced were suffering terribly living under the dictatorship and just too afraid to say so. If Segundo's parents tried to explain why they supported the Revolution, Arsenio would give an understanding nod and begin searching the apartment for hidden microphones.

It seemed that Medea and Arsenio believed that life under the dictatorship was very hard because the dictatorship supplied no kitchen appliances. They always brought more boxes of them than they could carry so that the family had to go meet them at the airport to help carry all the boxes. Then they had to find one of those big 1950s American cars for a taxi because the Lada did not have enough space for all of the appliances. They had fans and blenders and food processors and vegetable steamers. Arsenio would always be upset because the appliances from their last trip were not in use. Segundo's parents would look at him with sad and earnest faces and explain that the electrical system could not take the added load. Arsenio would nod in sympathy and then shake his head at a regime so despicable that they didn't even provide enough electricity for appliances.

But the truth was that they didn't want to use appliances. The importance of appliances was something Cubans learned from the Yumas. Everyone Segundo knew who had visiting relatives had appliances that they could trade for things they wanted. Segundo's best friend Silvio traded appliances for clothes, designer clothes—well, not really, but he thought they were—Chinese-made Armani suits and Italian silk shirts from Vietnam, all with designer labels occasionally misspelled. As in the "Versache" pants.

Segundo just kept all the appliances in their boxes. His mother argued that they should take them out of the boxes and spread them around the apartment when the relatives came. They tried that one year, but Arsenio did not appear to be fooled by the eggbeater by the sofa or the waffle maker in the bedroom.

Segundo preferred to keep everything packed away safely. He said that one day the Revolution would offer him an opportunity and he would need the appliances. Arsenio thought he meant an opportunity to go to America, but Medea thought he simply meant enough electricity. In reality he meant something entirely different. And he would just dream up appliances and they would find them. "We have no *nata* on our flans because we don't have a Mixmaster." Such was the reality of life in Communist Cuba—*flan sin nata*. The next visit, they came with a shiny chrome Mixmaster. It even said in embossed letters "Mixmaster." Segundo had not even known such a thing existed. It just sounded like an American name, so he said it. And here it was!

While in Cuba, Medea always bought several large Cohiba cigars that they hid in their clothes when they reentered the U.S., no doubt to be smoked by her husband, who was boycotting Cuba.

Fidel announced "a special period in time of peace." In a very long speech he explained that the Soviet Union was crumbling and Cuba was in for some very difficult times. For example, since there was no longer a Czechoslovakia, there was no longer a Czechoslovakian helicopter, and so there were no longer engineering jobs for Segundo and Silvio and their friends.

This happened shortly after Segundo married Esperanza in a small revolutionary service in which he promised to do his share of the housework. In truth, he did considerably more than his share. While Esperanza was working at the pharmacy he had absolutely nothing to do other than cleaning, straightening, and polishing their home. They lived in the house where he had grown up, with its high, splendid doorways, crumbling moldy walls, and tiled floor with only a few cracks. There was still room for his parents, and his sister had married and moved to Vedado.

The house was getting cleaner and better organized every day. But soon they wanted to have children and Esperanza said that it would not be good for children to have a father who did nothing but clean house.

"That is a counterrevolutionary attitude," said Segundo

with a smile. But it was clear that his wife, the first educated member of a family of black-sugar workers, did not find this funny. "Don't worry," said Segundo. "The Revolution will offer me a good opportunity very soon. I can feel it."

And it did. Things were changing. Policy on foreign currency was changing. The island was opening up for tourism. The Spanish were coming with Reconquista haughtiness, the French with great intellectual curiosity, the British on hard-drinking holidays, the Canadians were very affable, and the Scandinavians were very tall.

Segundo and Silvio went to the new hotel school. Silvio studied to be a restaurant manager, and Segundo? Inching closer to his never-spoken dream, he studied cooking. The instructor was from Spain and he taught Segundo how to prepare the local octopus in olive oil with red chili powder, which was a national dish of the instructor's native Galicia. Coming from the fishing port of Vigo, he taught Segundo many fish dishes, especially with olive oil and garlic. When Segundo completed his program he imagined going somewhere like the Hotel Nacional, where Silvio went, but instead he was assigned to a wealthy Basque from San Sebastián who had come to Cuba to develop hotels and restaurants with the Cuban state.

The Basque taught him to make dishes from food he brought in himself—salt cod with various sauces and little green chilies that had no sting, which he learned to grill and sprinkle with coarse salt from Guantánamo. The Basque ate every night at midnight in his apartment on Fifth Avenue near the Spanish embassy that was a six-story baroque palace. The apartment was new and clean-looking, unlike any place Segundo had ever been, and the kitchen was better than the one at the hotel school, though slightly smaller. The Basque knew everything about food and Segundo learned from him, but this was not the great chance the Revolution would offer him. That was still to come.

And then it did come. The government decided that people could run their own private restaurants in their homes. They were to be called *paladares*, delicious places. People gave up their family living rooms so that foreigners could eat real *picadillo* and *tostones*, while their children stared from the shadow of the doorway to see if foreigners ate differently. But Segundo wanted more and he had been a good revolutionary all these years and had contacts and this was his chance.

His "contacts," of course, was Miguelito, who had been working his way up in the party. "Miguelito," he said to his childhood friend, "I want to do a *paladar* in our courtyard. It is a beautiful space and I could make this place a real restaurant. I can cook Gallego and Basque food and Cuban. But you know, a real place for real people, you know? With a maître d' and a wine cellar. A place to be seen in Havana."

It was this last part that caught Miguelito's attention. "Yes, yes. This can be done. We should do this." He smiled his horrible crazy-fanged smile.

———

A truck arrived with huge earthen pots of low-sprouting palm trees for the tiled terrace. Segundo did not have to ask who'd sent them. Segundo and Esperanza put out most of the tables in the house, including nightstands, which they expanded with round sheets of plywood also sent over by Miguelito, along with white tablecloths to cover them. The tables were surrounded by almost every chair in the house, some folding, some stuffed, their own rickety mahogany dining room set, some of the claws at the feet cracked or broken like fossilized remnants of earlier life-forms.

This was his moment. The old porch off of the terrace was turned into a kitchen. There was no kitchen in Havana—not the Basque, not the school, or the Nacional—with as many appliances as Segundo's *paladar*. There was a steamer for the vegetables and an electric grill for fish and a toaster oven for additional oven space and an electric can opener for the beans, which he didn't use because he had an electric pot for slow-cooking soaked beans, and a food processor for making sauces and grinding up yucca roots for *croquetas*, a toaster for the toast rounds that he would serve with Spanish sausages and French pâtés. He had a rotisserie for chickens, which he would serve in a sauce made from garlic chopped in a food processor and sour oranges squeezed by his juicer. He even had an electric *tostones* masher because Aunt Medea once saw his mother flattening the banana slices with a bottle. In truth, Segundo found the bottle easier to use and a lot of banana slices were too flat after being smacked with the automatic *tostones* flattener. He had a blender for the daiquiris and a little beater, which Arsenio said could be used for beating the egg whites in pisco sours, but he still could get no pisco, which came from Peru, so he made rum sours with egg-white foam. And there was the Mixmaster for making cakes and the house specialty, *flan con nata*.

"Adé," Segundo called to the *babalawo* who now walked with a cane, his white hair flying out wildly so the top of his black head looked like a boulder by the Malecón with a wave spraying over the top. "I am going to have a restaurant," said Segundo. But the *babalawo* just smiled because he already knew. He knew everything that happened in the neighborhood. Even in "special times," Adé could get birds and goats for sacrifices, and he promised Segundo that he could always get him meat.

Two days before he opened, Segundo started cooking beans in the Crock-Pot. Then he decided to make some toast rounds. As he turned on the toaster, before the coils even turned red he heard a short puff noise, almost like a fastball landing in a catcher's mitt. Then there was no more electricity.

"Where is Miguelito?" Segundo, who was beginning to sweat in his white chef's uniform, asked Adé, who pointed down the block. Segundo made his way down the narrow street, clinging to the crumbling walls to let smoking cars lurch past with a rumble like percolators about to squirt coffee. And, to his horror, at the end of the block, in an ornate building with a balcony over the front doorway missing half its stone balustrade, was a sign welcoming customers to the Paladar de La Mulata. She had already opened and was serving chicken, *congri*, and *tostones* nightly to customers in her low-cut tight gown—so tight, extra rolls of flesh showed everywhere and her chest rose out of the bodice like the steep soft tropical hills of Pinar del Río. Even in the dark room he could see a row of white roots to La Mulata's black pulled-back hair, like a black frame with a white mat.

But Miguelito did not seem to see her flaws from his seat as she leaned over to afford him the best possible view while he sipped rum with a bucktoothed smile and a large Cohiba, the kind Fidel had decided not to smoke anymore back in some midlife health fad.

Ignoring this situation, Segundo walked up to Miguelito as though he were alone and told him about the electricity.

Miguelito puffed rich clouds of smoke far bigger than he was and simply said, "You need more power." He gave the word "power" a special puff. "I will take care of it."

"But when?" Segundo could tell that Miguelito was playing suave for the Mulata to see.

"It's done," he said, as though dismissing Segundo. But as he walked out into the white-hot sunlight Miguelito followed him and, looking back nervously at La Mulata, said in a whisper, "Look, I am your customer. Do you understand?"

Segundo nodded uncertainly, so Miguelito exhaled smoke

and rolled his eyes at his old friend's thickness. "I intend to eat on your terrace. I will be seen there every night. It will be my place. If people need to talk to Miguelito, like you just needed me, they don't chase down the street. They come to your *paladar*, where they will find me dining on champagne and caviar."

"Caviar?"

"Yes, make sure you have it. And champagne."

"How do I get caviar?"

"The Russian commissary. It is all arranged. Everything is arranged. Even the electricity."

Segundo went back to his house, passing Adé on the way. Adé winked at Segundo. *What a world,* thought Segundo. *The Mulata winks at Miguelito and the* babalawo *winks at me.*

Segundo told Esperanza what had happened, and this was really the turning point for the *paladar*. Esperanza had not been very interested in the *paladar* until she learned about La Mulata. It was just as Che had warned. The moment you introduce private enterprise you introduce ruthless competition. Esperanza went to Silvio, who still had good clothing connections, and got him to find her a very tight satin—maybe polyester—red gown, which she tailored to the shape of her body, her black satin skin set off by red satin cloth. She would be the waitress.

That afternoon seven men in uniforms the greenish brown of overripe fruit came from the Ministry of the Interior and hung wiring—three hung and four sat and sipped the bittersweet *cortaditos* that Segundo offered as a way of testing his coffee machine.

After they left, the terrace had a web of sagging black wires. Segundo was in the kitchen when he heard a scream that sounded like the last outrage of a tough old man. He cautiously went out to the terrace and at first saw nothing unusual. He looked up to make sure his new wires were all still hanging, and there, in utter silence, staring at him, were five very large shiny coal black birds perched on the wires. *Cuervos,* he thought. Ravens. What should he do? They looked too large and too dangerous for him to enrage them in any way.

Miguelito came by for another *cortadito* to have with his cigar. Segundo pointed out the *cuervos,* but Miguelito, relighting his Cohiba, insisted, *"Cornejas."* Crows.

"No," Segundo insisted. "They are too large to be crows."

Miguelito ended the discussion with a sharply pointed glare and then ducked his head to work on relighting his cigar.

Segundo understood. They were crows. It was the official decision of the party. Crows.

Then Miguelito's small black eyes—crow eyes, it suddenly occurred to Segundo—grew bright. "It can be the trademark of the restaurant. You can call the restaurant"— he paused for a moment and then wrote the words on the air with his cigar—"Paladar de Cornejas."

Segundo felt an anger rise within him. He thought he could smell Esperanza's fury, listening out of sight in the next room. They had chosen the name already—Paladar de Esperanza. Esperanza liked it because it matched Paladar de La Mulata. But Segundo liked it for its other meaning, "the savoriness of hope."

"If we call it Crows, people will not be prepared for how big they are. People will be afraid," Segundo weakly argued.

But Miguelito dismissed the argument in a cloud of humid smoke. "That's the way crows are in Cuba. Cuban crows are very big. *Paladar de Cornejas Cubanas.*"

So the name was settled.

Adé had a 1957 two-tone Chrysler, turquoise and white, that he used to go to ceremonies and to gather sacrificial animals. If he nursed the push-button gears carefully it could get up to a good speed. Segundo borrowed it for shopping. He drove along the Malecón, where the waves were splashing onto the road that morning. The fish was being delivered, but he had to go out to his old neighborhood in Miramar where the Basque lived, past all the fine diplomat residences on Fifth Avenue, past the Chinese embassy, and turn onto a street of small houses surrounded by chain-link fences. At the end of the street was a small organic farm, just a few acres planted by his friend Mariano, who became a farmer like his grandparents after he lost his job at the helicopter factory. Segundo bought fragrant fresh-picked herbs and small bright tomatoes and a bag of bright red little round *chucha* peppers that were not nearly as fiery as they looked, and long green plantains for *tostones*. On the way back he bought oranges from a covered outdoor market in Vedado, where good revolutionaries crowded into the abandoned homes of bad revolutionaries who had wormed their way to Miami. The market, heady with the perfume of ripe guavas, had great piles of plantains and onions and oranges and some meat that was not as good as Adé could bring him.

From there he could walk past a row of rotting mansions to the Russian market. Several people stood in front of the closed door as though some event was about to take place. Some men would knock on the door; it would open a crack, but they would not be let in. Segundo thought he must have the wrong place. "Is this the Russian market?" he asked a very tall, dark-skinned man who had just been turned away at the door.

"Yes, just go knock at the door."

He did, and a blond woman came to the door. She did not look like she was really blond, but she did look like a foreigner. She asked what he wanted and he explained that he was Segundo Montero and Miguel Debrazos had sent him. The instant he pronounced Miguelito's name the door was opened. Inside was a very small store selling American toiletries and some foreign liquors and a few Russian items— all on closed shelves behind counters. They did have caviar, both red and black. Miguelito had not said which color he liked. The red, the cheaper one, at fourteen pesos for a four-ounce tin, was expensive enough.

He bought Esperanza some American shampoo in a white bottle, called Dove. It was odd the way of late everything seemed named after birds. He should ask Adé about this. He bought a bottle of red vermouth to make Americanos because he had a reservation for ten Yumas. *Do americanos really drink Americanos?* he wondered.

He was very excited about this reservation. He had never met real Americans who weren't born in Cuba. Two years before he had been excited because the Baltimore Orioles were in the country to play the Cuban national team and the Basque had Segundo cook a meal with three of the players as guests. But these Americans turned out to be born in the Dominican Republic. This night, he thought, he would be cooking for real Americans.

He asked the blond woman if they had any pisco from Peru. They didn't.

Segundo ripped along the fish's belly, cutting fillets while thinking about Miguelito. He had found some Catalan champagne, some Cava for him to drink with the caviar. The important thing was the tall Spanish crystal champagne flute he had found for him to drink it in. It was, after all, the glasses that made it champagne. He had learned that in hotel school.

Miguelito insisted that he be served by the maître d', Silvio. Segundo could not decide if this was because Silvio was looking so elegant or if it was at last revenge for having

called him a beaver all those years ago. Silvio had found a
white tie and tails complete with gold studs, high-collared
white shirt, white tie. He looked like the men at the clubs in
the pictures before the Revolution. Esperanza in tight red
satin, it seemed to Segundo, was one of the great sights of
Havana. The American shampoo had not worked, made her
hair look as though it had received an electrical shock. But
she wet it and pulled it back tight on her head, which was the
exact way La Mulata always wore her hair.

Everything was ready. The fish was filleted. A sauce with
garlic and *chuchas* and herbs had been puréed in the food
processor. The small American fryer was heating oil to
exactly 85 degrees centigrade, which he had calculated to
be exactly 185 degrees on the American dial. The toast was
toasted. The chickens were slowly spinning in the rotisserie. The sour oranges had been juiced. The beans were in
the Crock-Pot. The daiquiris were in the blender. The octopus was steaming. The *ropa vieja*, which used to take his
mother five hours to make, was in the pressure cooker and
would be ready in another twenty minutes. The *nata* was
whipped for the desserts. The flan was in the electric flan
maker. He even had some dough kneading in the bread
maker. The electricity was holding up, and of course the
crows were lined up on the wire.

Yumas, Segundo had been informed, are always on time,
and it was true. At exactly eight o'clock the ten of them
arrived in flowered shirts and those five-peso straw hats
they sell in Habana Vieja and the bright rose faces white

people get when they come to the tropics. They were exactly what Segundo thought they would be, and they followed like ducks as Silvio ushered them onto the terrace. He thought that they might enjoy seeing the appliances in his kitchen. He might show them after dinner.

"Look at the ravens," a woman with pleasant fleshy exposed arms squealed from her sundress.

"No, Madame," said Silvio in the correct English he had learned in hotel school and a perfect voice that Segundo have never heard before. "Those are Cuban crows."

"Are you sure? They look like ravens. Are they dangerous?"

"Not at all. They just sit there."

"Why?"

Silvio, who had been well schooled in revolutionary dialectic, thought for a second and then said, "Because that is their place."

Miguelito entered in a puff of pastel smoke. He was wearing a white linen suit, a kind that had not been seen in Havana in some time. It was the look Miguelito said he wanted, though it seemed surprisingly pre-revolutionary. But then again, so was caviar and champagne. Silvio had found it for him. It looked several sizes too big and the left padded shoulder drooped down. Only the red suspenders—another Silvio find—saved his voluminous pants from unseemly disaster.

Silvio greeted him at the door. "Good evening." It was the best he could do. Miguelito had hoped for a *"señor,"* but this was, after all, just Miguelito. Silvio ushered him to a corner table he had picked, a mahogany table with a round marble top that Segundo and Esperanza used to use for family photos in their upstairs living room. It was placed in the corner by the largest potted palm so that Miguelito could be partially hidden behind the palm with clouds of cigar smoke marking his spot.

A couple dressed in practical clothes as though they had just been camping came in. When Segundo took the reservation he had hoped by their accent in Spanish that they were also Americans, but now they were speaking French and insisting they were from Canada.

Silvio told the large American table that their waitress would be out right away.

Esperanza made her red satin entrance. As she walked across the terrace every eye followed her, even the crows. Was she going to dance? To sing? To embrace a lover from some hidden recess on the other side of the room? Her heels clip-clopped across the tiles. It was hard to believe that she was only going to wait on a table. She offered them all Americanos to start, and the eagerness with which they accepted made Segundo smile, watching from a small kitchen window. He was right. That was what Yumas drank.

While Esperanza took orders at other tables Silvio brought Miguelito a chilled bottle of Cava and a crystal flute and went to the kitchen to prepare the caviar. He arranged toast on a turquoise plate and piled the coral-colored salmon eggs like polished topaz cascading over the plate. Segundo even had a silver caviar spoon left behind by the family that had abandoned this house before his family moved in. It was a subject of much laughter when he was a child and the family would imitate Aunt Medea in reverse—"*gusanos pobrecitos* living in Miami forced to eat their caviar with no spoon."

As Silvio was bringing out the caviar, two British couples walked in with no reservation. Segundo based his day's shopping on the reservations, but surely there was some extra. Silvio presented the platter to Miguelito, at the same time working out in his mind an elaborate ritual about squeezing the four in even though they had no reservation.

Suddenly a hoarse scream echoed through the terrace and all the customers looked up. All of the crows fluttered their wings and a few issued short squawks. One of the British men apologized in diplomat Spanish for not having reservations and said they would call next time. Silvio tried to tell them they could stay, but they were gone.

"It's a whole damn murder of them," said a large American with an enormous broiled red-balled head barely covered by his too-small five-peso straw hat. One of the people with him, a gray-haired American woman, still beautiful in one of those off-the-shoulders tops that Cubans hadn't worn in a long time, though, Segundo thought, maybe they should, looked up uneasily at the row of birds. "Why do you say 'murder'?"

"That's just what they're called," said the large redhead.

"Why?" she insisted,

"That's just what they're called. A pod of whale, a pride of lions, a murder of crows."

"Are they dangerous?"

"No," said Segundo. "They are really ravens."

"Ah," said the big broiled head from under his little straw hat. "Then it's an unkindness of ravens."

This was what the Yumas were like. They were all experts on something. Their government would not let them come to Cuba unless they were an expert doing research. Segundo tried to decide what kind of experts they were. Clearly not ornithologists or bird-watchers because they did not appear to like birds and they didn't know a raven from a crow. But they could be biologists. But Segundo decided that they were linguists. The one with the big red head looked like a linguist. Wasn't that a linguist's head?

"Well," the woman said, and smiled uncertainly. "Unkindness is better than murder."

"Are they dangerous?" asked a small worried man in a lime-colored guayabera, who was with the Americans but spoke Puerto Rican Spanish.

"Why do you say that?" asked the American woman next to him with the bright white lines on her shoulders from having worn a different dress in the daylight.

Just then several crows let out a scratchy howl. The Americans all looked up uncertainly. And that was it. They finished their meal with hats on, casting nervous glances at the birds on the wires, the murder of crows.

Night after night, usually at about eight-fifteen, the crows would squawk and the customers would become uneasy. They even tried not opening until eight-thirty, but

still about fifteen minutes into the service the oily black
birds squawked.

Reservations were canceled, diners left without dessert.
Sometimes customers came in and changed their minds
and left. Esperanza sometimes heard them mention "La
Mulata." There was another restaurant at the end of the block.

What did the crows want? Why did they come to his
paladar? Just like Segundo's team, they lined up every
night, waiting for customers that didn't come. So it wasn't
the customers that drew them.

Segundo consulted with Adé, who just smiled and nodded. Then Segundo handed him a rolled wad of twenty-one
peso notes. Adé offered to slaughter a dove in the dining
room in the presence of the crows, but since this might also
be in the presence of customers and he did not think that
Yumas would be understanding, he declined this offer. Adé
shoved the bills into the pocket of his baggy Romanian blue
jeans and winked. What would he do?

Miguelito, whose gods were not African, consulted with
the government. He was informed that Segundo was not
allowed to harm the crows. However, they did furnish him
with a piece of equipment, a crow repeller. A green government truck delivered this machine and it looked like it had
been left over from Soviet times, which is to say that it was
very large, it was made of blackened steel, and it looked
like the perforated barrels of several large-caliber machine
guns stacked vertically and sprouting metal wings at several
heights. When plugged in—another drain on electricity—it

emitted a sound like the creak of a rusty door hinge, but one continuous creak. The crows didn't mind it, but the customers did, driving the few he still had away.

After two weeks the only customer at the Paladar de Cornejas Cubanas was Miguelito, and his patronage also seemed uncertain—not that he paid for anything, anyway. The Paladar de La Mulata down the street was so busy that reservations had to be made at least a week in advance. One day La Mulata was leaving Adé's and ran into Miguelito on the narrow street and smiled and winked at him exactly the way she had twenty-five years earlier. "You should eat at my restaurant. I have the best chicken in Havana."

"I don't eat chicken."

"What do you eat? I can make it for you."

"I only eat caviar."

She smiled and stared at him. Her nose was almost touching his. He could see the dried, folding skin under her brave chin. She whispered, "I will serve you caviar on my naked breasts and you can lick it up all night, one egg at a time."

"Actually," he said awkwardly, "I prefer it just on a plate."

The Cuban crows left the *paladar*, whose name was changed to Paladar de Esperanza. Soon reservations needed to be made a week in advance. The crows perched instead on the broken balcony over the entrance to the Paladar de La Mulata, which made people hesitate to enter, even if they did have reservations. Her one loyal customer was Miguelito, who dined on caviar in her living room restaurant every night. Segundo could not help laughing. It was Miguelito. For some reason the crows followed him.

One night—one of those lonely nights with a starless sky and fog meandering in from the harbor—as she brought him his caviar in an otherwise empty living room she said, "Listen, Miguel."

And he did, because no one had called him that in a very long time. "Miguel, why don't you come upstairs with me."

Miguelito nodded and she climbed the stairs and he followed, placing his hands, fingers spread wide, on the globes of her celebrated *mulata* ass, which he had been wanting to do most of his life.

The birds outside started squawking, but Miguelito and the Mulata didn't care. Alone at last with their goal in view, the birds flew in and glided onto the little table in the living room, standing in a circle around the plate of caviar. After some small disputes about who got to stand where, they took turns pecking at the glowing coral-colored eggs on the plate one by one. The entire murder ate.

GLOUCESTER

The Science of Happiness in North Shore Frogs

But there is trouble in store for anyone who surrenders to the temptation of mistaking an elegant hypothesis for a certainty.

—Primo Levi, *The Periodic Table*

▼ ▼ ▼

Frogs are not really happy," explained Doktor Grete Adlgasser, Opal's mother, who knew these things. "People think they are happy because they look like they are smiling. But that is just the shape of their mouth so that they can uncoil their tongue very rapidly to catch flies."

"Why do they catch flies?" Opal asked.

"That is their food," her mother explained.

"So when they get one, it must make them happy," said Opal triumphantly. For a second she felt as though she had won.

But of course she never wins, and her mother answered, "It doesn't make them want to smile." Her father, Herr Doktor Heinz Adlgasser, concurred. "Why would a frog smile?" The idea seemed to make him smile, and Opal was pretty sure this wasn't just to catch flies.

Opal's parents were always right. It was an established fact. Her mother was a biologist and her father a physicist. Her mother taught at Harvard in a building Opal liked to visit only because they had most every kind of flower reproduced in glass standing in bloom forever delicate as the real ones. She didn't visit her father at MIT.

They were both famous. Her father, who championed string theory, had won a Nobel Prize for his work on the slowing of time for muons in motion. He had explained this many times to Opal, but she didn't understand it and didn't want it explained again.

In the summer they left Boston for their hundred-year-old stone house with colored glass windows like a church in the woods on the North Shore. It was a good place to be in the summer. As soon as you left Boston, or at least when you got past tough and grimy Chelsea, the world turned green and wooded and seemed to be filled with ever more wildlife, as though they had come from wilder parts of New England to summer in the North Shore just like Bostonians. There were more and more rabbits, brave little animals that dared to come out because the grass in the fields was so good to eat. Opal loved the rabbits, but they were too quick and they ran when they saw her. There were also black bears and coyotes, which Opal's mother said had come to eat the rabbits. Opal's mother had reduced biology to who eats and who is eaten. Opal never saw a bear or a coyote, but sometimes she would hear strange high-pitched dog howls and she hoped the rabbits heard them, too, and knew where to hide.

In addition to the bears, coyotes, and rabbits, the Adl-gassers' friends were drawn to the North Shore in the summertime. Some were men like Franz Heidler, who had won the Nobel Prize in chemistry for his work with nucleic-acid proteins and came all the way from New York. Some were women like Erna Hoff, who had possibly proven or disproven something about quarks. Erna liked Opal and thought of herself as someone who liked children, though she had none of her own. With an arm around her—which made Opal nervous—she explained to Opal all about quarks, how it was a particle with a strong force; how there were six different kinds; how they came in red, green, and blue; and how her concern was the blue. Opal nodded politely but in truth had no idea what a quark was other than it being something they all liked to argue about.

And there was Berndt Kaidel, who worked on special relativity in quantum mechanics and was on the threshold of proving Einstein wrong about the constancy of the speed of light, except that a man in Finland claimed he had already disproven Kaidel.

A great deal of their discussions were about Kaidel's theory, which Opal didn't understand any better than quarks. Her parents and their friends would probably be shocked to know that she didn't even understand Einstein's theory, let alone Kaidel's argument against it or the Finnish argument against Kaidel.

The scientists never brought their spouses unless they, too, were German scientists. They were all German scientists from good German families that had fled the bad Germans, except that there were always rumors about eighty-five-year-old Heidler. They sat comfortably in the thick upholstered furniture in the dark-wood living room and discussed the speed of light while sipping expensive imported fruity wine from long, slim, green bottles.

The only nonscientist in the house was Opal. She was eleven years old. It was assumed that eventually she would be a scientist, too. She never argued with this, but she found it hard to believe because though they were all speaking English, she could not understand anything they said. And they never gave her a taste of their wine, either.

She wondered why they always spoke English, since they were all German. The only German she ever heard was between her parents when they were talking about her. She knew this, first of all because she kept hearing the word "Opal," which seemed to her a ridiculous misstep for people who were always described as "brilliant." But also, she didn't tell them, but she could understand some German.

Opal spent her summer in the pool. She had eight bathing suits so that there was always a dry one. Some were one-piece, some two-, different cuts and shapes, but they were all one hue or another of green. She insisted on that.

The pool was in a shady gardened area with tall twisting trees and winding vines. When she first walked out, the frogs could see that it was she and they were always glad to see her. They were smiling. As she came closer it was harder for them to make her out, but they followed with their eyes and they knew that Opal had come. One would float toward her, showing only his eyes above the water.

Sometimes she would hear a coyote in the distance; sometimes she would see the last white fluffy trace of a grazing rabbit. Sometimes, especially later in the day, she would see a raven circling overhead. Her mother said that the raven was just waiting for something to die and then he would call his friends. Opal asked if he would hurt the frogs and she just shrugged, which was a Germanic "maybe." But the raven would leave when she came, which might have been another reason why the frogs smiled and were happy to see her.

She would swim the length of the pool with one of the frogs. They were strong, fast swimmers, but she was a lot longer, so she could keep up with a frog.

Once on the other side the frog would stretch out his arms and legs and float, keeping just his eyes out of the water. Sometimes Opal would reach from underneath, palm-up, and lift the frog out of the water. He was not worried. He would let her do it. The frog felt so small but powerful in her hand—like something concentrated and vibrating with life. It was a good feeling.

One day after she had tried to listen to Erna Hoff try again to explain quarks to her, she wandered sadly to the pool and looked at the frogs. There were two. Sometimes there were three or four, sometimes only one, but this day there were two—both smiling at her.

Suddenly she remembered all the stories from her childhood—"and then the princess kissed the frog . . ."

He wouldn't have to be a prince. After all, she wasn't a princess. But she just wanted a boy she could go out to the pool to talk with and escape the quarks. Would it work? She could try. She slipped into the water in her green two-piece and waded over to the resting frog, slipped her hand below and scooped gently upward until the frog, green and shiny and coiled with energy, stood, knees bent, in her palm.

She looked closely at it, trying to determine if it was male or female. She would have to ask her mother sometime how to tell. If it turned out to be a girl to talk to that would be fine, too. But maybe it would work only with a boy? Or was that the kind of prejudiced thinking she had learned to reject in her school in Boston?

She brought her hand to her face and pursed her lips and kissed the frog on the lips. Its lips felt hard against hers. But it did not even move, didn't jump away, just crouched in her hand and smiled. Nothing else happened. She wondered how much time this would take.

The next morning Opal was anxious to get to the pool. She noticed while brushing her teeth that she was looking very pale and she worried that her mother would think she was sick and not let her go to the pool. But no one really noticed her at breakfast. They were arguing Einstein. Kaidel pointed out, "Einstein never called it relativity, he called it invariance."

"Never, Berndt?" Opal's mother questioned.

"Don't you see, dat vas de mistake. Invariance and relativity are not za zame sing."

Opal slipped away to the pool. She really was very pale-looking, but fortunately no one noticed. In fact, as she stepped into the water her legs started looking so pale they were almost greenish. There were three frogs in the pool and a fourth under a broad leaf at the edge of the pool area. She was certain that one of them had to be the one she had kissed and yet there was no sign of "metamorphosis." In her mind she pronounced the word with a German accent to sound more scientific. This was her experiment. She might even start to keep a log the way scientists do.

Days went by and still all the frogs remained frogs—exactly the same. Her color still didn't look good, she was more greenish than ever, but her parents still had not noticed. They were busy with "the quarks," as Opal increasingly referred to their guests.

Then one day on the steps as she was about to leave the pool she did a deep knee bend and leapt out of the pool in a way she had never done before, landing on the tiles with a strange slapping sound. She looked down and saw that her feet were more than twice as long as they used to be and her long toes were all connected. She had webbed feet.

What had she done? She was frightened. She'd better go show her mother.

It was hard to walk now. Her big flat feet were making sucking and slapping noises as she walked into the house. Opal knew she could get there more efficiently by jumping, but this was a little disturbing and she did not want everyone's attention.

"Dis is nonsense," said Heidler, the energetic octogenarian, the fuzzy white crown around his shining bald head shaking so that he looked like a symphony conductor in the throes of Beethoven. "You biologists always talking about what is and isn't hardwired. There are no choices. The physical world shows us this. If you take acetone peroxide and you add heat you get a big boom. It will explode every time. It does not decide to explode."

"Yes," said Opal's mother with forbearance. "But with animals there is an element of choice, just like human beings have choice. We don't know how much choice an animal has."

"You know what Nietzsche said, Grete? We invented choice so we could have guilt!"

But suddenly Grete shrieked, "Opal!"

Finally she noticed, Opal thought.

"Opal," shouted Grete. "You are tracking water all over the living room!" She ran into the hallway closet and came back with Opal's turquoise-and-white rubber beach thongs. "Here, put these on."

How does she imagine this will work? thought Opal. *Just look at these feet. You are confronted mit ein physical impossibility,* Opal thought to herself in her mock German accent.

But Grete slipped them on and they fit the same as always, and a confounded Opal just walked out of the room as the quarks continued their discussion.

Every day Opal looked more like a frog, but no one noticed, no one except the frogs, who smiled more every time they saw her. For a while she was afraid that it was a mocking smile, but frogs are very welcoming and she could swim with them and jump with them and even take her turn grabbing flies because she now had a long, sticky tongue that unfurled from the front of her mouth, making talking almost impossible. What did it matter? She had no one with whom to talk, anyway. She learned to croak and often exchanged croaks, both the deep ones and the higher-pitched one. She would float on her belly in the pool with only her bulging eyes breaking the surface. Sometimes she would hop right through the living room, but the quarks never noticed.

It was fun, really.

One afternoon in the living room her mother turned to her father and said in German, "Heinz, have you noticed how much happier our Opal is of late? She always has this big smile."

Opal understood exactly what she said and she smiled, and no matter what her mother thought, it really was a smile.

IDAHO LOCAVORES

A Trilogy of the Sawtooth Wolf

The roaring of lions, the howling of wolves, the raging of the stormy sea, and the destructive sword are portions of eternity too great for the eye of man.

—William Blake, "Proverbs of Hell"

▼ ▼ ▼

Part One: Hunger on the Big Wood River

Everybody wants to eat someone. A flock of ravens, black and hungry, flew out of the Sawtooth Range and picked up the winding trail of the Big Wood River, where the wolves would lead them to more food. The high ridges were still too frozen and snowbound to provide much food for hungry elk or moose, and they had wandered down to the stands of thin white aspen and black-barked cottonwood that filled the floodplains, where the first buds of spring could be eaten. There the wolves were waiting.

Jack Bondy walked along the bank, not looking for the ravens or the elk. Little black bugs, midges, were hatching, a mysterious birth on the surface of the river. As he walked his boots sank into the soft unpacked snow, good skiing snow, he thought. But he would not ski today because it was March 31, the last day of the winter fly-fishing season on the Big Wood River, and rainbows were coming to the rippled icy surface because they wanted to eat the midges.

Jack Bondy was the only one who was not trying to eat. To the others along the Big Wood, he was the only incomprehensible one. He was not allowed to keep the trout he caught this time of year, so he was not after food. All winter

long he had been trying to catch one rainbow, who seemed to just laugh at his carefully tied flies. He had vowed to get this fish in his net before the season ended.

He had had the fish on the line twice this winter. The first time, the guides on his rod had clogged with ice and the fish had broken away before he could strip any line. The second time, just three weeks before today, the fish leapt out of the water, trying to run as he set the hook. Bondy could see it was a female, fat with eggs, and maybe twenty-five or more inches long. While Bondy took in these calculations—only for a second—she unhooked herself and swam off. "I'm going to get you," Jack Bondy swore to himself. He saw her two other times. Once, she was just a shadow, but he was sure it was she. But she wouldn't rise. She wasn't hungry. Another time she was holding up, working her fins to stay still in a pool so clear he could see her pink stripe. She might be even bigger than he thought. He tried several flies, but she wasn't interested. He streamed a yellow nymph so close it almost bopped her on the nose, and this got her attention but the nymph was moving too fast in the current and she didn't follow.

If he caught her today and released her, he could catch her again in the summer when she would be even bigger. Every time a fly drifted past her she made a decision. She knew what would happen if she chose the wrong one. But she had to eat. With each choice she grew a little smarter. He could get smarter, too. That was the importance of having choices.

Bondy sidestepped the elk droppings as he walked along the bank, stepping onto the slippery river rocks in a few places to cast. The elk had retreated up to a low ridge and looked down at him. He had caught one of the midges the day before and held it up to the sunlight, and a slight blue glow could be seen in the underbelly of the little black bug. So he had tied little black flies with a touch of blue down and had tied one on his line after a big yellow stone fly, a silly-looking thing that some rainbows were actually swimming up to just below the surface to eat.

He walked along the bank, occasionally stepping into the slippery rocky-bottomed river, looking in all the deep pools he knew. Two black mergansers, their red beaks sticking out like fishing tackle, flew low over the river in tight formation just above the shining surface, banking their wings to take the bends in the river. They, too, were looking for fish, but Bondy could see that they weren't having any more luck than he was.

The trout had turned brilliant because they were ready to spawn, which was why the season was shutting down. They were hungry, rising all around him, with a flash of colors as fleeting as a dream. He was standing in a black-and-white world—gray sky, white mountains, black cottonwoods, white aspen, slate-colored water—and that split second of rainbow was dazzling. Its only matching color were the bright red willow twigs coming up thick and at odd angles along the black-and-white banks like the crests of angry fighting cocks. But unlike the willow, the trout had color for only a second until they plunged into the cold, clear water and turned dark again, indistinguishably green against the rocky riverbed, vanishing so that you could never be certain that you really saw it.

His legs were held by the cold hug of the river against his waders. It was not so much his cold legs he worried about, it was his feet. Already some toes were numb. When he lost all feeling he would have to leave because the rocky bottom was slippery and he had to be able to step skillfully around the big rocks. If he fell he would have to leave and get out of his wet clothes quickly.

When his cast was right, trout would hit his midge the second it landed, as though trying to catch him by surprise and steal his rod. When he held on, they swam off furiously. He would give them a little line, bring them in, unhook them, and watch them swim away. Most of them were small, brash young trout who would know better by next year.

Bondy chose a favorite spot where the Warm Springs ran into the Big Wood. The beavers had been there and had knocked three cottonwoods into the river, built a little home with the twigs and branches, and stripped the bark to feed the family. The beavers had left the three logs white and shockingly naked in the stand of black-trunked trees. Dams always change rivers. Now the cold, rushing slate-gray water of the wrongly named Warm Springs charged into the Big Wood, gurgled angrily as it hit the logs, swirled past them, and rushed along the Big Wood, creating a deep and quiet pool on the other side of the log where a trout could rest in still water and feed on the midges that swept past him in the current. Bondy could cast just on the edge of the shallow golden water and the deep green. This was the spot.

He was not looking for a brash young trout, though he hooked a few more of them. His quarry had size and experience and, no matter how hungry, never rushed to pounce. Bondy gingerly waded into the river, feeling the slippery rocks through his waders with his still-nimble toes, tying a fresh midge on his line, inching into casting position. He saw her now, at first just a shadow, maybe a rock. But then it moved. It was she.

He backed toward the bank so that she couldn't spot him. She stopped moving. She hadn't seen him. He worked at an angle so that she wouldn't see his shadow.

Still undetected by the trout, he was being watched by a pair of keen yellow eyes—a gray wolf was hunkered in low in the beaver hutch, watching. There were no more beaver. The wolf, known in the pack as Nose, had taken care of them the day before. He crunched them in his jaws one by one— first the papa, then the mama, then the young one. The beavers were not quick enough to get away and for Nose it was an easy hunt. He didn't need any pack mates.

Wolves had not been hunted in the Sawtooth and White Clouds for more than forty years and Nose had no memory of people as dangerous. But Lord and Lady had a tremendous fear of them, not from their own experience but from genetic memory of poisonings, cowboys roping and dragging wolves to death, terrible things—they warned the pack to stay away from humans because they were extremely dangerous. As soon as the wolves picked up the human scent they hid, except that there were dogs with human smell and the wolves found these animals agreeable and would sometimes let them run with them.

Nose, of course, listened to Lord and Lady and so when he smelled a human, he too hid. But now, for the first time, he could watch one up close. He watched the human with fish all around him trying to do something foolish with the long stick and Nose couldn't help wondering, *How dangerous could they be?*

Lady had five pups that needed food. Nose ate Papa beaver, who was larger and he did not want to have to carry. Instead he brought back Mama for the pups. This day he had come back to get the young one that he had buried and frozen. The ravens who had feasted on the remainder of the papa beaver were back for more. But now there was a fisherman.

Bondy dried off his flies by whipping his line back and forth, prescribing graceful elongated circles in the air over the river. Then with a flick of his wrist the line straightened out and the fly landed on the seam between the two colors of water—the fast green and the slow black. The fly drifted deliciously off the ledge in the river. Below, the big rainbow studied the passing midge. She was always hungry when she was ready to spawn, but something told her to pass this one by. Something about this one reminded her of those other ones, the bad ones that had nearly yanked her out of the river.

She saw a midge she liked and she leapt and ate it and she retreated back to her spot in the pool. All afternoon Bondy drifted his feather midge past her and she was never fooled by it, leaping up for the right midges, letting Bondy's pass.

Hidden in the beaver dam, yellow eyes flashed side to side as Nose watched the human, spellbound, fascinated.

He detected an elk smell, which at first he attributed to the droppings along the bank. Then he caught a glimpse of a cow on the ridge—several of them. He would deal with them later with the pack. For now he was watching the human. Overhead, the ravens were doing the same thing. They didn't know what the wolf was going to do, but surely it would lead to food. Wolves always lead to food.

Bondy did not see the wolf, did not sense him watching. It was unfortunate, because everyone was talking about wolves and he really hoped to one day see one.

It started to snow and the wind brought in colder air and Bondy's toes were numb from the cold through his boots and waders and he reeled in his line and walked off. The trout rose for another midge and landed with a splash. Bondy pretended not to hear it. The first day the Big Wood reopened for spring he would come back and get her. But for now the truth was that he had not eaten breakfast and he was getting very hungry.

Nose came out from his hiding place, leapt in the river with his jaws open, and crushed the trout, snapping her backbone before swallowing her whole, eggs and all. Nose would go tell the pack about the elk who had moved from the ridge, but all the while, Nose was thinking that these humans didn't look all that dangerous. They couldn't even hunt down a fish.

▼ ▼ ▼

Part Two: Sheepish in Sun Valley

I n his heart, the Lord did not fear humans. After all, they were the ones who put him in power. He was just a beta wolf in the north when he was captured. At first he was terrified of their cages and their strange smells. One thing all wolves agreed on, humans smell bad. But they treated him respectfully and brought him down here, where he could start his own pack and rule. They were gentle creatures full of kindness. They put a collar on him with a radio signal and he didn't like wearing it. At first he would rub his neck against fir trees to try to get it off, but in time he was used to it.

If he even looked at a human he would see the disapproving face in the Lady. The Lady was not a pure gray Canadian wolf. She was partly from a line of Rocky Mountain wolves, and within her nerves and synapses she carried memories of the bad times when they were tortured and beaten and poisoned, when wolf hides hung from houses and almost everyone was killed. She wanted the pack to stay away from the humans.

So when the pack was together, such as on big hunts,

when they took elk and the time they got the moose, they all avoided humans and their smell. But now the Lord and a lot of the boys and men had a sense that they were a big pack and didn't have to fear anything. By summer, when the pups were grown, they would be nineteen. This was a pack that could rule the mountains and even have a presence in the valley.

Sometimes late at night they would go into Ketchum. They would wait in the moon-sparkled cliffs at the edge of town until all the strangers had gone back up their mountain to rest up for another day of sliding down it—why?— and the locals would finally stumble out of the Pioneer and the Sawtooth and go home. Nose would watch these oafish stragglers and he couldn't help thinking that if the pack ever wanted to take a human, they could get one of these at night. He wouldn't do it, of course. Even he was not crazy enough to attack a human. Besides, they smelled so bad. But he had a good strategic mind and he could never resist thinking about possible lines of attack. He couldn't help thinking that he had the mind of a leader.

When the last light went out on Main Street in Ketchum, the male pack, ten of them, would gallop through town so fast that even if a human did see them he couldn't be sure. Malcolm saw them one night on his way home and shook his head and thought he must be drunk, which in fact he was.

After they ran through town they might keep going straight to the sheep fields, where there was easy food. The Lady had warned them about this meal, but she ate it anyway. To most of the pack it was better than elk, which could hurt you with a hoof, and definitely better than moose. They had gotten a moose last year and the giant had nearly killed half of them. Surely some of them would have died if Nose hadn't grabbed on to the moose's nose, the trick for which he was named, and held on until the others could get its haunches, belly, and finally tear out his huge windpipe. Sheep was better, even if it carried traces of human smell and even if sometimes it was necessary to fight off dogs that smelled human.

The pack could grow because there was plenty of food, and sometimes, when they were all well fed, instead of going straight at the end of town they would turn left and run up to the mountains where the humans slid in the daytime. It was empty there at night. There was nothing to hunt except an occasional rabbit because the slopes smelled entirely of humans. But the wolves liked to play there, leaping and wrestling. Then they would run to the top of the highest human mountain, where there was a building that was always empty at night, and they would have a good howl and for just that moment, the human mountain was theirs.

Tom LaMotte, hosting his Hollywood crowd in his villa, would stop the party, shsssh everyone, point a finger and pose the way he did in that thriller shot in Alaska, and whisper in his melodious baritone, "Wolves."

Clement Stedlick, in his low-roofed glass-and-concrete home cantilevered on a high ledge of mountain, would look up from his more or less empty computer screen and out at the moonlit slopes and feel haunted but not inspired, which is what he was hoping to feel.

In their three-room house, Cathy, the high school science teacher, who loved nature and thought all the talk about the dangerous wolves was an exaggeration, turned to her husband and with her classroom authority pronounced, "Just coyotes."

Etxegarray, out on his sheep ranch, eyed his gun rack longingly.

Tom LaMotte walked into Annie's, the brightest star in a celebrity crowd. In his silver ski suit with cobalt trim giving a reflected glow to his perfect body, he looked every inch the action hero he was supposed to be. Annie was known as a locavore, which Tom had quipped, "Sounds like a kind of wolf." The crowd all laughed, not that it was funny—they had all heard disturbing rumors about Sawtooth wolves wandering into Sun Valley—but because it was Tom LaMotte. Annie was trying to cook with local products, an effort that had won her awards in national food magazines. The breakfast specialty was fresh eggs from Carey, trout—steelhead, since rainbow could not be taken—and fresh mountain herbs. Spring was late, but there was always rosemary, and she had found thickets of thyme and even a few spring onions in the lower valley fields.

"Skiing today, Mr. LaMotte?" Annie asked as she hurried up to show him to the best table.

"Tom. It's Tom. I thought I'd try Baldy. I hear some of their expert trails are a pretty good ride."

"The best in the world—they say. I've never been on them."

"You don't ski?"

"Not on those trails. It's straight down to Ketchum."

"No," he said confidently, but not understanding that Annie had been joking, "you stop before that. You should let me take you sometime."

After breakfast he drove his red Porsche, which he had been able to rent, special order in advance, in Boise, to the nearby lift station to get a carriage up Baldy. He didn't really like heights very much, and in moments when his compartment would swing gently over a deep, snow-filled gorge, he felt queasy. When he got out at the top stop, he pretended not to notice all the skiers in designer sweaters and well-styled nylon noticing him. Clutching his skis and poles, he made his way over to the most infamous trail. His boots hurt his legs. How could this be right? The expert shop in Los Angeles had insisted they were a perfect fit, but they hurt. When he got to his trail he took his position with his poles ready to shove off. The trail dropped straight down. It looked like he was about to slide off the edge of the earth. He looked around to assure himself that he was alone and then said in his deep film voice, "No other takers today, huh?"

No one could hear him, but he just wanted to try out the line. Then he turned his feet sideways and began wedging his way down the slope, step by step. But it was even too steep for this. He could feel his entire body sweating, which, he calculated, would not look good, especially with his makeup. He looked around one more time to confirm that he was alone and then sat on his muscular posterior that had been so prominently displayed last year in the action feature *Dark Run*. It had not done that well in American theaters but had earned a fortune in the home market and in Europe and Asia.

He popped his skis out and held them along with his poles and worked his way down the steep trail seated, using his legs. He calculated that by the time he got down to where the other skiers were the trail would become more reasonable and he could start skiing.

But it was not true that he was unobserved. Yellow eyes

were following him. Nose could not help but think that if he ever wanted to take a human, this would be the one. The way he traveled sliding on his back, completely exposed, he could pounce and tear his throat out in a matter of seconds—not that he would ever do such a thing. It wasn't allowed. He lay comfortably in the snow, his thick fur protecting him from the cold wind that blew the hairs in the wrong direction. The $4,000 LaMotte had paid for skiwear was not nearly as impenetrable, but fear kept the movie star warm. Nose had to get back to the pack. Legs, a lean woman who worked for the Lady, would be there, and he liked her and she would not be happy if she smelled human on him.

Every day just before sunset, Cathy, the science teacher, would struggle into a blue Lycra running outfit that kept her warm and revealed the body her students only dreamed of. Her husband urged her not to go.

"There are wolves out there."

"You just read that. Nobody ever sees them."

"Fish and Wildlife brought them. And the pack gets bigger every year."

"Name one person who has seen a wolf."

"I hear them every night."

"Coyotes."

"And are coyotes killing the sheep?"

"Maybe."

"And the elk and moose? They aren't American wolves. They brought them in from Canada. And they're really aggressive."

"That's silly," she said, and chuckled as she trotted off toward the trail. "Since when are Canadians more aggressive?"

Just like the Lady, Etxegarray's fears and beliefs were embedded in him from the memories of ancestors. His father had been born on a small farm on a slope of the Pyrenees, so steep it seemed you could fall off, above the little river town of Arnéguy. The farm was so close to the border that the family was not sure if it was in France or Spain. Nor did they care. They were Basques and spoke their ancient language and raised pigs and chickens and sheep and grew some corn for feed with beans planted in between the rows and they made strong and flavorful cheese from the pungent milk of sheep that grazed on the purple-and-gray scrub of the high mountains. With black-and-white dogs they guarded their sheep against bears and their home against officials from Paris and Madrid.

When Etxegarray's grandfather died the older brother took over the farm and his father went to America, where he found work herding a hundred thousand sheep in Idaho. He had never looked after more than fifty in Arnéguy.

There were bears and he occasionally shot one. He tried to hunt the wolves, too, but he could never find them. He knew they were there only from tracks in the snow and the remains of the sheep they killed. A ranchers' association was paying bounties for dead wolves. You could just cut off the nose and bring it in and get twenty dollars, which was a lot better than the five-cent bounty on magpies. Magpies were good to kill because they ate the eggs of ground-nesting birds. You could kill dozens in an afternoon, but you made more money with one wolf nose. There was also a bounty on coyotes. It was a kind of golden age when you could get paid to kill.

Still, no one could get wolves. Etxegarray's father started filling the carcasses of dead sheep with strychnine, which he could buy in Twin Falls. Then he saw wolves. There would be four or five dead ones near a sheep carcass. This was why the Lady, who had the gift of memory, did not like the pack to return to a kill. She wanted them to take what they could at the moment of the kill and not go back for the rest.

Etxegarray, unlike the Lady, did not have a memory of all this unless, like a wolf, the memory was there without his knowing it. When Fish and Game wanted to reintroduce wolves, he opposed it by instinct. And he continued to oppose it and argued that the packs were getting too big and there needed to be a hunt to "better manage the population."

Being a locavore chef, Annie had close relations with the local ranchers and farmers. But she did not want to get involved in their fight about wolves. She was an easterner, and she found it exciting to live in a place that had "wild wolves." "Wild" was a very important word to her and often appeared on her menus to describe both plants and animals—wild trout and wild thyme and wild berries.

Annie's current menu included the delicately flavored spring lamb from Etxegarray, and she also bought cheese from him. But she was wary of the big idea he had brought to the restaurant. "It's not that everyone is going to start cooking up wolves," Etxegarray argued.

"I wouldn't think so," said Annie. "They're a protected species." That was when Etxegarray remembered that he was dealing with an easterner.

"Look," he said. "You just make up the recipe. Publish it in the paper and people will start thinking about wolves as prey, not as innocent victims to be protected."

"But aren't they innocent victims?"

"Wolves?" Etxegarray laughed. "The only thing the wolf cares about is killing. He's a killing machine."

Dag Olsen came through the door with a pile of newspapers.

"Here's your *Times*," said Annie.

Clement Stedlick, who came down every morning to read the *Times* with a double espresso and hoped that someone would say something that he could use, said, "I thought they were supposed to come in at seven."

Dag Olsen, a large, thickset man, made thicker by a red plaid wool coat, walked over to Clement Stedlick, seated with a fountain pen and a notepad next to his now empty espresso cup, and stared down at him with his glacier-blue eyes and ten-day stubble on his broad face from chin to crown. "You the one I heard was complaining?"

"I like to read the *Times*. Why are you so late?" said Clement in a voice he tried to make friendly-sounding.

"You think I need this? I make twenty-seven cents a paper. Look at my truck." He pointed through the window at a red pickup truck. "Goddamn deer hit me. How many papers do I have to deliver to get that fixed?"

"I don't know."

"How many do you think? And you're going to complain. I'll just stop bringing them."

"I'm very grateful that you bring them. I've been wanting to thank you." Clement stood up to shake Olsen's hand, but he wouldn't take it. Clement still held up his smile. "It's great that you do this. Everyone appreciates it."

"Just stop your complaining," said Olsen, and he walked out muttering, "Fucking goddamn deer."

Annie could not help laughing, and she said to Etxegarray, "You worry about the wolves while poor Dag gets attacked by deer."

Etxegarray smiled. "I dream of a world where the sheep can attack—where sheep eat wolves."

"If sheep ate wolves," said Annie, "you would herd wolves and complain about sheep."

Clement dropped his *New York Times*, twisted the cap off his fountain pen, scribbled in his notebook, paid his check, and left.

Back in his glassed-in house he wrote:

The wolves were milling restlessly. The wolf dogs seemed nervous.

Six sheep had come down from the mountains. They were big and fat and had great woolly coats and would not be satisfied until they had smothered a few wolves. Terror showed in the wolves' eyes.

Etxegarray was driving out to the ranch when Juanito sauntered up to the road on horseback and waved for him to stop. The ground was still hard from winter and made a crusty sound against his tires. Juanito spoke to him in soft Peruvian Spanish, which Etxegarray, whose father had taught him Basque but not French or Spanish, could not quite make out. Juanito was so wrapped in his purple-patterned blanket that it looked and even sounded like a blanket was speaking to him. Juanito had something to show him, and Etxegarray followed the horse through the snowy brush on foot. The snow was melting in the field, but it was not easy going, and finally he climbed up on Juanito's horse to go the rest of the way through the gray and spiky winter sagebrush.

Etxegarray felt a primordial fury rise up in him as he surveyed the scene. The snow was splattered brown with old blood. Four gutted, partially eaten sheep were lying on their sides. Etxegarray shook his head at the wastefulness of wolves. They didn't even come back for the rest of the meat.

Juanito was pleased that he had this evidence to show him. He lived in a small trailer on a mountain and could hear the wolves all night. He was terrified but did not want to say so because he did not want to go back to Peru.

Against a rise, the clay-red snow was churned up where there had been a huge struggle and there was Apollo, Etxegarray's stately white Great Pyrenees guard dog. He had tried to defend the sheep but had been overwhelmed. There must have been a lot of them. One had torn his nose clear off his blood-soaked face. "The nose," said Etxegarray. *What kind of animal takes noses?* he thought, not even remembering his father's stories of the twenty-dollar bounties for wolf noses.

I t was about this time that Annie started noticing that Leopold was missing. Leopold was a fluffy white Maltese. He was part of the restaurant. All the customers knew Leopold, petted him on the way in and out of the restaurant. Leopold had a piece of green carpet that he rested on near the door to make himself available for customer pettings. But Leopold had not been seen in three weeks and Etxegarray was the first of several people to suggest to Annie that he had been eaten by wolves.

"They eat dogs, you know," Etxegarray heartlessly pointed out.

It was only one week later that the *Idaho Mountain Express* ran her recipe:

CIVET OF WILD WOLF

Any part of the wolf will work for this recipe, although haunches are recommended.

Cut the wild wolf meat into cubes. Place in a large earthenware bowl. Cover with red wine from Oregon or Washington and two ounces of local cider vinegar (available in Bellevue). Add wild juniper berries and wild rosemary (both found on the outskirts of Sawtooth National Forest—no harvesting in the forest), eight black peppercorns, and a minced garlic head from Hailey. Add four drops cold-pressed virgin olive oil. Let stand in a room that is not overheated for two days.

Fry cubes of Idaho bacon in a large pot with cold-pressed virgin olive oil. Remove wild wolf meat and pat dry. Dust in unbleached organic flour. Fry meat in bacon and olive oil. Add marinade and stew slowly for three hours until liquid is dark and reduced. Add one shot brandy and flame it. Add half a cup heavy cream (the local cream will be at its best in about one month). Cook a few minutes on high heat, until sauce is thick. Garnish with local wild green onions.

"There," Annie said in a vengeful voice. "You can't get much more locavore than that." And she noted with satisfaction that she had used the word "wild" six times in the recipe.

But it was probably a mistake. Her customers were not ranchers and did not find animals that they had raised from birth ripped apart in an open field. Her locavore clientele were the kind of people that in Idaho were known with increasing frequency as wolf lovers. After all, wolves were locavores. Many stopped going to her restaurant, which in turn meant that she had to reduce her order from Etxegarray. He regarded this as one more example of his business being hurt by the wolves. But he told Annie not to worry. "First time they eat a skier they will all be back, demanding you put the dish on your menu."

Clement Stedlick was not angry about the wolf recipe. He was just too busy on his new book to come down for his morning espresso and newspaper. Dag Olsen bragged that he had scared him off. But it wasn't that. It was the new book. Already that morning he had written . . .

Buck took one look at the nervous wolves, looking like they were about to bolt.

"Damn greenhorn's spooking the wolves," he shouted, and went looking for young Billy Burnett. And there he was with his big gray sweater with cable stitching.

"Get that damn sweater off. Don't you know wolves are afraid of wool?"

"But it's freezing."

"You ever see a wolfman with wool on? Get a fleece. Now get that thing off before the wolves bolt and we spend half the winter trying to round them up again."

"But it's cold."

"Who ever said wolfing was going to be easy?"

Clement sipped his coffee—not nearly as good as Annie's espresso, but he couldn't stop now. *This was good,* he thought. *Different, weird, good.*

Rumors were spreading. People were warned to keep their dogs and children inside. There were stories of missing children who had been, depending on who was telling the story, either eaten by wolves or adopted by them. No one could name exactly who these children were. Then there was a story about a schoolteacher in Alberta who had been killed by wolves. Since there is no documented case of a human being attacked by an unprovoked wolf in the history of North America, many people did not take this story seriously. But it resonated with Cathy's husband, who urged her not to go running anymore. Cathy laughed. "Even if the story is true," she said, "it wouldn't mean that wolves had a particular taste for schoolteachers."

The evidence was mounting in the Fish and Game office in Boise, where the heads of dead wildlife decorated the walls, that the wolf reintroduction may have gotten out of hand and there might be a need for a wolf hunt to control the population. Included in the evidence was a noted decline in deer and elk populations. This could lead to a decline in income for the agency, since they lived off of selling hunting tags. Surely the sale of tags for a wolf hunt would be highly profitable. They decided to hold hearings in Boise.

They hamstring the animal and leave it for dead," said one rancher. "Sometimes they don't even eat them. They just like to kill."

There were a number of biologists on hand to refute such testimony, but that didn't stop ranchers and frightened citizenry from spinning their yarns. Annie told the story of the murder of Leopold, despite the fact that there was considerable evidence including snow tracks pointing to a cougar as the culprit.

Rogers, who represented Sun Valley, said, "One mauling of a skier would destroy the community's most important industry."

Etxegarray smiled with approval.

It was pointed out that no skier had ever encountered a wolf, and Rogers argued, "Not yet. They are a slow and careful creature. They are up there stalking them, and sooner or later they will make their move."

"Not likely," said Armsby, a handsome brunette in tweed, who was a biologist for Fish and Game. "Wolves avoid human contact, and places like Dollar Mountain and Baldy are so overrun with humans, to a wolf they just reek of human, so that no wolf would want to go there."

Allen, a filmmaker from California who wore thousand-dollar hand-tooled cowboy boots, talked of his experiences on his documentary in which he got to know wolves, raised pups, kissed and played with them. He talked of how intelligent, affectionate ... He was an outsider and nobody really cared what he thought.

The Reverend Higgins chastised in a gentle demeanor. "I hate to use the word, but this is really blasphemy. God created a kingdom of animals and for us to decide that one animal does not have the right to take its place is like saying that God made a mistake and we know better and will correct his creation."

This was followed by silence while the wolf opponents decided how best to respond. Then Etxegarray, a good Catholic who did not have to listen to the Reverend Higgins, stood up and said, "God didn't put these wolves here. Fish and Wildlife did. And the wolves are a very aggressive foreign strain."

"That's right," shouted Blaine, a neighboring sheep man. "They're not even American. They were brought in!"

This, of course, made Etxegarray uncomfortable, since the same could be and had been said for him. But he continued, "The reintroduction program is a good program, and I support it. But—"

"But," interrupted Harwood, another rancher, "we don't need the federal government coming in here and telling us what kind of wildlife to live with."

Such statements were enormously successful at Sheep Association meetings, but Etxegarray did not think they belonged at this hearing, which could very quickly get out of hand, and then an opportunity would be lost. "But we are talking about a large and aggressive strain of a dangerous predator and we are being overwhelmed. How many of you feel safe letting your children play outside?"

Cathy, the science teacher, spoke. "You say we are overwhelmed, that there are too many wolves." She was nervous at first and a slight quaver could be detected in her voice, but as she spoke she slipped into her classroom style and felt increasingly comfortable. "But let me ask you something. How many people in this room have ever seen a wolf? Show of hands. Who has seen them?"

Necks were strained as people looked around the room for raised hands. The long, thin arm of Malcolm was sticking up, and everyone hoped that she wouldn't call on him.

But she did. "Malcolm," she said in her classroom tone.

"I see them late at night sometimes."

This was sad.

"A whole herd of them galloping through the center of Ketchum, right down Main Street, heading for the East Fork. It's like they are taking over."

Poor Malcolm, everyone thought. He hadn't been right since his wife ran off with that ski instructor from California.

The Fish and Game Commission authorized a limited wolf hunt throughout the state of Idaho. Many opponents, including Cathy and the Reverend Higgins, predicted a "wholesale slaughter," but few of the people who took out licenses had ever hunted wolves before. Etxegarray cleaned his rifle and polished it with great affection, and went out for the first six days of the hunt, stalking the slopes where wind whistled in pine needles, the great horned owl whispered its call, and magpies giggled. He saw elk trails and one swift little fox but not a trace of a wolf.

Few of the other hunters found wolves, either. Some got a fleeting glimpse but didn't have a shot. No shots were fired in the first twelve days. It turned out that it was harder than anyone realized to hunt a wolf. The hunters grew frustrated and desperate. Any shot was worth a try. Blaine thought he saw the blue streak of a wolf through the woods and fired at wolf height, hitting Cathy in her hip and dropping her immediately in intense pain.

Cathy healed but never went running again. Wolf opponents often named her as "a schoolteacher who was attacked by wolves." She soon learned that it was useless to try and tell the truth. In Montana, though no one knew her name, it was sometimes said by opponents of the wolf program that wolves in Idaho had mauled a schoolteacher. She received several requests for interviews to describe her ordeal being attacked by wolves. Her response that she was shot by hunters and not attacked by wolves usually ended the discussion. Often she was dismissed as a "leftie" or a "wolf lover," neither of which disturbed her since they were both true.

Etxegarray, ignoring the facts of the case, still thought it would have been better if the wolves had attacked a skier rather than a schoolteacher. After all, teachers had no importance to the economy.

Dag Olsen announced that his truck had been attacked by a pack of wolves while he was delivering the paper. He wanted $200 to tell his story, but no one paid it. An anti-wolf group in Stanley found him, and they managed to get him $20 to talk to a local online newspaper and another $40 for a cable channel in Mountain Home. But no one really believed that wolves attacked trucks and he wasn't a sympathetic victim. He looked meaner than a wolf and his backers became concerned that he was actually drumming up sympathy for the wolves. Etxegarray saw his television interview and shook his head. "Can't they just get a god-damn skier!"

The hunters did manage to get a few wolves, including two from the Big Wood pack. They were both male, of course, since the females all believed the Lady's warnings. They got the Lord. They weren't supposed to shoot wolves that had radio collars, but on the last day of the hunt Harwood, who had never got off a single shot, got the Lord in his sights. He could see the collar, but it was too perfect a shot, and he fired and said it was an accident.

Without the Lord, the pack was breaking up. The Lady wanted a small pack with fewer wolves to feed now that the humans were aggressive and dangerous again. Nose decided to pair with Legs and try to form his own pack.

The pack gathered one last time for a howl for the Lord. They climbed twelve thousand feet to the top of Hyndman Peak and howled sad songs. Nose held his head higher than the other wolves and no one challenged him.

Clement Stedlick was still in his glassed-in house late at night, working on his new book. When he heard the howl, he was writing:

> *He had the ewe in his sight—a big black woolly one. She bleated long slow "bahs," pleading for her life. But this sheep had smothered more than fifty head of wolves and Buck was not going to let her go.*

Clement paused and rubbed his chin. He thought, *This is going really well,* and then rubbed his head. *Or am I just crazy?*

But there was no one to answer him other than a distant howl from another mountaintop.

▼ ▼ ▼

Part Three: Night in Stanley

There was nothing Hal Benson could do about it. The notes suspended in the frozen air echoed off the Sawtooths, a mournful unknown language, a grim call to arms that he could feel running along his limbs. The howl of a killer about to kill. Hal pulled his thick down quilt over his head.

Hal knew they were out there, the sons of bitches sent by the government—the government and the Communists over in Blaine County. But what could he do.

It was March already, but the thaw was late. There was still ice on the wide curve of the Salmon River. There had not even been enough melt to drive the water fast. Life was still hard up on the jagged icebound slopes of the Sawtooths. He used to take six or seven trips up there. The hunting was good and so was the money. Now the elk were all gone. The wolves ate them all. Hardly anyone even asked for trips anymore. They could go other places where the government hadn't planted wolves.

He got a wolf tag last fall and had been stalking the sons of bitches ever since. He liked to call them sons of bitches, quipping that it was literally accurate. For months he

stalked the steep, rocky slopes and never saw one. Then, when he did, the son of a bitch hunkered down low and he couldn't hit him.

He liked hunting with his old Winchester. A lot of his customers complained because it had a kick like a moose, but Hal said that anyone who wanted to hunt in the Rocky Mountains should be able to take a punch in the shoulder. But with the wolves he kept firing, swinging the bolt, firing again, but somehow he couldn't hit one. For a large animal they were very fast, faster than elk. Now he had ordered a semiautomatic that fired the same .308 Winchester cartridges. It might not be legal, but no one was going to follow him up to the high country where he was going to hunt the ledges. Everyone in Idaho knew about SSS hunting—shoot, shovel, shut up. Or he could claim that he was attacked. You can do anything if you are attacked. You can toss hand grenades if you have them. Next time he saw one of the sons of bitches he was going to keep spraying until he dropped him. Hell, he might be able to get a whole pack. Just shut up and bury them.

That had been the plan, but now they were coming down for him and he just had his bolt-action Winchester. He thought for a moment about a shotgun. No, he would stick with a hunting rifle.

He got Henry, the fat, white, fluffy Persian angora, in and wouldn't let him out. What chance would he have—a fat, slow thing who only wanted his belly rubbed. The wolves could take down mountain lions. Henry didn't even hunt mice anymore. His only exercise was prowling at night, and now with the wolves around Hal couldn't let him do that. He was going to get even fatter.

And there was Davey, the little white Highland terrier, too small to have a chance. Davey loved to explore along the snowy bank of the Salmon. But now Hal didn't dare let him wander. Now he had to walk him on a leash—on a leash here in Stanley as though he were a city dog. You couldn't have dogs or cats or children out anymore. He warned everyone. Sooner or later someone was going to get eaten. Some people listened, especially in Stanley, where the hunting had vanished. But a lot didn't because there were all those fool biologists going around telling everyone that a wolf won't attack a human.

Hal had deconstructed the word "bi-ol-i-gist" with such slow venom that if someone did not know the word they would gather that a biologist was something hideous.

Lying bastards. He was going to take his .308 one day and shoot one of them. He swore to God he would. They were the menace. They brought in the wolves, big killer wolves from Canada, and then told everybody they didn't have to be afraid.

"Why would they do that?" he would ask at the meetings, and then explain in a loud, hoarse whisper, "Because they work for the fucking Democrats!" And then he would look around the room with his hard gray eyes just daring someone to contradict him, and when they didn't, while he had their attention, he would add, "Them and the Communists."

A lot of the men would grumble in agreement. Then he would continue. "They wouldn't bring them into Colorado. Why not? Because they've got plenty of Democrats and Communists." The men would grumble in agreement again.

"First they eat all the game to starve us out. Then when they don't have any more fresh meat, they're going to come down and get us."

He warned everyone, told them to get ready, but not many listened. Already up north a couple of children had been eaten. You weren't going to find it in any newspaper, but Hal had ways of finding these things out.

It was such simple goddamn science. Anyone who knew any biology at all could see it. They had plenty of biologists in Canada that knew. But they could shut them up. Hell, if you couldn't figure this out, you weren't any biologist. He explained it all the time. The wolves had just about eaten all the ungulates—the elk, deer, and moose. That's right, they could take down a thousand-pound moose. Two would grab the front legs and then one would jump up and tear its throat out. You didn't see moose around anymore. You didn't see any ungulates. They could even go out on the ledges and get the bighorn sheep. Hal himself had gotten only one bighorn, ten years ago, by climbing up to a Sawtooth pinnacle and crawling on his belly to get the shot. Damn thing almost dropped off the ledge, but he got it and it was hanging high on the living room wall right now. But the damn wolves took them down all the time.

Now they were going to start on people. It was simple biology—the survival of the fittest, and we weren't the fittest. It was a matter of time before they ate a few, but when they started to find human skulls gnawed down to nothing but white bone, that's what it was going to take before people would listen. He almost wished it would happen so people could see. He fantasized about who he wanted eaten—a biologist? The governor? The Fish and Game commissioner? Or, even better, that environmentalist woman from Boise.

He had seen the victims—sheep, elk, deer. Sometimes there was nothing left but bones, head and feet picked clean—the bones scraped bare. Sometimes they would just eat a choice organ or two and leave the rest for the ravens to pick over. That's why the ravens liked them. But once you have seen a wolf kill—seen what they actually do—you don't love them anymore. Even the Communist wolf lovers in Ketchum and Boise would change their mind after seeing that. And some day when it will be human remains, that will change everything. Fish and Game will come in by helicopter with machine guns.

One of these days a wolf pack will come down right into town. They probably had already been here casing things out. Wolf packs have advance men who check out new killing fields and report back. They were here now. Tonight. Maybe the whole pack.

Hal knew the wolf pack was in town because while he was walking Davey, the dog was acting very nervous. There was a raven screeching from a black cottonwood branch, calling to his friends, and by the time they were going in there were five or six of them, big black birds shouting from the big black trees. You could see the evil. Hal looked around where the snow was still fresh for wolf tracks. He couldn't find any wolf tracks, only dogs', but that didn't mean a thing. Wolves knew how to cover up their tracks—another thing Hal knew for a fact that the biologists kept denying.

He could not settle Davey down. After they got home his little pads kept thumping on the high-polished ponderosa pine floors. Henry seemed nervous, too. They knew. He stared anxiously at the door.

It was a bright night, a full moon that silhouetted the ravens on the branches. Clouds were moving in, but the sky still had a big clear hole where the moon was shining. Hal could smell the snow coming.

He realized that he needed to secure his house. Of course, the biologists would say that a wolf would never enter a human home. But ranchers have found their tracks right outside their homes, and once a wolf pack decided a human was their prey they would stop at nothing. He loved his house, which he had built himself back when the hunting was good and he was making a lot of money from the wealthy people who came to hunt the Sawtooths and maybe fish or raft on the Salmon while they were here. The days before the government brought in killers from Canada to destroy them.

He built the house from local woods and blue and yellow jasper from up north—everything perfectly fitted by hand. As he pulled the lever by the fireplace, a clever construction he had devised himself to close the damper and block off the chimney—originally from birds—he thought that it might have been a mistake to design a house so low and flat. But at the time there were no wolves and no need to worry about them getting on the roof. They could be on the roof right now. He listened for footsteps above, but of course they wouldn't make any.

One thing he had done right was build thick wooden shutters for the windows, though he had to go outside to close them. He grabbed his Winchester and slid the bolt to make sure he had a cartridge in the chamber and started for the front door.

"Where are you going?" his wife, Kate, in a cranberry-colored chenille bathrobe, asked while yawning and rubbing her head.

"I've got to close the shutters," Hal said.

"What for? And what's the gun for?"

"The wolves. They're here."

"Really? Where?"

Hal smiled at her naïveté. "You don't think they're going to show themselves, do you?"

Some snowflakes were beginning to swirl and hop in the wind. "It's starting to snow," she said.

"Yep," he said. "I'll be right back." And he went out and closed all the shutters and locked them with their bars. Each time he finished one he grabbed his rifle and looked around. But hard as he stared into the darkness with his steely gray hunter's eyes he could see no sign of them. He massaged the barrel of his Winchester and muttered quietly, "That's okay. I know you're there watching me. I'll watch you, too, you son of a bitch."

It was dark now. But the snow on the ground glowed from the blue moonlight like iridescent paint.

When he got inside, Kate was turning on lights and complaining about how dark the house was with all the shutters closed. "A nice moonlit night, too."

"Snow will block the moon soon. I can't take chances."

"With the wolves?"

"With the wolves."

Moving to the kitchen to turn on more lights, she said, "A lot of people are starting to think you're crazy."

"Yeah. What do you tell them?"

Kate didn't answer. She could feel them drifting closer to the things they shouldn't talk about.

They both knew that there was a time when she would not have questioned him about the shutters.

Still, he would protect her. He wouldn't fail her on this. Not on this.

The wolves were howling. You couldn't hear them as well with the shutters closed, but they were getting closer.

"They're near the house," Hal said.

"This is ridiculous," said Kate.

"You don't hear them?"

She stood very still with her head cocked as though one ear was better than the other. Then she shook her head in disgust, put on her fluffy turquoise slippers, and marched to the fireplace, where she gathered dried branches that they used for kindling. She struck a long match that they kept in a pail by the kindling and lit the bundle.

"What are you doing?"

"Wolves are afraid of people and afraid of fire," she said.

"What biologist told you that?" he sneered, but it was too late. Kate flung open the door and walked out into the snow with her torch to get some wood. She finally showed him what she really thought—out with a torch to face the wolves alone, leaving him and his useless rifle inside. The minute the door was open, Henry, who had been denied his nighttime prowls for months now, ran out in something between a run and a waddle. He was soon out of sight.

"Henry!" Kate shouted. But Henry had disappeared into the dark. Kate looked with her torch that was burning down very quickly, and worse, now Davey, who missed his leash-free cavorting, ran out the door and headed down the road that led to the Salmon River.

Suddenly there was a noise, a screech. It could have been a raven, but Hal knew that it was poor Henry that the wolves had gotten. "Son of a bitch," he cursed, and grabbed his Winchester and a handful of .308 cartridges and ran outside, so enraged that at first he didn't notice that he was barefoot in the snow. He thought of going back for shoes, but there was no time. They were going to get little Davey. But as Hal pranced farther, light-footed in the freezing snow, he saw a red glow on the ground. It was Kate's burned-out torch.

And then he saw Kate; she seemed to be sliding through the snow on her back. Had she fallen? And then he saw one raised foot. It was in the mouth of a wolf that was dragging her away. He couldn't see if she was hurt. But her arms were flailing, trying to grab on to something, so she was still alive.

Hal charged forward, his Winchester steadied on his hip. But as he got closer he saw them. There were four. At first he saw only yellow eyes, but then he saw their canine silhouettes. They were much larger than dogs—incredibly large. He had always said that they had brought in giants from Canada. Then he realized that there were three more behind him. He could see their gray-and-black fur. None of them were moving, but they knew they had him surrounded. He cursed himself for having not yet picked up the semi-automatic from the gun shop. But he could still do this in one shot if he was a good enough hunter. His only chance was to find the alpha male. If he could drop the alpha with one chest shot to the heart, the others might back off.

There was a large male standing off to his right. He was the alpha. He stood there like an infantry commander about to give an order. Hal raised his Winchester and had the chest in his sight. It was an easy shot because the alpha, unlike the others, was sitting on his haunches, exposing his chest. He wasn't hunkering low or running away this time. He had him. He felt the curve of the trigger on his index finger and inhaled. He almost smiled at the sureness of the shot, except that his feet hurt in the snow.

In the next instant the rifle was not in his hands and he was on the ground. He felt shooting pain traveling up both his arms. His wrists were held in the jaws of two wolves.

They were too strong. He couldn't move. He saw the yellow eyes of the alpha moving closer. He couldn't help wondering if they were going to scrape their bones clean or just eat a little and leave the rest for the ravens to pluck. One thing was certain: when whatever was left of them was found, that would be the end of wolves in Idaho. He had defeated the wolves, but they had also defeated him.

The alpha moved forward. He was standing on Hal's chest. But it was surprising for such a large animal how light-footed he was. Hal had his chin pressed tight on his chest to cover his throat, but he knew it wouldn't do any good. He had failed, he thought. He had failed Kate, and that was the final truth. He knew that no matter how hard he tried to protect it, the wolf was about to tear out his throat. That's how they killed. The wolf's breath, smelling vaguely of fish, fogged his view in vapor. He could see a nose like a big ripe black fruit move closer to his face and a wide-open mouth running along a long muzzle, looking as though he were smiling. The smile got bigger. Hal could see long ivory fangs about to rip him. A paw as big as half his face landed roughly on his forehead and pushed his head back. The wolf was so strong that Hal could not even struggle. He let out one last scream while he still had a throat. But it was too late. No sound came out.

Then he heard a shout.

It was Kate. "Jesus Christ, did you just hit me?"

Hal turned his head and opened his eyes. Kate was lying

next to him in the bed. Henry was lying on his chest, on his back, hoping Hal would rub his belly.

"Why'd you hit me?"

It took him a second to find his voice.

"I'm sorry. I don't sleep well with those damn wolves howling."

"I don't even hear it."

"They're there, though. Trust me on that." He rubbed Henry's belly and Henry purred.

NEW YORK NITPICKERS

At last, I have a future. I could see no future in Diego Martin, or anywhere else on the beautiful hopeless island of Trinidad. But now I am in America, where people are smart-smart and rich-rich. And I am in New York, where people are alchemists who can make money out of any little thing. I don't want to be, as they say, a nitpicker, but there is one problem and I have to admit that it is starting to bother me.

This town is infested and the people all have bugs in their hair.

They have some bugs, tiny little hair louses that you can hardly see. But they have a lot of eggs, nits, and if they don't get rid of them they turn into lice. I see some children who are crawling with them. From there they crawl onto their parents. Then onto everyone else. But not onto me, because I stopped them. I shaved my head. A black woman with a shaved head can be fashionable, especially with big gold hoop earrings. It is better if you have one of those fine egg-shaped heads. I have more of a melon head, but that doesn't matter; I am one of the few women in New York who is sure to be absolutely louse-free.

It's one of those things you are not supposed to talk about. I know it is the land of the free and all that, but there are a lot of things you are not supposed to mention even though everyone knows it. It's like white people can't dance.

We know this but don't say it. So another one is that black people have prettier heads than white people. A black man with a shaved head is far more beautiful than one of those big pale eggs. And a white woman with a shaved head is too horrible to ever speak of. But black people look good without their hair and they would be wise to shave it off.

I should explain or people will think I'm crazy. This goes on, this business of the invasion of New York City by lice, but not that many people know about it. They walk around infested and with bug-ridden children and they don't even know. The two things no New Yorker will ever admit: falling for a scam and having bugs in their hair. Falling for a scam is worse, so sometimes even when they have the bugs they won't come to me because they are afraid it's a scam. That is if they even realize they have bugs. They walk around scratching their itchy heads, trying on hats, sitting back on furniture and leaving their bugs to crawl on someone else. How can anyone try on hats? Why do the stores allow it? Everyone walks around like the problem isn't there. They don't admit it because no one wants to be thought of as a carrier, a contagious person.

And they think that being covered with lice is a poor-people thing. And being poor in New York is never acceptable. But in my experience they are all rich and infested. In fact, I am beginning to think that lice prefer rich people. I know they like clean hair. People shampoo with special potions that cost dizzying amounts of money, a good example of how New Yorkers can get rich on anything, and they wash and wash until their fine hair shines—and it's still full of lice eggs. They have just made their hair more attractive to lice.

The truth is that lice, just like a lot of folk, are more drawn to rich white people than poor black ones. It's just a fact. That is the kind of hair lice like. Rich white people feel bad for poor black kids and spend money so they can spend time in the summer in special camps. But they send their own kids to nice, nice camps for ballet and music and fancy sports like fencing and tennis and lacrosse, and then when they come back the parents send them to me because their hair is alive with lice. The poor black kids who went to the special poor-black-people camp? They come back and their hair is fine.

Back in Diego Martin, we had all kinds of bugs. They crawled up the bushes, along the ground, into your house, and sometimes a child, especially those more out in the bush, got lice in their hair. Not too much. Not like in New York. We always heard that the Indian people in the south were infested with them. But it wasn't too bad in Diego Martin. If someone got them, they went to my cousin Enid. She was the lice expert. There were always women with strange kinds of obeah who knew how to deal with one problem or another. There was Sharon Williams, who people always went to with love problems. My cousin Enid was the one you went to when you itched. Then Enid moved to New York. I can see why some white people might think it is a scam.

Enid kept writing me to come join her in New York. She had a job. Everybody in New York had jobs and made good money, she said. At the time all I had was selling mangoes near the Savannah in Port of Spain, which was an Indian job and had no dignity and, worse, made no money.

So I followed Enid to New York and I quickly saw that it was a dirty place and a buggy place. Diego Martin had insects, but it wasn't buggy like New York. I mean, the people weren't buggy. I truly hate bugs. I'll show you what I mean. There is a plant, a green vine that crawls up on everything in Diego Martin. It will cover your house if you don't chop it back. They call it passion fruit, but a real Trini boast, the plant doesn't produce any passion fruit, only an occasional flower at the end of a vine of big green shiny leaves.

When I left for New York I took a four-inch stalk of the vine from our house, a little piece of Diego Martin. I had to hide it from the American official at the airport, buried it in my underwear and women things, where he would be embarrassed to look too carefully. When I got an apartment in Harlem, in the heart of history, I bought a big pot and some dirt and put the stick in a glass of water for two weeks until it got white root tentacles and then planted it in the dirt and I started getting a green vine that grew and grew just like in Diego Martin.

But it wasn't Diego Martin, it was New York, where everybody profits from everything. In this case it was cockroaches, ugly blackish-brownish fiends, that couldn't pass up the shiny sticky sap from the new leaves. I hate bugs. I chopped down the vine and threw it out and that was the end of my piece of home.

Enid was making good money working for the Jews. The company was called Licefreee, and yes, she was back in her old trade. In New York they called it a nitpicker, and her big idea was for me to be a nitpicker, too. It was too late to go back, and so Enid trained me. The money was good. The other Trinis were making nothing looking after children, but Enid and I were making it by the cartload picking bugs out of their hair. You used this special shampoo and then you combed every strand with a fine metal comb and you could get sometimes six hundred nits and more than a hundred full-blown lice out of a single head. These New Yorkers were crawling with them. It was disgusting.

This all took place in a big room. New Yorkers do not waste space, so this room was unusual in how much empty space it had. The walls were white and there were eight white chairs like the kind in a beauty salon but with lots of space between them. There was also a chair that looked like a fire engine and another that looked like an airplane. These were to make it fun for small children, but so far I haven't seen any children who think this is fun. A head takes two or three hours.

The only thing on the white walls was a little proverb in a glassed frame above each chair. My chair got "Life is not measured by the number of breaths we take but by the moments that take our breath away."

So far, nothing in my New York life was taking my breath

away. What I missed most about Trinidad was light. This is a dark town. My apartment building was only a few feet away from the next one, so alley gray was the only daylight that came through the two windows in my two rooms with sills that were peeling like something left out in the rain. The narrow streets of Midtown where I worked were surrounded by tall buildings like a dark trail in a rainforest. Occasionally I found a broad avenue that got sunlight or one of those perfectly aligned east-west streets at the moment of sunset, as red in the mango sky as the end of a Diego Martin day. But most of the time the large room where I picked nits was actually the brightest, cleanest spot I had. You had to have light to find the eggs.

I was spraying myself with peppermint because the brochures we gave to families said that peppermint kept lice away. The Jewish owner, a nice-looking woman with a full body named Leslie, laughed at all my questions about catching the lice. "They can't fly, you know," she would say with her pleasant dark-eyed smile. "The day lice start flying I'm quitting," she said, and she and Enid and the Jamaican women all laughed. I kept spraying peppermint just the same.

Then I started noticing certain precautions. Jews are smart-smart. They had some obeah thing on the doorway to keep bugs away, but that wasn't the important thing. As I examined Leslie more closely I realized that *she wasn't wearing her real hair.* It was a wig. Not only that, but when her husband came by he was always wearing a hat and he never took it off. This New York is as hot and wet as Diego Martin in the summer. It felt like you could squeeze your hand and come up with water. Made people loose and wilted with as little clothes as possible. It was a sexy season. It made my bald head shine and it made me feel sexy. But this Jewish husband kept on his black hat and his long black coat and stayed covered while his wife wore a wig. The Jews were not going to get infested.

One night I was in Diego Martin under a hot yellow sun and everyone was sweating and shining except Leslie, as dry as could be under her big hair wig. In that dream, as often happens in dreams, I did something I had been wanting to do. I snatched Leslie's wig right off her head. Underneath it you could hardly see her real hair through the piles of nits. Lice were crawling all over it, some of them falling off onto her shoulders.

I woke up kicking my legs in the bed as though I were running lying down. The big Trini sun was only a lightbulb I had left on. My smooth melon head was wet as a fruit in the morning field.

I liked my melon. I must have looked all right like this even without a good egg shape, because men asked me out all the time. Only, if I told them what I did they didn't ask me again, so I learned to keep quiet about my work. I didn't blame them. Would you go out to dinner with someone who had spent the day picking bugs out of people's hair? Picking bugs out of white people's hair is not a decent job for a self-respecting black woman. So I never told anyone. Enid would tell everyone and her boyfriends lasted about three minutes after she told them. I never said a thing. If I were forced I'd say that I was "a hairstylist."

Still, the money was good-good. Their babies grew up and didn't need nannies, restaurants closed, and stores were replacing cashiers with machines, but if you saw what I've seen you'd know that the lice business is never going to die out in this town.

When I went out with a man, I couldn't help looking through his hair. I would study it while he was talking, which they didn't mind because there is nothing a man likes better than a woman who stares at him like the miracle had just appeared while he is talking. But sometimes I would sift through their hair while they were making love to me and one time I found a nit. It was sickening. I didn't want these New York men and their thick hair. They would say sweet things to me and I would look back and see only lice.

But then there was Howard.

Howard was tall, a nice tamarind-husk brown, a smile that stayed in his eyes. He had a condition he was born with. He had not one hair follicle. Not on his body, his head, his brow, his eyes—I mean, nowhere—just smooth and brown. You'd have to feel sorry for the lice that landed on Howard.

Back in Diego Martin there was a famous calypsonian who got rich from all his records and built a special house and brought in tan couches of Italian leather. Those couches were so smooth, felt so nice, that when I was a little girl I used to go over there just to sit on one of them. Howard reminded me of those supple, smooth Italian leather couches. I loved to rub his smooth, tan head and run my fingers across his brow where his eyebrows should have been and touch the tan, smooth muscles of his chest.

Meeting Howard was one of those breathtaking moments by which life is measured. This one I was not going to lose, so of course I absolutely was not telling him what kind of work I did.

"What do you do?" he asked.

"How do you mean?"

"Do you have a job?"

"What do you do?"

"You first."

"I'm a hairstylist."

"Really? Where's your place?"

"It's around. What about you?"

Howard smiled. So it became a game. Who was going to confess first. I didn't think Howard was hiding anything. He was just trying to force me. I almost slipped one afternoon.

We were walking by a hat shop. It was a fancy hat shop for fancy rich heads. Men's and women's hats. Felt, velvet, straw, sisal, feathers, ribbons, and veils. Hats that stood up. Hats that flopped down. Everything. All the fancy rich came into the shop to try on the fancy rich tops. And you know what fancy rich people have on their heads. And that just spread it from one person to another. "Disgusting," I growled.

"What is?"

"The way everyone tries on hats, not knowing what was in the hair of the last person."

"What would be in their hair?"

Howard was staring at me the way you might look at someone telling you about an experience with three-legged green people from another planet. I knew I was getting into deep trouble. It was like the pitch lake back in Trinidad. This is a lake of natural asphalt. They say some New York streets are paved with it. It is deeper than the height of thirty men. It is asphalt, so you can walk on it, but on a hot day you start to sink. Once you start sinking they say the harder you try to save yourself the faster you sink. I was on a pitch lake now and struggling hard and sinking fast.

"No, there's nothing in the hair. It's just I love hair so. Nothing I love more, and the hats . . ."

I am not sure what I was trying for, but looking at hairless Howard, I knew I had made a big mistake. But then he smiled and started laughing. He thought the mistake was funny. There was something a little strange about Howard.

I was growing cautious about this man with no hair who wouldn't talk about himself. One day on my way to work I thought I saw Howard off to the left. Was he following me? I took the 1 train to Times Square, the 7 train to Queens, a taxi to Brooklyn, and as I was grabbing the F train back to Manhattan I saw a shiny tan globe in the distance—Howard's beautiful head. He was following me. What bothered me worse, he was really good at it. Was he some kind of spy? CIA or something? But why would the CIA be interested in me?

That was when I realized it. The only reason Howard would be spying on me was if he worked for the immigration people. Was Howard going to get me thrown out of the country? It was hard for me to believe, but there it was. Or was I wrong? Maybe he wasn't following me. I caught him only that one time and it was only a quick look at the top of his head. In all of the millions of people in New York, there could be another head like that. But I am a professional about heads.

The smart thing would have been to stay away from Howard. But I couldn't. If your life is to be measured in the moments that take your breath away, how can you afford to walk away from one?

So there was now something tragic, ill-fated, about our relationship and it showed. Not in him. He was the same, same smile, same laugh. But in me. I think I even enjoyed the tragedy of it. Finally he asked me what was wrong.

"Why won't you tell me where you work, Howard?"

"All right," he said resolutely. "I will. Then you have to tell me what you do."

I agreed, though I was not certain that I would really tell him the truth. I guess it depended on what he did.

He took us on the Lexington line to the Upper East Side and we walked down Madison Avenue with windows full of jewels and furs and dresses for movie stars—mostly showing people what they could never have. You never saw anyone walk into these stores. Were they just there to tease?

Howard stopped in front of a store. It was that hat shop. And it was full of customers—well-dressed women trying on one hat after another, just spreading their lice. And there was a sign, a small sign that I hadn't seen before—"Howard's Haberdashery." It was just printed along the awning where you wouldn't think to look. All the really hip shops and restaurants now hid their name so it was hard to find. When you can't find the name, hide your wallet. It's going to be one of those stores that you walk in and they look at you like you killed a relative or something. They only want a kind of people that have too much money to think about. I know those people. They came into my shop every day with bugs in their hair.

Howard had been trying to show me his shop before, but I had been too dumb. What was I going to say now when he asked me about my shop?

"Howard," I said.

"Beautiful, isn't it? I've had it for seven years."

Wasn't there something in the Bible about a seven-year plague? "Howard, aren't you worried about health concerns?"

"Health concerns? What health concerns? It's a hat shop."

"But I mean, all these women you don't know trying on hats and then putting them down and the next one trying on the same hat and you don't know what's in their hair."

"This again." Howard smiled his smile. "Don't be such a nitpicker."

A feeling of panic shot through me. How did he know?

HAITI

The Leopard of Ti Morne Joli

▼ ▼ ▼

Izzy Goldstein felt in his heart that he was really Haitian, although no one who knew him understood why he felt that way.

"Izzy, you're Jewish," his mother would say with sorrow showing on her brow as she examined the vodou artifacts displayed in his Miami Beach apartment. He had a particular affection for Damballah, the snake spirit, and there were steel sculptures, beaded flags, and bright acrylic-on-Masonite paintings of snakes. He had thought of getting a terrarium and keeping actual snakes, but then there would be the responsibility of feeding them.

His original connection with Damballah began when he became convinced that the spirit was Jewish. True he was a *lwa* of Haitian vodou and of African origin, but when not a snake, he was often portrayed as Moses and there were several richly colored chromolithographs of Moses holding the Ten Commandments on Izzy's wall that he had bought in Little Haiti. This was little comfort to his mother, because Moses was shown with horns. But even worse, from his mother's point of view, was the other Damballah poster in which he was depicted as Saint Patrick dressed like a Catholic cardinal with a Celtic cross and snakes at his feet.

Izzy argued that the name Damballah ended with an *h* and that Creole words never have a final *h*. Hebrew words, on the other hand, frequently do. His mother did not find this argument convincing. He also had an *ason*, a gourd covered with a net of snake vertebrae, that he had bought in Little Haiti, and had the habit of shaking when making a particular point, to the general annoyance of friends and family.

Also in his apartment was a picture of an admiral. This was in fact Agwe, whom Goldstein tried to consult regularly because he was in charge of the sea. The sea was important in his life. He had learned to sail in small boats, handling a mainsail and a jib across Biscayne Bay, running to one causeway just so he could go beating in the wind to the other end of the bay. He tried to get away from the sea by going to college in Wisconsin, but after three semesters he dropped out and joined the merchant marines and spent five years on freighters across the Atlantic.

Five years of that was enough, and he was back in Miami, trying to find a direction for his life.

Damballah offered fertility, rain, and wisdom. It was only the last of these that interested Izzy Goldstein. Back in Miami, he kept reading about Haiti. Then he started to go to Little Haiti, eat *griyo* and *bannann peze* in the restaurants and learned about vodou. He even started going to ceremonies late at night. He wanted to be possessed by a *lwa*, he wanted Damballah but would have accepted whichever one wanted to take him. Only, it reminded him of that period before his bar mitzvah. He wrapped himself in his tallis, closed his eyes, and bobbed his body up and down in rhythmic rapture as he recited ancient Hebrew and Aramaic, languages, to be honest, he understood even less of than he did Haitian Creole. But no matter how hard he tried, the Hebrew god did not stir within him, and now neither did the *lwa*s.

At the lunches in the little restaurants, at the late-night ceremonies, at the clubs where groups played *konpa* and merengue and the people danced so perfectly while hardly moving at all, he asked, "What can I do for Haiti?"

No idea came to him. There was no wisdom from Damballah. The *lwa*s were as silent as Yahweh. Until one day . . .

A 110-foot rusted Honduran freighter was for sale for so little money that he could buy it with the money he had saved from the merchant marines with enough money left over for the repairs. The engine needed only a little work, which he could do himself, the shaft was straight, the screw was almost new, and he had to spend only a small amount on scraping and repairing the hull. A forward pump needed a little work. And then Izzy Goldstein was captain of a freighter.

He was going to name it *Damballah*, but then a better idea came to him in Little Haiti on a block of two-story yellow buildings shining hot in the Florida sun. He could form an organization that brought relief to Haiti on his freighter. What kind of relief? Doctors? Medicine? Food? Tools? What should he bring them? He went to the Jeremie, a little bar where he could find his friend DeeDee.

DeeDee, whose real name was Dieudonné, was a light-skinned Haitian with graying hair. He kept moving back to

Haiti and then back to Miami, back and forth as regimes changed and he was in or out of favor. DeeDee took him to a lawyer in a gleaming white office on Brickell Avenue. The lawyer's name was Smith. He was tall and lean and had his hair slicked back in that way that had become fashionable for men with that kind of straight hair. He was from that rare group known in Miami as Anglos. An Anglo was a negative grouping. If you did not speak Spanish and you weren't black and you weren't Haitian and you weren't Jewish, you were an Anglo. Smith wore powder-blue-striped seersucker, and this worried Izzy. He never trusted men who wore seersucker suits. Izzy was surprised that a lawyer who specialized in Haitian clients would have such a luxurious office, but whatever reservations Izzy had about the lawyer were laid to rest when the lawyer told him that he was not going to charge him. "I'll just do it for Haiti."

Wasn't that wonderful. The lawyer showed him how to establish a nonprofit organization with tax-exempt status and a fund-raising program. Izzy called his organization National Assistance for a New Haiti and had the letters NANH painted on the hull of his freighter. Haitians pronounced it like the Creole word *nen*, which means "dwarf" and made them laugh, but Izzy Goldstein didn't know anything about that.

What he did know was that thousands of dollars from concerned Americans was contributed to NANH, and with that money DeeDee loaded the freighter at night. He said it was too hot during the day. When they were set to leave,

Izzy was surprised to see his deck stacked high with used cars, bicycles, and even a few Coca-Cola vending machines.

"I don't know, DeeDee. Is this the kind of stuff that they need in Haiti?"

"They need everything in Haiti," he said with a big sweep of his arms. "Even bicycles."

"But shouldn't we bring medicine?"

"We are gonna do that, too. But you have to be careful with medicine."

"How do you mean?"

"Not everybody is happy to see white people come with medicine." Izzy looked worried. He didn't like being reminded of his color. "We will go to Ti Morne Joli and Madame Dumas will explain everything, man," said DeeDee with a reassuring smile. The lawyer had talked about Madame Dumas also. She was going to be important for NANH.

They pulled up the anchor and made their way around the curve of the Miami River into the bay Izzy had always loved and set a course for Gonaïves, Haiti. In the pilothouse Izzy Goldstein was too excited to sleep. Help for Haiti was on the way.

When Haitians die, which happens every day, it is Agwe's work to carry them across the ocean back to Africa. But Agwe did not always have to do this work. In ancient times, when Haiti was still connected to Africa, life was much easier for Agwe and, in fact, for all the old lwas. *In those days all the* lwa *and all the animals of Africa could easily walk to and from Haiti. Haiti had lions and elephants and tigers and giraffes and leopards. The forests were thick with vegetation and the tree branches were heavy with every kind of fruit. But that was in the old days.*

Gonaïves looked white in the hot sun with a black sky behind it filled with rain that would not fall. It was even hot at sea and it got hotter as they approached the stone-and-cinder-block ramparts.

Below on the quay was chaos. There were trucks and cars but mostly large handcarts and children chasing them, hoping for something that dropped. The port official boarded and Izzy Goldstein told him it was "the NANH from Miami," and the official, hearing "the *nen* from Miami," smiled. Izzy supposed that the man was laughing at his French. The official said something in Creole and Izzy looked confused and then he said in very good English, "How much are you gonna pay to dock here?"

DeeDee took over and Izzy was led by a deckhand down to the teeming, sweating crowd, and in the middle of it he was introduced to the most beautiful man Izzy had ever seen. Jobo was tall, broad-shouldered, and lean and muscular, and his skin had the satiny luster of burnished wood, perhaps a very dark walnut. He led Izzy to a perfect, polished white Mercedes that clearly did not belong there in the ramshackle port.

Jobo seemed a pleasant young man, there was a sweetness to him, but when he sat in the driver's seat and turned the key, he was transformed. With his fist he pounded ferocious blasts of the car horn and left no doubt that anyone in his way would soon be under his tires. The crowd parted and they were on their way, climbing only slightly as they left the steamy dilapidated city and entered the last green village on the edge of a bone-colored Saharan landscape that rolled on and on like a sea.

Again Jobo honked the horn insistently in front of an iron gate, which, to the great excitement of Izzy, was fashioned into a swarm of black metal snakes. A boy appeared and with every ounce of his small body managed to push the gate open. The car drove into a lush tropical world of ponds and fountains and green and orange broad-leafed plants and drooping magenta bougainvillea and coral-colored hibiscus sticking out their tongues suggestively. Rising above this forest were high-pitched roofs and wide balconies.

They got out of the vehicle and stepped up to a wide, high-ceilinged porch with a tiled floor and large potted plants. Between two lazy banana bushes was a tall cage about two yards square. Inside was a leopard, lean, with angry yellow eyes and ears cocked back and fur like silken fabric in black and rust and ochre. The cat was pacing back and forth, as though exercising to keep in shape. Overhead, a palm crow whined its *"cao-cao"* plea that made people straighten up so the bird would not mistake them for dead and swoop down for a peck. Izzy did look weak at the moment and he did not know to straighten up. He was hoping someone was about to offer him a tall, cold drink.

When Haiti was sent away, many of the lwas—including Damballah, Èzili, Legba, and Agwe—went with Haiti, but most of the animals stayed in Africa. However, Èzili kept one leopard because she could not resist beautiful things. She wanted to keep the leopard the same way that she kept closets full of beautiful dresses and fine jewelry. The leopard tried to run away, and so she kept it in a pink jeweled cage.

Jobo ushered Izzy inside, holding open a large glass door that did not fit with the rest of the house. Once inside, Izzy's body instantly hardened to a tense knot. It was as though he had walked into a refrigerator, possibly a freezer. He was not sure but thought he saw traces of vapor from his breath. A furry red creature glided toward him, speaking the same formal and emotionless French of his ninth-grade French teacher who had always called him Pierre because she said there was no way to say Izzy in French.

"Bonjour, bienvenu. Comment allez-vous," she said with a smile made of wood. She was wrapped in a thick red fox coat. Her body stuck out at angles, a hard, thin body. Her

straightened black hair was swept up on her head. She wore shiny dark purple lip gloss with an even darker liner. Her green eyes were also lined in black, which matched the carefully painted polish on her long nails filed to points as though for weapons. All this dark ornamentation on her gaunt face made her skin look pale with a flat finish, like gray cardboard.

On one finger was a very large emerald that was close to matching her eyes, and when she held her long hand to her face the stone appeared to be a third eye. She would have been attractive, except that everything about her seemed hard. Even her face was bony. Maybe, Izzy thought, she understood this and wore the fur to try to appear softer.

She turned to Jobo and ordered him in French to fetch a cold bottle, which was what Izzy wanted to hear. To Izzy it seemed odd—here he was trying to learn Creole—that a Haitian would speak to another in French, even though Jobo answered only in Creole. Izzy soon realized that she also spoke nearly perfect American English. So who was the French for? Even when she spoke English she punctuated everything with *"N'est-ce pas?"*

Jobo returned with two very long crystal champagne flutes and a bottle of champagne, which he opened with the craftsmanship of a well-trained wine steward. It was cold and bubbly, with a flush of rose like the blush on her protruding cheekbones, though probably more natural.

"Pink champagne, *n'est-ce pas?*" she said. "Don't you love pink champagne?"

"Èzili's drink," said Izzy, who knew that Èzili loves luxury and her favorite color is pink. The smile flew off her face like a popped button, leaving Izzy to wonder what he had said that was wrong.

She offered him a building near the port that he could use as the NANH warehouse, although when he said "NANH warehouse" she smiled. She could also provide a staff for distribution of the goods he brought in so that he simply had to bring goods in and the rest would be taken care of. She asked nothing for this service, simply explaining, "I am Haitian and I love my people." He was moved, but he thought he detected a certain angry glow in Jobo's eyes while she was speaking.

"All I ask, *mon cher*..." She paused, and he thought maybe she was going to ask about aid to a favorite cause. Which in fact, may have been the case. "Gasoline, *n'est-ce pas?*"

"Gasoline?"

"Mais oui. Beaucoup, beaucoup. I will tell you how many barrels."

"But, ah—Madame Dumas?" He was so cold his teeth were chattering as he tried to speak.

"Oui," she said softly like a kiss.

"How do I justify spending relief money like that?"

"Ah-bas, c'est tout correct, n'est-ce pas? It is an operating expense, *n'est-ce pas?* It's for my generators." And she moved her green eyes across the ceiling. "This takes a lot of gaso-

line, *n'est-ce pas?* And then there are the freezers for the meat, *n'est-ce pas?*"

He supposed that she was keeping meat for the village, and that would be a worthwhile thing to subsidize. Far safer than leaving meat out in this tropical heat. Although you could keep food fresh forever in this living room.

"As a matter of fact, I am going to buy a freezer compartment for your ship. You can bring down meat."

"That is a wonderful idea. Put some protein in people's diets."

"Eh, *oui,*" she said in a distant philosophical tone. "Jobo, this reminds me. Feeding time." She put on a pair of French horn-rimmed sunglasses. And then she said something in Creole that Izzy didn't grasp, though it sounded like something about his shirt, which he then removed as he went out into the heat.

She smiled at Izzy and said, "He is too beautiful for clothes, *n'est-ce pas?*"

Izzy nodded, unsure of how to answer.

"So it's all arranged. My man is paying them off so you can unload right now."

"Paying the . . . ?"

"All taken care of," she said merrily, with a gesture like washing her hands. He was informed that he would be staying in Madame's house, which he did not feel entirely comfortable about, but he had no other ideas of where to stay.

He was put in a room as cold as the living room, with

carved wooden panels and a ceiling fan for which there was no real use. The air-conditioning could not be turned down or off and the windows did not open. But the bed was equipped with fluffy goose-down quilts imported from Austria.

Izzy went outside to warm up. Jobo, with a large ring holding many keys, was coming from a wooden shed with a package. He stepped up to the porch and over to the leopard cage. He unwrapped the package and took out what looked like two sirloin steaks. Izzy assumed he was mistaken about the cut, but the steaks were nicely marbled. All the while, the leopard paced, stopping only for a second to snarl. The animal was dangerous, and Izzy could see claw marks— parallel lines on both sides of Jobo's shirtless back.

"Jobo," said Izzy. "Is there some kind of a ceremony I can see?"

Jobo showed a sweet smile. "You want to see some real voodoo?"

"Yes, exactly."

"I can arrange it, but it is *koute chè*."

"How expensive?"

"*Anpil. Anpil.* I will take you to Kola."

"Kola is the *ougan*?"

"He's a *bòkò*. He can fix it. I'll go talk to him now." And with that, shirtless and with claw marks showing, he walked down the driveway and out the gate of iron snakes.

Izzy sat on the porch, watching the incessant pacing of the leopard. The cat had one of the steaks in his mouth but he didn't stop moving, not even while eating. Izzy thought about the vodou priest named Kola. Did that mean a line? A queue? It must mean something.

The leopard pleaded with Agwe that he did not want to be locked in a cage and asked to be taken back to Africa. But Agwe said, "I can only take spirits back after they die."
"Then kill me. I want to go back," said the leopard.

Haitians like nicknames. Dieudonné was called DeeDee, Ti Morne Joli was always called Joli. Madame Dumas was LeChat, the *bòkò* was Kola, Jobo was Beau. And Izzy? Everyone in Joli called him Blan.

"What is this Blan up to?" asked Kola, a short stocky man with a powerful body, shirtless, like Jobo, sitting under a leafy tree, on the stripped-bare engine block of a long-dead car. All the other parts had been sold and someday the block would be, too. He dug in the earth with a trowel and pulled out two small green Coca-Cola bottles, felt them to see if the ground had kept them cool, dusted them off with his thick but skilled fingers, and handed one to Jobo.

Jobo smiled. "What do Blans want? He wants a vodou ceremony."

"A vodou ceremony?" Kola's face had a wide, toothy smile. He rubbed his belly. He was proud of his belly because he was the only one in Joli who had one. "*San dolar.* Tell him there is a nice ceremony for a hundred dollars. For one-fifty I can show him something special."

Jobo nodded.

"But what does this *blan* want? Is he bringing *blan* doctors and their medicines?"

"No, I don't think so. But I wanted to talk to you about your medicines."

"You need a powder, Beau?"

Jobo looked at the ground and shook his head.

"Do you have money for my powders? What do you need? A rash, a headache, a fever, the stomach? What would you like to do?"

"You know my aunt's baby died today?"

"I know."

"Do you know how much meat Madame LeChat has? Do you know? *Anpil, anpil.* Three big freezers. It all goes to that cat. If she died, everyone in Joli could eat meat for three weeks."

"Yes, but for a great lady like that, that *koute chè.* Do you have that money?"

"No. But if I did, you could help me?"

"It would cost less to kill the leopard. Then she wouldn't need the meat. Maybe you could take it."

"I don't just want the meat."

"What do you want?"

"*M vle jistis.*"

"Ah, justice. Justice costs. Justice is very expensive."

Izzy was pacing the porch, almost the same strides as the leopard, but he didn't realize it. Something about that leopard pacing made him restless. That and a harsh cry from upstairs from time to time. "Jobo! Jobo!" Finally she came downstairs and out onto the porch. The light from inside was shining on her. She was wearing a long silk shift and he could see that there was no shape to her body—just long and thin. He also saw through what was left of the makeup that she was a bit older than he had first thought.

"Have you seen Jobo?"

"He went to the *ougan* to arrange a ceremony for me."

"The *oun*?"

"Kola?"

"Ah, the *bòkò*, Kola." Then her emerald eyes darted past him. It was Jobo coming back. Izzy sensed that he should retreat to the other end of the long tiled porch.

"Jobo," she called out. *"Jobo, viens ici! Viens!"* She spoke in that melodious high pitch used by Frenchwomen when calling their pets.

And he did come and she put her arms around him, her cardboard gray hands looking bright against his black back as she dug her black polished nails into his skin.

DeeDee, can you help me?" asked Jobo.

"What do you need?"

"Money."

DeeDee laughed.

"I need to pay for something very expensive. Just one time I need some money. I can work."

"Why don't you ask the *blan*?"

"This is not *blan*'s business."

DeeDee understood and told him that he was loading a shipment of mangoes on the NANH late that night.

"I'm not sure I can get away at night."

"Late late. I am paying very well for this particular shipment—of mangoes . . . Give her a lot of champagne."

"Mais, oui."

DeeDee paid off all the port officials with money from Madame Dumas, and the NANH untied and set her bow northwest to round the peninsula and head to Miami. The mangoes helped the ballast, but the freighter was still sitting a little too high in the water. They had to hope there were no storms. Izzy was surprised when he inspected that the mangoes were just piled in the hold without any crates. "It will take forever to off-load," he complained. DeeDee shrugged.

Then Izzy noticed they were off course, but DeeDee explained that they had to make a quick stop. "To take on more ballast?" asked Izzy.

There was no answer, but DeeDee was busy navigating. They dropped anchor by a reef—a strip of white sand and a grove of palm trees in the middle of the turquoise sea. Izzy saw nothing heavy to load on the boat.

Then the crew lifted the cover off the hold and Izzy was astounded by what he next saw. Haitians came crawling out from under the yellow mangoes, like an infestation exposed to the light. Men and women, one child of about eight. They were almost naked, one man was completely naked, and they staggered up, their limbs stiff and their eyes blinded by the hot light. They were hurriedly helped to the beach on their uncertain legs. There were eleven of them, including three that were dragged and appeared to be dead.

Shouting erupted in Creole. Arms flayed the hot air angrily. They were saying, "This is not Miami. You took our money." Some pleaded, "Please don't leave us." But DeeDee insisted that this boat was too big to bring them in and that small boats would come tonight to drop them on the Florida coast.

Izzy was angry and fought with DeeDee all the way to Florida. DeeDee's answers made no sense to him. "Why are we doing this?"

"Because we can't bring them into Miami."

"Why were we carrying them at all?"

"They needed the help, Izzy."

"I have to tell the Coast Guard. They'll starve in that place."

"No. It's all arranged. Boats will come for them tonight."

"They said they paid. Who got the money?"

"The mango growers."

They tied up on the Miami River. But they could not go back to Haiti. There was a coup d'état. Little Haiti was intoxicated with news. A new government was being formed. There were curfews. There was rioting in Port-au-Prince and Gonaïves. In Gonaïves a mob attacked the NANH warehouse, took everything, and then tore down the building, a chunk at a time, with rocks and machetes. People were singing a song as they worked, *"Pa vle gwo nen"*: We don't want the big dwarf. After a day all that remained of the two-story building was a few steel reinforcing rods sticking out of the ground.

DeeDee vanished and it was said in Little Haiti that he was now an official in the new government. Izzy hadn't realized he was involved in politics. He had never seemed interested in anything but commerce. Then a man approached Izzy alongside his boat on the river. Izzy recognized him. He was usually in Bermuda shorts with an "I love Miami" T-shirt, a Marlins hat, and a camera. But this day he was wearing a suit and showed Izzy something that said he was an FBI agent.

Kola had a new Coca-Cola cabinet. It was red-and-white metal with a glass door. A stray rock from the riot had dented one side, but the glass door was intact.

Of course, it didn't keep anything cold, because Kola

had no electricity. But it was a good cabinet and he kept it behind the temple and stored his bones, herbs, potions, and powders in it. His Coca-Cola was still in the ground where it was cool.

Soon Madame Dumas began experiencing something completely new to her. She started to sweat. Even in her air-conditioning she was sweating. It poured out of her forehead and ran down her fine cheekbones, and from under her arms down her sides, a rivulet flowed to the small of her back, and from under her breasts sweat soaked her stomach. Her pink silk shift had turned cranberry with wetness. And as the sweat poured out she became weaker and weaker—while Jobo watched.

Madame Dumas collapsed on the living room floor and crawled to the table where she kept her sunglasses to cover her eyes. But she could not find the glasses. She looked up at Jobo with her arm reaching toward him. "Jobo, *aide-moi.*" Help me.

He only stared at her.

"I need a doctor."

"I can't get a doctor. The roads are closed. The coup."

"Oh, yes, the coup," she muttered, as though there was a secret irony to this that only she could appreciate. "Then the *bòkò.* Can't he make a powder to fix me?"

"*Mais oui,*" Jobo answered, appreciating his own secret irony.

"*Vas-y.* Get something!"

Jobo left and did not come back for hours. When he did, Madame Dumas was not sweating anymore. She was stretched across the cool floor tiles—dead.

Jobo unceremoniously removed all her clothes and carried her out toward the leopard cage. He opened the door to the cage and dumped her on the floor. The leopard, who had not been fed in three days, was so startled that he stopped pacing. He walked over to the body and sniffed it as Jobo started to close the cage. Suddenly the cat leapt over Jobo, knocking him over and off the porch, and went into the bush, over the wall in graceful flight, and was never seen again. He might have run to the arid desert in the northwest and managed to find a way to survive there. Or maybe he ran along the Artibonite River to hide out in the mountains above the valley, where many Haitians have also hidden.

The leopard had left Jobo with the question of what to do with the unwanted remains of Madame Dumas. While he was contemplating this dilemma someone started clanging the locked iron gate. Jobo ran down and saw Kola framed in black iron snakes. He explained that Madame had a family that wanted both the house and the body. They wanted to bury it in France, but Air France had suspended flights because of the coup d'état.

"Eh, *oui*," said Jobo, who had never seen an airplane close up, with feigned comprehension.

"*Poutan!*" shouted Kola, raising his stubby index finger to make a point. "However," he translated, carefully pronouncing his English syllables, "I told them if they want to come get the body in a week or even two, I can use magic to keep the body in perfect condition."

"Magic?"

"*Mais oui*. And you have that magic in your house. It is the magic of meat."

Now Jobo understood. "And they will pay?"

"*Gwo nèg koute chè*," Kola said. You have to pay a lot for an important person.

Jobo smiled, "*Anpil, anpil dola?*"

"*Anpil*. Very expensive."

After Kola left, Jobo went back to the cage and picked up Madame. She still had not stiffened much. He emptied one of the big top-loading freezers and dumped her, where she landed in a most undignified pose and was petrified in ice just as she was to be thawed and served up properly by magic at the right time.

Jobo was right. Once the freezers had been emptied the people of Ti Morne Joli ate meat for three weeks. Many became sick because they were unaccustomed to such a rich diet. But it was not likely to happen again.

It was Damballah who finally confronted Èzili, bribed her with dresses and bracelets and pink elixirs until she set free the leopard. The leopard ran and ran and ran as though he could run all the way back to Africa. But there was the ocean there now. He ran so hard that he turned into a man.

That was the first Haitian and that is why Haitian people always struggle so hard to be free.

I want to talk to my lawyer," said Izzy.

"I think you need a new lawyer. He's been arrested. Seems you were just a small part of the operation."

Izzy thought, *They arrested the Anglo. Isn't that something? They got the Anglo.* Then he said, "Why do you say that the goods were stolen? Everything was paid for."

"We were watching you. What tipped us off was that you had Coca-Cola machines. You can't buy them. Only the Coca-Cola Company owns them. You're not the Coca-Cola Company, are you?"

COYOTE

The coyote is a living, breathing allegory of want . . . lives chiefly in the most desolate and forbidding deserts, along with the lizard, the jackass-rabbit and the raven, and gets an uncertain and precarious living, and earns it.

—Mark Twain, *Roughing It*

▼ ▼ ▼

Part One: Stalking in New York

What this grim, ungainly, ghastly, gaunt, and ominous
   bird of yore
Meant in croaking "Nevermore."

—Edgar Allan Poe, "The Raven"

I f he wasn't so old-fashioned, none of this might have happened. They were all cutting across Putnam County, heading east toward Connecticut for some turkey hunting. They had done this before. Only, he was different from the others. He was a little smaller and not at all like the new coyotes that were moving into New England. They all had wolves in the family, and he did, too. His grandfather was a wolf—his father's father. But he took after his mother who was pure coyote. He was small like her and he didn't like moving in crowds and didn't want to hunt with a pack. As far as he could tell he was faster and smarter than most anything he wanted to eat, and he preferred to travel alone and live by his own wits, which was the old-time coyote way.

So as they headed east toward turkey land he spied a raccoon off to the right and ran after it. He easily ran it down

and ate it. Later he found its mate and ate her, too. That night he feasted on a small white-tailed doe. Why did he need to belong to a pack?

It got better and easier as he got into Westchester. This was stand-up territory. Stand-ups were the one animal he always avoided. They were very slow, but they were smart and knew a lot of tricks. It always seemed to him that stand-ups thought like coyotes. But they had a lot of dangerous equipment. No animal had as many different ways to kill you as a stand-up.

Now, down in the stand-up land where they built huge nests there were still plenty of raccoons, rabbits, deer, and a lot of dogs and small cats. But the stand-ups put food out in barrels—meat, fruit, vegetables. There were a lot of things you couldn't eat. Metal and paper, but the barrels were also so full of food that he didn't have to hunt if he didn't feel like it.

It was a good place, and he declared it some nights on a black rock with flakes of schist that sparkled in the moonlight. Some of the more knowledgeable people who knew a coyote howl when they heard one would shudder. The dogs all knew and tried to tell their owners, but all the barking only served to help cover up the coyote howl.

And then one night after howling the coyote trotted through paths and roads without seeing a single stand-up and he came to a wide, empty bridge and trotted across until a stand-up came out of a very small hut and made strange high-pitched sounds and held out a paw toward him.

This seemed strange, some kind of trick, and he ran quickly past her.

Joyce Canara thought it was strange, too. She did not know much about wildlife, since she had only been out of the Bronx two times to Queens to apply for her job unless you counted her tollbooth, which was technically on the Manhattan side of the bridge. But that dog was not just a dog. There was something tough and wild about it, like certain boys when she was in high school that had a look and you knew to stay away from them.

She had been on this toll for only two months and she didn't like being there at night even though there were two other night toll collectors and a policeman on duty. Since there were no cars coming she went up to each of the toll collectors and the cop and asked them about the dog but no one had seen it. This confirmed her fears. She could be mugged, murdered, or kidnapped and the others wouldn't see it.

She told the cop, a ten-year veteran who had worked his way to this easy night job, which he intended to sleep through until he got promoted to an easy day job, that "a wolf just entered Manhattan."

"A wolf," he said, without believing her.

"Yes, a wolf. I just saw it. You should call someone."

He shrugged, his palms up, as though pleading to a god, and with deliberate slowness, just to let her know what he thought of her emergency, he called Emergency Services and reported that the toll collector "claims she saw a wolf run across the bridge into Manhattan."

This is how it begins, thought Arthur Mintz. And then he added silently, *Or really how it ends.*

He was standing in front of the refrigerator, door open, staring at the well-lit contents, hoping something would remind him of why he was there. He could not even remember walking to the refrigerator or even opening the door, which must have been a very recent event. He had no idea what he had come to get.

It would get worse. His beautiful Anna, whom he married forty-eight years ago last February 16—Anna who was so much younger than he, who looked up to him and admired him—Anna would one day realize that she was now married to a fool. Once she knew, his life was over.

There was a soft nudge on his left calf. It was Freser, the red-and-white Cavalier Prince Charles spaniel, chubby and round as a seal. Freser had mastered the trick of flipping his leash off its hook and carrying it in his mouth when he wanted a walk. Arthur clipped the leash on his collar and they walked to the door. With weather like this, taking Freser for a long walk was the best part of the day for both of them.

He knew exactly what the weather was like because the windows were wide open. Anna insisted on keeping the windows open. She said that it let the "smell of aging" out. She said it as though it were his smell, but in truth she was trying to keep the smell off her because, though younger than Arthur, she could feel old age nipping at her heels, too. That was why Arthur angered her. Arthur knew that she was right about the windows, that there was a certain smell to old people's apartments because they did not open the windows. Opening and shutting windows was too much of an effort, but also old people did not want strong winds blowing through their home, disarranging things and creating disorder. Arthur was already having that feeling. After all, it was hard enough to remember where things were without the wind moving things around.

But once your apartment got that smell, people could smell old age on you, and you were dismissed and there was nothing to do but wait for the end. When you die in New York you are simply freeing up valuable real estate and so everyone looked forward to your demise.

Then he heard a door open in the hallway. It was his neighbor across the tiled hall—the only other apartment on the first floor. He would not risk another encounter with her. He dropped the leash and shuffled to the stuffed corduroy chair and sat down in the dark room, where he could face an original Rauschenberg, his sigh vibrating his lips with a sound like an old engine shutting down. A tenacious sense of self-preservation told him to wait for the neighbor to leave the block.

Freser, whose heart was set on a journey, amused himself by holding the raven in his teeth and shaking it while growling. Did Arthur care anymore? Just let him have it for a toy. When he bought it, it was thought to be worth something, though he paid only $70 at an auction. Supposedly it was used to promote Alfred Hitchcock's movie *The Birds*.

Arthur used it for years as a prop for his Edgar Allan Poe reading. He would sit in this same chair with the raven perched behind him and all the lights turned off. He held a flashlight and shined its beam upward so that only his face—shadows where the highlight should be—and the beady-eyed bird could be seen. The hushed atmosphere seemed spooky as he recited the stanzas, and his son listened, spellbound until the very last.

> And the Raven, never flitting, still is sitting, still is sitting
> On the pallid bust of Pallas just above my chamber door;
> And his eyes have all the seeming of a demon's that is
>   dreaming,
> And the lamp-light o'er him streaming throws his shadow
>   on the floor;
> And my soul from out that shadow that lies floating on
>   the floor
> Shall be lifted—nevermore!

By the time Arthur got to the last word, his voice was a harsh whisper—"nevermore."

The son felt that sweet sense of fear and sometimes irrationally commented that their bird also "never flitted," though he wasn't sure what that meant. But he pretended to know. The fun was in pretending.

Then one time when David was fourteen and in a whiny, unpleasant mood, Arthur took the flashlight and raven and prepared to start his performance and David said, "Oh, Dad, that's so corny."

The funny thing was that Arthur found the word "corny" to be corny. Nobody said that anymore, did they?

But now, as Arthur thought about it, it was not that moment standing in front of the refrigerator with a confused expression, it was that earlier moment when his son cut him down with an obsolete word that was the beginning of the end of his life. Soon David was off to school never to return, Arthur and Anna's life's work gone. Other parents talked about how their kids would come back with their dirty laundry, but David, it seemed, had learned how to do the laundry himself—a dread of every parent, no doubt.

There is a stench here, thinks the coyote. The streets, the cats, the rats, the dogs, the food barrels, it all has that same stink. It is the smell of stand-ups. The coyote had always known that smell. It is the smell of trouble. This might be the biggest stand-up pack in the world. The coyote was beginning to understand that he was wrong about stand-ups. They were not at all like coyotes, individuals who lived by their wits. They were like wolves, working in highly organized packs, obeying the laws of the pack, operating together. Even if they weren't as smart as he had thought, they were even more dangerous.

But he had learned something else. Where there are stand-ups, there is food, endless supplies of it. First there were the barrels where the stand-ups tried to hide their food in paper and plastic and metal. And near the barrels there were always rats. Rats were everywhere he went. Whenever he felt a little hungry he could eat a rat. The birds were slow and easy to catch also, especially the gray oily ones. And there were squirrels and not enough trees for them to hide in. And lots and lots of cats. And dogs. The dogs were meatier than the cats, but they often came attached to a stand-up. If you caught them by surprise, the stand-up would often let go and you could run off with the dog. But one time the stand-up held on so tightly that the coyote had to let go and run off. It was a big meaty one, too. But he had to be careful of stand-ups and not draw too much attention or he would have the entire pack coming after him.

He probably shouldn't howl. But he couldn't help himself. At the end of days like these he had to rear back on his haunches and let loose with a few notes at least. What a place. The coyote didn't ever want to leave.

Nevermore. Nevermore. What did the raven mean by that? What did Poe mean? Arthur used to think about this frequently after reciting the poem, but he hadn't thought of it in years. A strange thing, memory. What had he been looking for in the refrigerator?

When you live in a New York apartment, everything changes the instant you go outside. There is a momentary shock just as quickly forgotten. First there are the smells. For Arthur and most New Yorkers it was a single composite smell that they thought of as New York. To Freser and other dogs, and now a coyote, New York had an endless variety of distinct scents to track down. No wonder Freser so looked forward to his walk. The smell that New Yorkers called "New York" was a blend of sour milk, rotting vegetable, creosote, cigarettes, a harsh molasses burn, and gasoline. Other smells were added, depending on what was going on at the part of the block where you happened to be standing—the heady vapor of diesel heating oil, a simmering paella, a stale puddle, espresso, or the white smoke of burning oil from an older car whose rings were worn.

The same was true of the noise. It was a roar created by tires on hard top or clanking over heavy metal plates, horns, sirens, the ball bearings on the casters of carts and dollies pushed down the sidewalk, the growl or purr of engines, the insistent clip-clop of determined women wearing crafted shoes like tiny hooves of delicate horses, the screams and giggles of children, airplanes whining in the sky and the rapid thumping of helicopters, the machine-gun slamming of jackhammers, people shouting, dogs barking—for humans, all fused into a single urban roar, but for dogs and coyotes, a long list of sounds to be investigated and evaluated.

Late the previous night it seemed that all the dogs in the neighborhood had joined in on a howl. Even Freser contributed with his high-pitched and unimpressive voice—something he never did.

Freser was happy, waddling merrily, sniffing everywhere, researching the prospect of something to eat. Occasionally he would stop to inhale a scent. If Arthur stopped, he would nuzzle his ankle. Freser had reduced life to the search for food. He almost never found any, but Arthur would occasionally slip him little cubes of orange cheddar cheese so that Freser could maintain the illusion that life's promises are fulfilled. Maintaining that illusion is the secret of happiness. And so Freser was a very happy dog. Freser's joy was infectious so that Arthur felt that he, too, got a great deal for a small amount of cheese.

Arthur happened to notice that they were on the corner of Perry and Washington. He didn't think anything of this in particular, but then there was dryness in the throat, a sense of panic. Arthur had lived in Greenwich Village for almost forty-five years. July 1 would make forty-four years, Arthur recalled. And yet he still found the streets confusing, the way they darted off on angles so that parallel streets crossed. But where was his street?

Now he could feel the panic in his chest. But then he got it. Barrow Street. Where was Barrow Street? Barrow and what? If he could just get back to Barrow Street, he was certain he could find his way home.

This had happened to him before and it would be all right as long as Anna didn't find out. He had a GPS on his cellphone. He only had to put in his location, which he could get from street signs and his destination, and it would get him home. Barrow and . . . what?

His task was further complicated by the fact that he had forgotten his glasses and could not read the small screen. But he could get by. Then the screen went black. His battery was out.

Freser had felt his panic and now he was panicking, too—whimpering, pulling on the leash. He wanted to go home. But how to find the way home? Then it occurred to Arthur that Freser could find his way home. He was so fat and unathletic, surely he was getting tired. He was tugging on the leash, which he rarely did. All Arthur had to do was let him lead the way.

In a soundless bouncing trot, the coyote was following, head down, fluffy tail dragging, ears at half-mast, trying to look unassuming and unthreatening, which was his style. His sharp yellow devil eyes, like the scope on a sniper's rifle, were fixed on the red-and-white dog pulling a stand-up. This was perfect, the coyote thought—the scared little dog and the stand-up who wasn't paying attention. How did stand-ups survive? They had no sense of danger. The frightened dog would be an easy snatch. The coyote put his head down and his haunches high, ready to pounce.

At the Emergency Services Unit, B. K. Mullan was assembling information in his computer. B.K. had become a master at this, completely modernizing the unit. Everyone called him B.K., and no one knew what it stood for. There were a lot of jokes about it standing for Beast Killer. B.K. did not find this funny, because his job was to capture animals alive.

There was that one time with the python, but B.K. admitted that he didn't understand snakes. And the ocelot had barely survived, but that was just because he didn't realize how much smaller than mountain lions they were. He was not making that mistake again. He was supposed to be looking for a wolf, but it was more likely a coyote, and that could be one hundred pounds smaller.

There were an increasing number of reports of missing pets—even more than usual. There were calls about a "weird-looking dog." Several callers said they saw a coyote. Even more said they had seen a wolf. They received more than two hundred calls about dogs howling at night. One woman said she had been walking her retriever on Central Park West when a wolf jumped out of a bush and grabbed him and dragged him away. A man reported seeing a wolf eating birds and squirrels in Riverside Park.

Then there was the mauled pit bull. At first B.K. had thought it was a call about a pit bull mauling. They got calls all the time about pit bulls attacking other dogs or people. But this was different. The pit bull was the victim. He went to see it. This dog, with tooth punctures on his face and shoulder, was clearly not attacked by a wolf. He would not have survived a wolf, but also the angle of attack was different. A man described the animal leaping above the grass to pounce on squirrels and mice, a typical coyote move. This was a coyote.

After several days of entering information into his computer he had his conclusion: it was a coyote who had entered Manhattan from the West Bronx across the Henry Hudson Bridge. It had moved down the West Side and would currently . . . currently be . . . near the dog run off the West Side Highway at about Houston Street. He checked his equipment and got in his van.

A nna saw Arthur and Freser and was about to walk up to them when Arthur did a sudden and strange thing. He darted to the side of a brownstone stoop and stared out.

What was he looking at?

It was that new girl who moved in across the hall.

Anna had never spoken with her, and for a long time Arthur hadn't, either. But he was curious about her, curious about her fabulous shoes. She left her shoes outside her door just across the hall from Arthur's door. This told Arthur that whoever had moved in, she was not a New Yorker. She was not worried about someone stealing her shoes. And they were probably expensive shoes. They were gold, or purple or chartreuse, with matching jewels. Some had spiral straps that wrapped up the leg. All of them had very long heels, sometimes thick and sometimes so thin it was hard to believe anyone could balance on them. In his occasional more honest moments Arthur had to admit to himself—he never discussed it with anyone else—that there was something vaguely erotic about the idea of some woman leaving clothing that she wore at night, exotic intimate clothing, he thought, in front of his door. Every morning one pair was left out from whatever she had been doing the night before. Arthur wanted to steal one of the shoes—just one—to teach her a lesson, he told himself, though he knew that wasn't the truth. He wanted to steal a shoe just to have it. He did not know why. Was it to have a part of an incredible nightlife she was experiencing with her shoes? Why did she leave them out, anyway? In time, it was a morning ritual. He would walk Freser and, opening his door, he would wonder what shoes she had left. Freser was interested, too, and once grabbed one in his mouth. Arthur had to kneel down and take it away. Then he panicked, imagining that she would open the door at just that moment with him squatted down, holding one of her shoes. He quickly tossed it to the ground.

He never saw her but naturally imagined her to be tall and shapely, with sleepy eyes and cascading curls of satin-sheened brunette curls.

Then one morning there she was. He knew that would ruin it. She was a thin, not particularly shapely, short, tough-looking young woman with her hair unnaturally black and streaked with purple. But he had to admit that there was something sensual about her even if it was only the tragedy of self-mutilation. She wore a short skirt and a sleeveless halter and was in the process of putting on thick-heeled copper-colored shoes. A green, red, and blue floral design was tattooed on her shoulder and flowed down her sinewy arm. Her flat, pale stomach and back had a partially exposed tattooed Asian scene involving elephants and tigers and forest leaves. The colors were vivid against her white skin, but he couldn't quite make out the drawing with so much of it covered above and below. There was a vine or a snake that started at her ankle and rose to under her skirt. To where? Was her entire body covered in tattoos? He strained to see if he could confirm the design under her clothes.

"What are you looking at?" said an angry voice. One eyebrow was encased in so many rings it looked like a furry caterpillar emerging from a metal tunnel. Her eyes were strikingly light blue, perhaps striking only because so much black makeup encircled them that she had the stare of a frightened raccoon. There was something silver and bullet-like piercing a nostril and two silver arrows stuck out of her cheek. Her shoes were probably not that expensive, after all.

"Well?"

Arthur realized that he had spent an inappropriate length of time staring at her body and he felt embarrassed.

"Are you stalking me?"

"What?"

"Are you some kind of stalker? What do you want?"

"No. I live here."

"So why are you stalking me?"

"I live here. I could just as well say you were stalking me."

"What! Me stalking you!"

Arthur was surprised by the angry reaction, but then he realized that this was not a good thing to say to a woman. "No, I just was . . ."

"Listen. I carry a can of mace in my purse and my cell-phone is set on nine-one-one. I can call the cops. It's illegal to stalk."

"I wasn't stalking. I just . . ."

"Stalk. Gawk. It's all illegal, you fucking pervert."

Arthur wondered what her idea of perverted was. Then he realized that he had been attracted to her because he thought she was a pervert—a person who did wild unacceptable physical acts into the night. With her shoes on or off? He didn't know why he thought that. Probably some unfair judgment. But he did know that men never won these things. She would go to the police and nothing he said would matter. He would be the sick old man. It was the "old" part that bothered him, that would bother Anna. It was perfectly okay to be a young pervert.

He and Freser walked past her to go outside. He would avoid her.

Now here she was and he did not want to appear to be looking at her, but he realized that he could follow her and find his way home. How did he know she was going home? She turned right on Charles Street and then left on Christopher. This felt like the right way.

What does he want with her? Anna wondered.

Freser was pulling on the leash, not wanting to follow her, acting agitated, making it harder for Arthur to follow undiscovered. Why did he have to act like that now? He was probably just reacting to Arthur's agitation.

The coyote found it was easy to follow undiscovered. Coyotes knew how to do this, and he trotted at a distance, thinking, *This will be so easy. Next time they stop.*

Arthur crossed Bedford Street and then realized she was

out of sight. He had lost her. Where did he live? Why couldn't he remember? He looked at the two- and three-story brick houses. Where did she turn to get back to Barrow Street? He must know this. He was holding his head in his hands and the coyote was about to make his snatch when they both heard a voice behind him. "Stalker!"

She had ducked down Bedford Street to fool him. "You are behind me," said Arthur. "You'd have to be the stalker. I was just going home."

"You are going the wrong way. You were looking for me."

Arthur realized that Bedford Street must be the right way. "I'm just going home," Arthur said.

"I'm not putting up with this. I'll call the fucking cops."

Anna could not hear them, but she understood now. At first she felt sick. They were having a lovers' quarrel right there. She didn't want to believe it, but all the signs had been there for months. Arthur had been very distracted. His mind was somewhere else. Was it with someone else? She didn't want to think that, but it seemed that way. And now she had the truth. After a moment of anger, she started to smile. She had misread everything. Arthur was not so old, so worn and tired as she imagined. And that meant that she wasn't, either. She should confront him about this at some point and act extremely angry. But not now. Make him endure his angry lover.

The smile still on her face, she turned and walked in the other direction even though this was away from their building.

An easy snatch, thought the coyote, as he slithered into position.

The girl reached deeply into her large black leather bag with the orange fringe and she pulled out a spray can, which she held in one hand, and held a cellphone in the other. "You know what I'm going to do now? I'm going to give you a face full of mace and then call the cops."

So this was how she was. Arthur couldn't help thinking that he had been right. Role-playing. Power. Sadism. She probably had special outfits. But he also realized that if the police came while he was gasping from mace spray, they would believe anything she said.

"What do you have to say now?" she said, her metal-studded lips curling up in a smile showing unnaturally white teeth. Did it hurt to smile with all that hardware?

"You know what I have to say," Arthur answered, bringing his face so close to hers that he could touch her eyebrow rings with his nose. And then in a hoarse whisper he said, "Nevermore."

While she stared back at him quizzically he turned down Bedford Street. It seemed right. He was heading home. He was close. At Grove, Freser yanked him to the left. *Freser knows the way,* thought Arthur. Freser wanted to go faster. He pulled on the leash. At Bleecker he pulled them left again and up to Tenth Street. After about twenty minutes of this Arthur realized that he was no longer in the Village. Where was Freser going? Where was home? He reached for his cellphone, hoping that it was not completely dead.

Suddenly something leapt at Freser. He moved out of the way. Something so lifeless he thought it was a fur coat, a very ugly brown-and-gray one, flopped on the sidewalk.

B.K. never missed. That's why they called him B.K. He had been getting phone calls with sightings all over the West Village. He picked up the coyote and carried it to his van. "Don't worry," he said to Arthur and the few other people who had stopped. "He's just tranquilized. We're going to release this guy out where he belongs."

"Can you tell me where Barrow Street is?" Arthur asked. But B.K. didn't hear him. He was always focused on his work.

Arthur picked up Freser, realizing what had almost happened to him. Was he just a self-centered . . . old person? "Well, Freser," he said. "Let's go home. You lead the way."

But when he put him back on the sidewalk it was clear that Freser, now free of danger, wanted to go back to enjoying the sounds and smells and was not ready to go home.

Arthur Mintz wondered how he would ever get home. "Nevermore."

The coyote had no such worry. Coyotes know how to travel long distances and they are never lost because they know how to smell and how to listen. He would wake up in a cage and then be taken hundreds of miles away. No matter where this one was released, he was coming back to New York. He liked it here.

▼ ▼ ▼

Part Two: Mexico City: In the Capital

> If death's the reason for love
> we love unfaithful passion
> love the defeated
> those eyes gazing into time
>
> —Bei Dao, "On Eternity"
> (translated by Yanbing Chen)

The stench of Cuauhtémoc was almost unbearable. This was saying a lot, considering all the garbage it competed with—the sweet and sour smells of things rotting and the bitter smell of anything they burned for a little heat at night.

Décima couldn't wait for him to be eaten. Already the coyote had pulled out a foot—the right one, she thought, but couldn't be sure from that distance. The coyote was leaning back on his bony haunches, Cuauhtémoc's foot firmly in his mouth, and pulling. Soon the coyote would have the whole body out and he could drag it off and eat it. The raven circling overhead croaked until another joined him.

Why, Décima wondered, did a raven always call in another one? Just less for him. The coyote would let him

have only eyes, anyway. Décima would have thought the
raven would have wanted both eyes for himself, but he
always called over a partner. Maybe it was like having
Lázaro. If you had a partner, you had to share, but you
couldn't survive on your own.

It was all Lázaro's idea in the first place. Look at him
now, perched on a stuffed black garbage bag in a valley of
cans, triumphantly watching the coyote at work through
his new green-tinted sunglasses with black plastic frames
and a gringo name printed on one stem.

It had been Lázaro's idea to leave Morelos. "Let's go to

the capital," he said. "There's money and opportunities in D.F. We will just die here in Morelos."

He was right, too. They had nothing there. Décima's real name was Decimoquinto, the fifteenth. She was their fifteenth child and they never gave her a real name because they hoped she would die or run away. Finally she did. With Lázaro. To the capital. Where there were opportunities.

Suddenly it was as though she were slapped. Lázaro covered his face. It was that smell, sweeter and stronger than garbage, the stench of Cuauhtémoc days after he died. They should have buried him deeper, but with no shovels it was the best they could do. And the coyotes could probably dig him up, anyway. This one had dragged him out and was pulling him away to eat. Décima would have thought he would be all bones by now, but he had gotten fat, almost like he was made of balloons. He looked ready to pop. One of the ravens had already started on an eye. That was why Cuauhtémoc had made Lázaro promise to bury him with his sunglasses. Sunglasses were important if you wanted to keep your eyes. Sometimes when you are weak and dying the birds don't wait if you don't have glasses. They had been friends and Lázaro had the decency to let him die with his glasses. But he wasn't going to bury him with them.

Not that Lázaro was going to be able to keep them. Jalisco would take them. They didn't know his name, only that he was from Jalisco and that he had a machete. A man with a machete could take what he wanted. Sometimes he took Décima. It was very quick from behind sometimes when she went off to relieve herself or if Lázaro went off to relieve himself. Lázaro pretended he didn't know, that he never saw, because there was nothing he could do and if he tried, Jalisco would kill him and then Décima would be his and he could make her do whatever he wanted. Jalisco was the man with the machete.

He needed a machete because he had something to defend. He had a house. His house was a wooden box about four feet by four feet by four feet. A few other people in the dump had boxes, but Jalisco's was made of wood.

It took only a day until Jalisco punched Lázaro so hard in the side of the head his sunglasses fell to the ground and one dark lens cracked and fell out of the frame. Lázaro was so angry he forgot all about the machete and charged at Jalisco, headfirst, like a goat. Jalisco swung his machete but was off-balance. It was not a good swing. It didn't take an arm off or anything like that—only a slight gash in the forearm with a small trickle of blood. But it was enough to remind Lázaro that you can't fight a man with a machete. Perhaps later. There were many bottles here and he could break one and cut Jalisco's throat while he was sleeping and get back the sunglasses.

For now, Jalisco could not get the broken lens back in the frame so he covered that side with a piece of cardboard that said *"Uvas."* It seemed like bad luck to put a sign over your eye that said "grapes," but of course ravens probably liked eyes better than grapes. The people around the dump who never knew his name anyway started calling him Uvas.

Jalisco did not find this funny but there is only so much you can do with a machete. Décima, who like the ravens could not read, did not understand this debate.

Lázaro and Décima never regretted their decision to move to the capital. Even if at the moment they were living in a garbage dump, this was the Distrito Federal, the city of Aztec kings. At first it did not seem like anything special, just the same kind of houses they had always seen. But then they got to broad boulevards with statues bigger than trees and buildings like palaces lined up in a row. Some buildings were entirely made of glass. This city was full of big caciques, important rich people, and all you had to do was somehow make a connection to something. If you could sell something, there were plenty of people with money to buy it. Opportunity was everywhere in the capital.

They walked along Reforma, the biggest avenue they had ever seen, and at a particularly promising intersection they turned right. They saw the U.S. embassy, which was large and white and clean, and they saw people with carts selling food. Décima thought that someday they could have a cart and sell steamed tamales, which she knew how to make because her family had her make them.

Lázaro thought this was a bit ambitious and maybe they could start with hot yams. *"Camote!"* he practiced shouting, the way the yam sellers did. They found a small covered market. This was a very good spot to ask for money because people seemed to feel generous when they were buying things. They could understand that. It would be fun to buy things.

But entire families of Mazahuas had established their places on the sidewalks near the market and they sat there, the women in bright skirts, the men small and tough-looking.

Lázaro knew from back in Morelos that it was a mistake to get in a fight with indigenous people. It was like they said about the iguana—once they bite you they never let go. So they moved a few blocks away and sat in front of a pink house with a gate, bougainvillea growing on their wall, rich and bright as the Mazahuas' dresses.

Every morning a woman who looked like a Mexican but dressed like a gringa would come out, stop, open her purse, and with long fingers with the tips painted to match the bougainvillea offer some pesos—sometimes ten, sometimes a nice tightly rolled fifty-peso note. They were making good money and hiding it in Lázaro's pants, which was not a good place, but after Cuauhtémoc died he took his boots, which only had a few holes and were too good to feed to a coyote and he could hide the money there. They were sure that soon they would have enough money for a *camote* cart. Such things were not impossible in the capital.

At first they spent the night in the neighborhood. The Mazahuas would return to their mountain village. They thought this would give them an advantage with the early-morning shoppers before the rest could get in from the mountains. But Lázaro and Décima started noticing at day-break the bodies of people who had stayed the night. One man was so badly beaten he probably would never walk again. Another was lying in a puddle of blood, facedown, his pants and shoes missing.

Lázaro had not journeyed to the capital to end up dead on some street without his pants. It was a Mazahua woman who told them about the garbage dump. It was a long way away but not as far as the Mazahua villages, and it was a place to spend the night. The garbage dump was not their idea of being in the capital. But they could see that they would not survive sleeping on the street in town. After they got the *camote* cart working, they would find other possibil-ities. This was only temporary. The Mazahuas, of course, were hoping they would never return. To a Mazahua, a mes-tizo from Morelos was no different from a gringo.

They could eat on the way. When the market closed in the evening, there was lots of food to throw away—soft black bananas, mangoes whose orange flesh had turned brown. Sometimes there was even old meat with not too many flies. They could not bring the food back to the dump because that would arouse suspicion. But they could eat it as they went or even gather scraps of wood and light a fire and cook the meat or even roast the old fruit or vegetables they got. It was far better than what you could find to eat at the dump. Life in the capital was going to work for Décima and Lázaro.

The machete wound in his arm was not healing. In fact, the entire arm felt numb. At first it was red, but then it turned a pale, dead-looking color and it started to smell like Cuauhtémoc. Lázaro knew what that smell meant. He had to take care of Décima while he still had some strength. He was growing weaker all the time.

Jalisco now had a blind spot on the side where his sunglasses were cardboard, and Lázaro came up on that side with the broken-off neck of a Tecate beer bottle and drew the jagged glass as hard as he could across Jalisco's throat. Jalisco hissed and red bubbles started bulging from his throat. As he fell onto a heap of vegetable peelings, Lázaro grabbed his sunglasses and then, leaning over him, forced his eyes wide open with his fingers and said, "You thought you could have Décima. She's going to watch the birds pluck your fucking eyes out. What do you think of that, you fucking asshole? Look. The birds are already up there." And at just that moment an angry shriek came from the sky. He hoped Jalisco heard it, but now he was dead.

Lázaro dragged him to the edge of the dump, pulling him by one foot like a coyote would do. The coyote was already circling, his big tail dragging, waiting for his meat. Lázaro only had to back off about fifteen feet and wait a few minutes and the coyote was dragging Jalisco away. In the distance he could see a big purplish-black bird swoop down and land on his face.

Then Lázaro went back to Décima and presented her

with the machete. He had thought of bringing her Jalisco's
box, but he knew she would not want to live in his house.
Now, with the machete, she could defend herself. "Now you
are the one with the machete," he said as he settled into the
garbage. They both knew that he would never get up.

He lasted four more days. He moved his arm slowly, as
though beckoning her. She came over and in a frail whisper
he hissed, *"Camote!"* He smiled and then he died. Then Décima took the machete and dug as deep a hole as she could—
maybe three feet deep. She chose a low, flat place, and when
the hole was three feet deep she had still not struck ground.
She removed all the money from his boot and shoved it in
the waistband to her skirt and placed him in the hole with
his sunglasses with the one cardboard side securely on his
head. Then she covered him with garbage and sat on a pile of
trash and waited. All her work was for nothing. It took the
coyote an hour to find him and twenty minutes to dig him
up and pull him by one foot. The coyote was going to get to
chew on Cuauhtémoc's boots after all.

"Adiós, mi amor," she whispered to the man who had taken
her to the capital, as the coyote dragged him away. It was
the first time she had ever called him—or anyone—*"amor."*

Now she had to go into town by herself. At least she had
the machete. But it seemed that people would give
money to a couple but not a woman alone. Perhaps it was
the machete, though she kept it hidden under her skirt. But

the finely dressed women gave her nothing. Nor did any passersby. At the end of the day she went behind the market, looking for food. She had not eaten in several days. There was a coconut and she took out her machete and opened it.

"Look at that," one man said to his two companions as they slipped behind the market. "A woman alone with a big machete."

The three men walked over to her and she knew she was in trouble, knew she should swing the machete, but she was too weak, too tired, too hungry. The men threw her to the ground and started tearing at her clothing. It didn't take them long to find her roll of money, all of the money she and Lázaro had saved for the *camote* cart. One man held her arms to the ground and the other held her legs, spreading them far apart. She screamed as loud as she could and one of them grabbed a clay water jug and smashed it over her head.

When she woke up a broken jug was lying next to her and someone was screaming. The money, of course, was gone, as was her machete. Her clothes were ripped. She wished the screaming would stop. She had a terrible headache. She did not know if they had done anything to her. She tried to sit up, but she was very dizzy and the screaming got worse. Objects slipped in and out of focus. She managed to stand up and she somehow staggered all the way back to the garbage dump. It took almost two days. When she got there she collapsed on a soft pile of cardboard with some tin cans. She forced herself to get up but could manage no more than a crawl on hands and knees. She saw someone and crawled toward them. The other person was crawling, too. When she got close enough she struggled to focus and made out two yellow eyes. They were not cruel eyes, not brutal. They were . . . wise. They were eyes of someone who simply knew what was going to happen.

Décima lay down and reached to her torn skirt and ripped off a strip of cloth that she wrapped tightly around her head and secured with a knot, which made her headache worse. But she had to cover her eyes. She lay down on the trash and hoped that she would die before the coyote took her. She just wanted the screaming to stop. She could hear the animal breathing. Her last thought was, *At least I didn't die in Morelos.*

SAN SEBASTIÁN

Begoña and the Bear

... because life is not a show, because a sea of pain is not a proscenium, because a screaming man is not a dancing bear.

—Aimé Césaire,
Notebook of a Return to the Native Land

Hunters have shot dead the last female brown bear native to the Pyrenees, condemning the species to extinction and causing an "environmental catastrophe" for France, the government said. Animal protection groups were last night concerned for the survival of the bear's 10-month-old orphaned cub which escaped unharmed, but which was barely weaned. His mother, affectionately known by game wardens as Cannelle (Cinnamon), was killed on Monday when a group of boar-hunters shot her in what they claim was self-defense.

—*The Guardian*, November 3, 2004

The last female brown bear native to the Spanish Pyrenees is thought to have died, signalling an end to the species.

Ecologists have expressed concern after it emerged
Camille, a female bear whose territory crossed the
mountains in the northeastern Spanish regions of
Aragon and Navarre, had not been seen since February 5.

The bear, who was thought to be around 20 years
old, has not been sighted and there had been no
reports either of attacks on livestock or on bee-
hives within her territory for eight months, leading
the Spanish conservation group, Ecologistas en
Accion, to conclude: "The bear is almost certainly
dead."

—*The Telegraph*, October 27, 2010

I t was time. The Joaldunak had not stamped the ground
to awaken it for spring, the wind still raced from the
steep scrubby cliffs down the sheer drop to the valley
and ripped through the village of a few dozen stone houses
that was Ituren. There were two bars, both on corners of the
narrow stone-paved streets, and Zubi Nabaroa sat on a
wooden stool in one of them under a row of hams hung by
their ankles. He tried to warm himself on his second glass
of hot coffee, sherry, and anise liqueur. This time of year it
took two glasses to warm up, but it always worked.

Once he was warm enough, Zubi would pack up his chorizos, for which the wealthy Basques of San Sebastián paid high prices on San Sebastián Day, January 20, when all the rich people were drunk and full of Basque spirit. The price of 500 grams of his chorizo in San Sebastián on January 20 would feed a large family for a week in Ituren. But of course, you didn't eat in Ituren the way you did in San Sebastián— all that baby eel, and *bixugo* fish with garlic, and stuffed spider crab, while in Ituren there was lamb and ham and chorizo.

Zubi made the best chorizo, which was why they paid those prices in San Sebastián. He raised his own pigs, black-and-white Basque pigs, which were the sweetest and easiest pigs in the world. This was not because they were Basque but because, like the Basque people, they had very large ears. Unlike the Basque people, their ears flopped over their eyes so they could not see where they were going. When your ears cover your eyes you take life as it comes. That was why they put blinders on horses. These pigs had good but short lives, eating copious amounts of local acorns and dying young to make chorizo. The chorizo hung from the trees all winter and was very hard—some said too hard, but that was how it was made.

When Zubi finally was warm enough—it took a third coffee, sherry, and anise—he wrapped his gray wool scarf tight around his neck, zipped up his fleece-lined leather coat, secured his big beret on his head to keep dry if it rained, tapped his walking stick against the stone corner piece of the building, hefted his bundle of chorizos to his back, and walked to the bank of the Ezcurra. The mountains weren't melting yet and the Ezcurra was only a rocky stream and it was easy to walk over her curving weedy bank. It would be more of a river when it turned into the Bidasoa. By following the rivers he avoided climbing mountains. Once he got to the mouth of the Bidasoa he would not be far from San Sebastián.

A raven shrieked in the sky and Zubi raised his fist and cursed. That son of a bitch wasn't going to steal his chorizo. But as he looked on a nearby crest he saw the rounded bulk and humped shoulders of a large brown bear. He studied the furry hulk. Was it really a bear? He had not seen one since he was a small boy. He remembered how the sheep men hated them and shot them anytime they got a chance. He did not blame them. The bears killed their sheep. How would he feel if the bears ate his pigs? But they didn't. He had heard that there were no Basque bears left. Everyone knew that. In the Basque-language press the passing of bears was second only to bicycle racing. He had seen a show about it on Basque-language television in one of the bars in Ituren.

He periodically looked behind him up in the mountains and usually he saw nothing, but sometimes he would see the bear. It was following him. No doubt after his chorizo. Zubi was not going to let him take the chorizo, his valuable annual supply for the fiesta.

But suppose the bear came down to take them. How

would he stop it? Just the black claws on his paws were longer than his fingers. Unlike the sheep men of his childhood,
he had no gun. What would he do?

When he got to bigger towns the bear would probably
leave him. Soon he saw the red tile roofs of Vera de Bidasoa,
a town with maybe three thousand people, some paved road,
and some cars. The bear would not follow him anymore.

He rented a room over a bar for the night—a small, clean
room with a red tile floor and dark oak furniture. There was
a simple wooden crucifix on the wall in which Christ looked
strangely comfortable hanging there. A lot of pilgrims came
through and stayed in the room.

Down at the bar, everyone was talking about Begoña.
Begoña was the most famous Basque terrorist still living.
She was said to be a leader of the most violent Basque
national group. It was also said that she had bombed several
locations in Madrid and assassinated a Policía Nacional colonel in Zaragoza. She was credited with three train station
attacks and numerous bank robberies. She was rumored to
have killed five Guardia Civil. She lured them into a hotel
room one by one and strangled each of them either before,
after, or during lovemaking, depending on who was telling
the story. She was said to be very beautiful, but that was not
certain, because no one knew what she looked like.

Begoña is a Vizcayan name from near Bilbao, and so it
was supposed that she spoke Basque like the people in that
far province. But she was sly enough to have changed her

dialect. Maybe Begoña was not even her real name. In fact, it is not certain that she was present at any of the crimes she was said to commit. According to one rumor she was really a man. She may have been in her early twenties, but some said she was in her nineties, a veteran of the Basque Army during the civil war.

A man drinking brandy early the next morning at the bar where Zubi was warming up with coffee, sherry, and anise told this last rumor. Here they made the coffee with too much sherry and not enough anise.

The reason everyone was talking about Begoña was that she was said to be going to the San Sebastián festival, no doubt to blow something up or assassinate someone. How could they find her when most of the town would be wearing disguises, either Napoleonic soldiers or chefs, or even a few oil sheiks, pirates, and frozen belly dancers.

When Zubi left town he looked up on the ridge and there was the bear waiting for him. He thought of going back to town and finding someone with a gun to shoot it. But he couldn't do that. This was probably the last Basque bear.

Zubi continued to see the bear from time to time, even as he got into more crowded areas. Walking along the highway between Irún and Errenteria, he looked up on the thick green carpet of the hillside and saw the brown rounded top of the bear. Just past the seaport at Pasaia, the bear was behind a rock. Zubi did not see it again and he safely finished the last downhill hike into San Sebastián, where he removed his large blue damp beret. There were a lot of Spaniards in San Sebastián, and it was a good idea not to look too Basque.

Though a hard, cold wind blew from the mountains with that clean, bitter scent of snow, the streets were filling up. The seventy-five *txokos*, gastronomic societies for men and a few women who liked to cook together, had all organized their march. A group was finely dressed in Napoleonic uniforms. They wore high leather boots over tight white breeches, a little too revealing for the figures of gastronomes. Then there were smartly tailored blue tunics with red-and-white piping and tall cylindrical Napoleonic hats. These soldiers marched in formation, beating drums in unison, first pounding the skins then beating the sticks together in a tinny noise then back to the drumheads with their deep-bellied thuds. They did this with great seriousness, not a smile showing on their faces, which were reddened by the grating wind and by the flush of alcohol to keep them warm. The shops they passed offered them drinks.

Each group of soldiers was followed by red-faced musicians and then a chef in white with a puffed-out toque on his head, conducting the group behind him with a giant knife or fork used as a baton. Then came women in kerchiefs and traditional working dresses and then chefs in white.

The women and the chefs answered the soldiers' drums with a battery of their own on upside-down buckets and pots. A loud battery of drums and then a response from a loud battery of buckets. Each flourish got a slightly more elaborate response. The Basques, who forget nothing, remember that when Napoleon's troops occupied San Sebastián the troops were constantly harassed by jeering unarmed women to their rear.

Drums echoing through the streets and off the mountains that stayed green even in the winter, they stopped for extravagant debates from drum to bucket in front of each police station and even the headquarters of the Ertzaintza, the Basque police. Captain Jenaro Anitua, from nearby Zarautz, stood on the balcony, a gallant figure in his black uniform and red beret, and waved to the drummers while several of the men from his antiterrorism unit, helmeted and masked, examined ruddy faces one by one, looking for Begoña, though they did not know what she looked like.

At Casa Pampl, the large elegant restaurant with two Michelin stars—some years he had three—owner Pampi Urabayen had just received word that the crabber had arrived. The tall, silver-haired man with a reassuring smile and a calm demeanor seemed uncharacteristically nervous. This was the night for *txangurro*. There was still afternoon light, blinding white sunlight exploding from behind dark afternoon clouds, but by ten-thirty tonight revelers would burst into his restaurant demanding *txangurro*, stuffed spider crab. It took some time and skill to locate and extract the meager white flesh of a spider crab without damaging the shells so they could be refilled and served.

He needed about sixty and had hired an extra cook, a local specialist, to do the crab. The crab were waiting, but where was the crabber? Finally he was told that the crabber had arrived—why so late?—and turned to leave his carpeted room and head for the room off of the main kitchen, where the crabs were waiting, to make sure the crabber had everything he needed. But Lore from the reservation desk ran up to him with a smile almost the width of her face and said, "Pampi! They're here."

Pampi thought for a second about checking on his crabber first, but he bounced up and down on his toes to change direction, grabbed a case of champagne, and ran to his balcony. This was his favorite moment of the day, and he jumped up and down with childish excitement as he heard the drummers approach.

"Ba-pa ba-pa ba-pa," pounded the soldiers. "Ba de dad a bade dat dat dat," answered the women and the chefs. Gently, one by one, Pampi tossed down champagne bottles. Chefs caught them against their soft bellies, which seemed designed for catching champagne bottles. They opened the bottles with loud pops that made the black-and-red Ertzaintza and the green Policía Nacional very nervous. But Pampi, who prided himself on the right drink for every moment, decided that it was too cold for champagne and ordered his staff to serve coffee with brandy.

They marched below—the French soldiers, the women, the chefs, the soldiers, the women . . . the bear. Yes, a large Basque brown bear. One of the spectators, a heavyset man with a thick black beard, shouted in a wet-throated voice, "Look, it's Begoña!" He let out a loud laugh, but no one else was laughing. The crowd released a collective shriek and turned to the rear. The bear panicked and lumbered out of sight down Trueba Street.

"This is strange," Pampi said to himself, but he did not have time to think about it any longer than that. He had to go check on the crabber.

Lore came up to him again, this time without the smile, and said, "Pampi, Colonel Gallego Gomez wants to talk to you."

It seemed to Pampi that this was the perfect time for a small glass of dry sherry, and he poured two glasses of amontillado, dry but golden and complex, shipped to him directly from a vintner in El Puerto de Santa María. He directed the colonel to a table in the corner of his still-empty restaurant. There was something stiff and squeaky about the colonel that resembled new leather. He even made that leather squeak when he moved, perhaps from his thick belt.

"What can I do for you, Colonel?"

The colonel, holding his glass to his perfectly trimmed black mustache and taking one sip, said, "Pampi can I take you into my confidence?"

Colonel Rafael Gallego Gomez was known as a torturer of extreme cruelty, a man who knew how to make people talk or how to kill them in slow, terrible ways, sometimes both. No one really wanted to be in his confidence. But what could Pampi do? Here he was. "Certainly," Pampi said with his charming smile.

The colonel squeaked his leather as he leaned closer and whispered, "Begoña is here."

Pampi looked alarmed. "Here in my restaurant!"

"No. Of course not. But here somewhere in San Sebastián. And it is my job to see that she doesn't leave."

"Listen, Colonel. I am all for that. All these stupid little acts of violence are ruining the city and ruining my business. Every time they do something there are a few tourists who will not come back. Tonight I can feed locals, but the rest of the year I depend on tourists. You have to get rid of these terrorists."

"I know that a lot of people come here with a lot of different kinds of politics and you hear things."

"If I hear something, I will tell you."

"Not the Guardia Civil. Not the Ertzaintza, me."

"You. Absolutely, Colonel." Then Pampi stood up. "Excuse me, but I have the stuffing of sixty crab to oversee for tonight. Why don't you come back later and I will serve you a *txangurro*."

"I hate crab."

"No matter," said Pampi. "What do you like?"

"Lobster."

"Come back about eleven. I will serve you lobster and champagne."

"Thank you very much."

And as the colonel squeaked toward the door, Pampi added, "Oh, and Colonel, please be careful. Begoña may have come here to get you."

The colonel's black mustache curled on one end. "I am here to get her." And then he walked out and down the stairs and out onto the busy streets, one hand on a squeaky leather holster, observing everything on the streets . . . listening to every word.

He turned on narrow Legazpi Street near the market. He could hear the drumming a few blocks away. He walked right by Zubi Nabaroa, who was displaying his chorizo—a quiet street ill-suited for commerce but where the city had told him to go. He had already sold quite a few. Colonel Gallego looked at him as though counting the pores in his skin. Zubi was glad he had taken off his beret.

Suddenly there was a deep asthmatic gurgling sound. It was the bear, closer than Zubi had ever seen him and looking very large, with a strong sour smell like the smell of nature disturbed. The bear, which, to judge from its size, must have been a male, spied the chorizo he had come into town for and stared at it with small, hard eyes. He moved toward the chorizo.

The colonel unsnapped his holster and pulled out his handgun and shouted something at the bear. Zubi could tell that it was supposed to be Basque, but he could make out only the word "Begoña." Then he repeated it in Spanish, a language Zubi did not speak well, but he knew the colonel had said, "Begoña. Stop or I shoot!"

Zubi did not find it odd that the Spaniard would mistake the bear for Begoña. Begoña was famous for her disguises, and Spaniards always imagined Basques to be more skilled than they were. Besides, the colonel knew that there were no more bears. But Zubi realized that the Spaniard was going to shoot the last remaining Basque bear. He grabbed one of his thick meter-long chorizos and swung it as hard as he could.

Zubi Nabaroa was a strong man. The chorizo struck the colonel in the head and he was motionless for a moment. Then he turned around and stared at Zubi with his small, dark eyes—very similar, it occurred to Zubi, to the bear's eyes. A small rivulet of blood trickled down from his hairline. Then he snarled and said, "Begoña!" and he staggered and reached for Zubi like . . . like a bear reaching for chorizo. What could he do? The colonel knew his face. Zubi smashed him again with the chorizo as hard as he could, and this time the head made a heavy thud different from the time before. The colonel crumbled onto the cold stone-paved street. The bear, much as he wanted the chorizo, had retreated as soon as he saw the gun.

P ampi!" shouted Lore from the dining room to Pampi, who was headed toward the kitchen. "Pampi, Captain Jenaro Anitua is here. He wants to speak to you."

With resignation Pampi made his way to the bar and poured two small straight glasses of dark reddish-amber *patxaran* made by a farmer he knew in Navarra who made it from tiny wild plums.

"Kaixo, Jenaro," he greeted the captain, who was wear-

ing his red beret jauntily to the side more like a soldier than a Basque.

"*Aizu, Pampi.*"

They sat and sipped *patxaran*, and the captain, as he always did when he sipped alcohol, started talking about Zarautz, where he came from. "You know," said the captain, "Zarautz has the most beautiful harbor in the world."

Pampi smiled.

"All right, it's not Donostia," he said, using the Basque name for San Sebastián to be polite.

"It's a nice town."

"I know a man in Zarautz who paints a painting every day of the same view past the beach of that big rock in the harbor. Every day and every painting is completely different. I'd like to live in Zarautz and do a painting every day."

"Do you paint?"

"I'd like to learn."

"So why not quit the Ertzaintza?"

"And then what do I do for money? My wife likes it here in Donostia. She shops and shops and shops." He took a deep sip of his *patxaran*. "So Pampi, we are friends, are we not?"

"*Bai,*" Pampi agreed in Basque.

The captain leaned forward and pulled his red beret down and whispered, "You can't tell anyone I told you this . . . Begoña is here."

"In Donostia!"

"*Bai!* You can imagine how the Spanish want her. We can't let the Policía Nacional or the Guardia Civil take her.

The Ertzaintza has to take her. That's why we were created. To show that the Basque could police themselves. We have to be the one to take her."

"What can I do?" Pampi whispered.

"I know you hear a lot here. If you hear something I should know, call this number. It is my direct cellphone." He handed him a handsomely engraved card. "Don't turn her over to the Spanish. We are here."

"Jenaro, you can count on my help—if I hear anything."

"Ezkerrik asko."

"You are welcome, my friend. Come by later and I'll serve you a stuffed *txangurro.*"

"Emm. I like *txangurro.* We eat them in Zarautz."

"I'll have one for you," said Pampi, remembering that he should check on how they were coming along.

Zubi Nabaroa, who wished he had never left Ituren, was sweating. He had killed a Spanish colonel and had heard what happened to Basques who did such things. He would be horribly tortured. He had heard stories of hot irons, electricity, partial drownings, even castration with a hunting knife. Better to die now than to fall into Spanish hands. Or he knew places in the high mountains where he could hide and never be found.

But wait! What was there to connect him to the killing? Only two things: the body and the murder weapon. Wasn't that about everything but the confession?

But the body could be hidden, and the murder weapon—he could sell it off to be eaten as soon as possible. After all, it was just a large chorizo.

Then he realized that he did not have to hide the body. It could be found, just somewhere else—not in front of his stand. An ideal place was close by—the market. The market was closed and anybody could have killed the colonel there. So he removed his six remaining yard-long sausages from the sturdy canvas bag in which he carried them. With a cloth he wiped the trickle of blood now dried black off the colonel's forehead so that he would look presentable. He then put the bag over the colonel's head and turned it upside down. Zubi thought he would fold him into the bottom of the bag, but he was becoming a little stiff. He put the chorizos in so that the bag had chorizo tops and two boots showing from the top, but no one was going to notice. Everyone was drunk.

When he got to the market he turned the bag upside down and peeled off the bag like unveiling a statue. The colonel was standing stiffly against a wall by a pile of empty boxes. Zubi stepped back and decided the colonel looked good standing there, he had looked a little stiff before he died and now was no different, and so he gathered up his chorizos and left.

He was careful to identify which chorizo was the murder weapon, a particularly hard and thick sausage, which made it too obvious when the police started looking through the sausages for the weapon. Of course, that was the one they would choose because it was the best one. It made the best club. But also, if someone knew chorizo, it was the best one. He should sell it to someone special, someone who knew chorizo and was sure to savor it—quickly.

Not all the chefs in all the *txokos* were drumming on the streets. Ander Elarregui, for example, wore neither his chef's uniform nor that of a Napoleonic soldier. A small man with wire-rim thick-lens glasses that suggested poor vision, he nevertheless was thought to be the best wing shot in Basque country. Every fall he went to Roncesvalles and hid in the pine woods where Basque warriors once waited to pounce on Roland and the French rear guard of Charlemagne. From there, through his thick glasses, he would shoot quantities of little gray-and-white wild pigeons, with which, not only according to his own *txoko*—Gastrotxa-peldun—but according to most everyone in Guipúzcoa, incontestably he made the best *salmis de paloma*.

Also not drumming was a thick sturdy man with a tangle of curly long black-and-gray hair called Marmitako. His real name was José Marie Lizar, but he made the best *marmitako* in Basque country. A *marmitako* is a fisherman's stew and there is no agreement on the ingredients other than that tuna must be included. Marmitako would never say what his ingredients were. Food was going this way. The rough, simple foods of fishermen and farmers were becoming the prized dishes of expensive restaurants. *Alubias de*

Tolosa, just a bowl of red beans, was a fiercely fought contest in Tolosa every year that Marmitako could never win, probably because no matter how good his beans, he was a Vizcayan in a Guipuzcoan contest.

But in truth Marmitako was not good at anything but making *marmitakos.* He had failed at every job he ever got, had not worked for several years, and was completely without money. Many said that Marmitako was not very smart. Some said that he was dumb. Ander explained that he just seemed that way because he spoke in Vizcayan.

Ander wanted to help him because he was married to Ander's sister. And he had a plan.

Ander was an executive at a downtown branch of Kutxabank. Ten months earlier he was promoted and given the combination to the large walk-in safe. This knowledge weighed heavily on him. He wanted to rob that bank and all he had to do was walk in and take the money. But if he did that they would know that he had done it because he had the combination. So the question was how to make it look like it was someone else.

Then, only a few days earlier, a solution came to Ander. The solution was brilliant, but it required a plan. Ander had not slept in days and his eyes were red. But so were everyone else's from staying up late and drinking. What gave him the idea was that he heard that Begoña was coming. With Begoña in town, any bank robbery would be blamed on her. That was assuming that no one saw him rob the bank. And that was why he needed Marmitako.

They built two bombs. Bombs were Begoña's kind of weapon. The two bombs had to be on timers set to the exact same time. One was a big bomb and one was smaller. This may all sound difficult, but Ander, who always had a mechanical gift, found all the information he needed on the Internet.

There were even a few helpful suggestions at what appeared to be a website from Basque terrorists. The bombs were built in boxes used to transport the large rounds of sheep-milk cheese that Basque farms produced, *ardi gasna*. He was even able to get cheese labels from local farms to put on the boxes. Ander set the bombs in advance to blow up in exactly two hours and forty-five minutes. Then Marmitako's only task was to leave his large bomb somewhere in the train station while Ander left his small one by the bank. Ander didn't need a bomb. He had a key. But a bomb would look more authentic. The train station would be bombed and draw all the police and no one would notice the bank.

And so Marmitako set off for the train station with a box of cheese. But twenty minutes later he was back at the corner bar where Ander was waiting. The bartender had bought some exceptional chorizo, large and hard, and cut it in paper-thin slices, which Ander was enjoying with a glass of *txakoli* that the bartender poured from high over his glass so that it would fizz. Marmitako tried to get Ander's attention, but the bartender was explaining to Ander that he bought the sausage from the producer, who came to town with it only this once a year, and that he was just around the corner from the market if Ander wanted to buy one. All the while Marmitako kept trying to interrupt.

"What do you want?" Ander finally turned to him.

Marmitako motioned for him to leave the bar.

"Did you plant it?" asked Ander.

"Not exactly," said Marmitako.

"What does that mean? The thing has a timer!"

"I know, I know. There's time. But something happened." Marmitako was speaking Vizcaíno and Ander was having trouble understanding.

"Calm down, Marmitako, and tell me in Castilian."

"Okay. I was carrying the box and I went by the market on the way to the train station and that colonel was there."

"Which colonel?"

"That Gallego from the Policía Nacional. He was just standing there staring right at me and he looked kind of funny and then I had a brilliant idea."

"Really, what was that?"

"There was a big pile of boxes. Cheese boxes with labels and everything. I think they were all empty. It was that stuff from the French side. Above Arnéguy. Nice strong flavor from the high pasture . . ."

"What happened to the bomb!" Ander suddenly shouted. Sweat made his glasses slide down his nose.

"Nothing. I just left it there with the other cheese boxes. Smart, huh?"

Ander stared at him. "Aside from the fact that a bomb in an empty market is not going to attract the attention of a bomb in a crowded train station, there is the fact that the location is all wrong. The train station would draw all the police away from the area, and the market will draw them all into the area where the bank is."

"It's okay. I know where to find it and the colonel is probably gone now. I'll go back and get the cheese and take it to the train station. There is still plenty of time." He was also thinking he could stop by and get one of those chorizos.

"Hurry up. And then call me when you have it planted. But be careful what you say over a cellphone."

"I'll just say that Aunt Karmele got her cheese."

"Perfect."

"Listen, Ander, maybe we shouldn't do the train station. A lot of people could get hurt there."

"Marmitako," Ander said, staring at him through his thick lenses that concentrated his red eyes into tiny penetrating lasers. "Do you want the money or do you want to be a loser all your life?"

Marmitako retreated with his wound. How could his friend talk to him like that? If he just got this money no one would ever speak to him like that again.

Ander waited at the bar with more chorizo and *txakoli*. Still waiting for his call, he moved on to grilled Guernica peppers with coarse salt from Vizcaya. He also took a nice little open sandwich with baby eels. The more he ate, the more he wanted one of those big chorizos to take home.

Time was running out. Wherever that bomb was, in forty-four minutes it would explode and he had to leave his by the bank. Why wasn't Marmitako calling? There was no more time. The fool had used up all his time and now he would not be able to buy a chorizo. He paid his bill and, with the box marked *"Ardi gasna"* under his arm, left for his bank.

Marmitako wondered, what if he went to the train station and there were people there he knew? Well, they were probably people who called him "a loser." Maybe he could find a spot at the train station where there were not a lot of people.

Walking quickly to the market to retrieve his package, Marmitako turned down Legazpi Street. The air was still filled with the pounding rhythmic debate of drummers, but this street was empty except that Zubi Nabaroa was still there. And he had two chorizos left. Marmitako thought of buying both and giving one to his friend Ander. But he had heard they were very expensive. But then, after today, what would he care about the price of chorizo?

Zubi was studying the man approaching him. He had the body of a peasant. Would this be the man to whom he should sell the murder weapon? But suddenly behind his prospective customer he saw the large figure of brown furry rolling muscle coming down the street. He pointed and Marmitako turned. Who does he see coming toward him but Begoña herself, dressed in a bear suit and looking angry. Everyone thought he was a fool but he was not tricked this time.

"I didn't know you would be so mad," Marmitako pleaded

to the bear. He was scared. "I thought you liked getting credit for these things."

The bear swatted with his huge paws and his long black claws and slammed Marmitako into the wall of a building. It looked to Zubi as though he were just tossing him out of the way. *He's coming for my chorizo,* Zubi thought. *Maybe I should give* him *the murder weapon.*

"Begoña," Marmitako implored, bleeding and struggling to stand.

But the bear threw him against the wall again and slashed with his claws and blood splattered on the wall. "Begoña, it wasn't my idea!" Marmitako screamed, and the bear, alarmed, lumbered back down the street with surprising speed.

Marmitako collapsed—dead.

Zubi groaned.

It was not good to have corpses in front of your chorizo stand. This one was a bit too messy to put in his chorizo bag, so he dragged it by the arms back to the market. The colonel was still there and looking good, though a bit too pale. Maybe if he dumped this one next to him they would think they killed each other, though the claw marks might be hard to explain. Maybe a desperate struggle? But as he dragged Marmitako to the colonel's feet, the colonel fell over, straight as a felled tree. It was as though he'd died again. Best to leave everything.

He returned to his stand and discovered that the latest

victim had left behind a box. It was a cheese. *Ardi gasna*. A sheep's cheese. Was it made in the high country, where the grazing is tough and the milk tastes strong, or was it made with the rich bland milk from the valleys? He preferred high-country cheese. He sniffed the box and couldn't tell, though he thought he detected a certain valley richness. He would look later. He tucked the cheese under his stool.

Ander, still angry about missing the chorizo man, wondered why Marmitako had not called him. Muttering to himself, he made his way to a safe position across the street from the Kutxabank. It was a commercial street and all the stores, including the bank, were gated closed. Ander placed his box in front of the bank. What if some passerby noticed it? He thought of unlocking the door and placing the bomb inside. But maybe they would be able to tell later. Better not.

There were still some drums and some trumpets heard around town, but then there was a very large boom. Ander was surprised at how loud it was. The other one was a long way away at the train station but sounded much closer. The front of the Kutxabank dissolved so suddenly that he didn't even see it fall. It just wasn't there anymore. He rushed into the building.

Captain Jenaro Anitua was in his black-and-red car. He received a call that someone had "blown up the market. So far they had found two dead and no wounded." Why would she blow up the closed market? Maybe she wanted to scare people without a lot of casualties. They did that sometimes.

He was about to turn on his siren and rush to the market, which was not far away, when he saw a small dusty man coming out of the Kutxabank, carrying one of those cheap brown leather shoulder bags. The man was so slight that at first he imagined it was a woman dressed as a man. Begoña! Some said Begoña was very small. But then the captain recognized the man. It was that man from the bank. Señor . . . Señor . . . Elarregui. He parked the car at an angle to block him, almost pinning him against the building.

"Señor Elarregui," he shouted as he got out of the car.

Ander struggled for words. "I was just . . . I . . . The front of the building is gone."

"I see that."

"I was checking for . . . for damage."

"What's in the bag?" said the captain, grabbing it from him.

He pulled the zipper, which made a high-pitched note. Looking inside, he estimated that the bills totaled more than one million euros.

In life there are some split seconds that take a long time and others that fly by quickly even though in real time they are both the same length. This was a fast moment. Jenaro liked the feeling of holding more than a million euros in cash. That was the only thing he felt. But it was a life-changing fraction of a second in which all his decisions were made. He smiled at Ander. Ander smiled back helplessly as the captain drew his handgun and fired several rounds into the street and in the wall of the building behind Ander. Some made sparks as they skidded off the stone. Others caused pockmarks in little bursts of powder.

With each round Ander flinched. But then the captain gave him another reassuring smile and Ander shrugged and smiled back as though to say "Isn't this silly?"

The captain nodded and raised his weapon and fired a single bullet into the center of Ander Elarregui's forehead. He fell slowly, still smiling. Even on the ground, looking up with the dark hole in his forehead, he was still smiling. Jenaro, realizing the wound looked too much like an assassination, shot Ander once in the shoulder and once in the chest. He reached down to rearrange Ander's face, but it had become a rubber mask that popped back into a smile no matter what he did. He took out his car keys, pushed the button, and his trunk flew open. He quickly deposited the bag under a pile of blankets that he and his wife and young son used when they went to the beach in Zarautz. Then he took out a Beretta—compact, a nice little Italian gun. He liked to shoot the Beretta, but it had no registration. He took it off of a young man he arrested on terrorism. Probably if police tried to trace it they could track it back to some terrorist cell. He quietly kept the gun because he had an idea that an unregistered gun would be handy someday, even though the young man was not convicted because no one could find a weapon. Jenaro didn't mind. The kid was from Zarautz and he knew his family.

Jenaro placed the Beretta in Ander's still-limp right hand, placed his finger on the trigger and fired a few rounds, and then let his arm drop. When the hand hit the ground the pistol stayed in his palm. This was a lucky day, Jenaro thought.

He called in the incident. Bank robbery in progress. Man and woman. The woman got away but the man stayed behind to cover for her, fired at him, and he had to shoot him. They would soon find out that he was a bank officer working for Begoña. She had infiltrated the bank. She was everywhere.

Zubi had decided that it might be dangerous to be caught with the cheese. Besides, isn't it bad luck to eat a dead man's food? Two minutes after he dropped the cheese off with the colonel, on his way back to Legazpi Street he heard a loud boom and realized that he had been right about luck.

That was it. He had sold every chorizo except the murder weapon. Of course, after what had just happened to the colonel's body, they might not be that interested in one little head wound. But he had heard that they had laboratories that could find out everything. He wrapped up his last chorizo and started to head out of town.

"Hey, you. Wait!"

Zubi turned slowly and saw an Ertzaintza captain running toward him. If he tried to run the man would probably shoot him. Could he be fast enough to club him? He would have to try. He couldn't let him take him. But when the captain reached him, almost out of breath, he said, "Any chorizo left?"

"Yes, one left." And he sold the captain the murder weapon, which, he was pretty sure, would soon be eaten.

It was late by the time the captain had cleared everything up and come to Casa Pampi for his *txangurro* with his lieutenant and his chorizo.

P ampi! *Kaixo!*" He was in a very expansive mood, talking and laughing and eating. By the time they finished their spider crab, Pampi had no more customers. But the Ertzaintza were drinking Rioja Alavesa Reserva and followed the crab with broiled garlicky *bixugos* and then ordered steak with roasted peppers.

The other customers were all gone and the kitchen cleaned, so Pampi sent the staff home and cooked for the two himself. After the steaks, they ordered cheese and brandy and took out large Cohiba cigars from Cuba.

"You know, Pampi," said Jenaro, puffing yellow smoke from his cigar. "It's amazing that for all that mayhem only two people died."

"Three."

"Ah, but Ander was one of them," said the captain a little too defensively. "Too bad about the colonel, though."

"Yes, a tragedy," said Pampi, and the two enjoyed their moment of insincerity together.

Frustrated, Pampi paced his empty dining room and back to the kitchen and then quickly back to the table. "My friend, I promised to help you if I could." The captain and the lieutenant looked up with perplexed expressions.

"Come with me." He led them to a back window in the kitchen. There was an odd tin-can sound outside, and when they looked out the window they saw a bear going through the garbage.

"A bear?"

"When did you last see a bear? Don't you know that bears are extinct in Basque country?"

"I thought they hibernated in the winter," said the lieutenant.

The captain paused for a minute and then his face became animated again. "Begoña," he said in a harsh whisper. He phoned his headquarters and said, "I have just spotted Begoña in a bear suit going through the trash behind Casa Pampi. I'm going to try to hold her, but send me help."

"What?"

"You heard me."

"How do you know it's not a real bear?"

"Don't you know the bears are extinct? And they hibernate in the winter!"

"Right."

"Yeah, Begoña's so smart. She didn't think I would know that," said Jenaro.

Pampi told him not to pay the bill, which he had expected, and he grabbed his red beret and his long chorizo and charged down the stairs. He sent the lieutenant for a shotgun.

He was not going to engage Begoña until the lieutenant or men from the station got there with larger weapons. The bear looked up from the garbage and studied the captain. Jenaro grew nervous and drew his pistol. The bear studied him. He grew more nervous.

"Don't move, Begoña, or I'll fire." He wondered where to aim, since the bear costume was obviously much larger than she was. Or was it? According to some rumors, Begoña was a giant.

The bear started moving cautiously toward the captain and he fired a warning shot in the air. But it made only an odd click and then he remembered that he had fired all the rounds in the clip. The bear came up to him and stood on his hind legs, easily more than a head taller than the captain, and growled and showed large yellow teeth.

This was one of those split seconds that took a very long time. The first thing the captain realized was that this was not Begoña. This was a real bear.

The next thing he realized was that he was about to die.

They would find the bag and the money, and his wife and son would get no pension. But maybe not, because most of the men under him were bright enough to just keep the money for themselves.

He remembered that he had stuck the chorizo in his belt like a battle saber, so in a last desperate attempt he drew it out and poked it at the bear. A chorizo, he realized, did not make much of a weapon.

The bear swatted at the chorizo and knocked it out of his hand. He bent over and put it in his mouth and, having at last gotten what he came for, the bear quickly trotted out of town.

Pampi gathered up the dishes from the policemen and put them in the kitchen sink and quickly went to the side room. The crabber was still there. The crabber removed his chef's toque and let long raven-black hair flow to her shoulders. Pampi put his arms around her and said, "Begoña." They kissed the kind of kiss that has been waited for a very long time and then, arm in arm, went up the back stairs to an apartment Pampi kept over the restaurant. Slipping out of their clothes, they made love for what was left of the night and then fell asleep at daybreak, woke up in the early afternoon and made love again. It was time for her to leave, but it wouldn't be difficult. No one expected her to still be in town. She had robbed a bank and assassinated the Policía Nacional colonel. The Ertzaintza could not help being a little miffed when they stated that they were the first ones at the scene of the bombing and the

Policía Nacional said no, that their Colonel Gallego was there first.

According to the newspapers, in the assassination one innocent bystander was killed, José Marie Lizar, aka Marmitako, so called for the excellent *marmitako* that he made. No one was sure of his secret, but it was thought that he grew a special pepper and also that he may have added some *patxaran*.

Begoña also robbed a Kutxabank and got away with 1.835 million euros. She escaped with the money, but Captain Jenaro Anitua of the Ertzaintza bravely faced Ander Elarregui, an officer of the bank who worked with Begoña and was an expert with firearms. Elarregui was celebrated for his *salmis de paloma*, a secret recipe involving flamed brandy and wild mountain mushrooms. The rest of the recipe is not known, nor is the whereabouts of Begoña and the 1.835 million euros.

The next afternoon Begoña took the Basque train to Hendaye and a French train to Hasparren and hiked to the farm in the flatlands of Soule that grew corn and gave her a place to stay in a Basque-speaking community in a forgotten corner of Euskal Herria, the Land of the Basques.

Zubi Nabaroa was relieved to leave Donostia—San Sebastián of elegance and beauty and festivals. All the way back to Ituren he looked for signs of the bear but never saw him again. Neither did anyone else.

Captain Anitua of the Ertzaintza retired from service and bought a huge nineteenth-century mansion overlooking the ocean at Zarautz. He took up oil painting. His wife occasionally came back to San Sebastián for shopping sprees big enough to become a Basque legend.

ABOUT THE AUTHOR

Mark Kurlansky is the *New York Times*-bestselling author of many books, including *Cod, Salt, 1968: The Year That Rocked the World, The Big Oyster, The Last Fish Tale, The Food of a Younger Land, The Eastern Stars, Ready for a Brand New Beat,* and the short story collection *Edible Stories*. He lives in New York City.

Mark Kurlansky is legendary for finding the big story in unlikely places.

Whether writing about fish, sports, or music, the *New York Times*–bestselling author reveals the fascinating natural and cultural history all around us.

by Sylvia Plachy

T381-0814

A deceptively whimsical biography of a fish.

Wars have been fought over it, revolutions have been spurred by it, national diets have been based on it, economies have depended on it, and the settlement of North America was driven by it. Cod, it turns out, is the reason Europeans set sail across the Atlantic, and it is the only reason they could.

Cod is a charming tour of history with all its economic forces laid bare and a fish story embellished with great gastronomic detail. In it, Mark Kurlansky brings a thousand years of human civilization into captivating focus.

A James Beard Award Winner for Excellence in Food Writing

"A charming fish tale and a pretty gift for your favorite seafood cook or fishing monomaniac."
                                                        —*Los Angeles Times*

They are Europe's oldest nation without ever having been a country.

Straddling a small corner of Spain and France in a land that is marked on no maps except their own, the Basques are a puzzling tradition. For centuries, their influence has been felt in nearly every realm, from religion to sports to commerce. Even today, the Basques are enjoying what may be the most important cultural renaissance in their long existence.

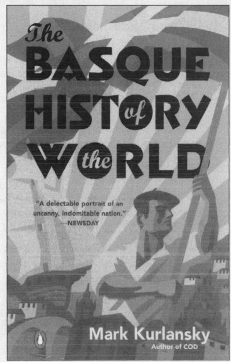

The BASQUE HISTORY of the WORLD

"A delectable portrait of an uncanny, indomitable nation."
—NEWSDAY

Mark Kurlansky
Author of COD

Kurlansky's passion for the Basque people and his exuberant eye for detail shine throughout this fascinating book.

"Entertaining and instructive...[Kurlansky's] approach is unorthodox, mixing history with anecdotes, poems with recipes."

—*The New York Times Book Review*

Until about 100 years ago, when modern geology revealed its prevalence, salt was one of the world's most sought-after commodities.

A substance so valuable it once served as currency, salt has influenced the establishment of trade routes and cities, provoked and financed wars, secured empires and inspired revolutions. Populated by colorful characters and filled with fascinating details, Mark Kurlansky's kaleidoscopic and illuminating history is a multilayered masterpiece that blends economic, scientific, political, religious, and culinary records into a rich and memorable tale.

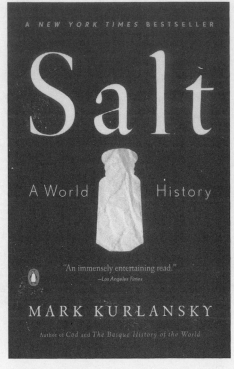

A NEW YORK TIMES BESTSELLER

Salt

A World History

"An immensely entertaining read."
—*Los Angeles Times*

MARK KURLANSKY

Author of *Cod* and *The Basque History of the World*

"The fascinating, indispensable history of an indispensable ingredient...a must-have for any serious cook or foodie."

—Anthony Bourdain

T384-0814

In this delightful collection, Kurlansky serves up a true smorgasbord by the world's most discerning gourmets and gourmands through the ages—from Plato on the art of cooking to Louis Prima at the pizzeria.

Choice Cuts offers more than two hundred mouthwatering selections, including M. F. K. Fisher on gingerbread; Pablo Neruda on French fries; Alexandre Dumas on coffee; and a vast variety by Escoffier, Brillat-Savarin, Waverly Root, Elizabeth David, A. J. Liebling, Ernest Hemingway, Virginia Woolf, Charles Dickens, Honoré de Balzac, Anton Chekhov, George Orwell, and Alice B. Toklas, among others.

Filled throughout with recipes, menus, classic photographs, and Kurlansky's own original drawings, *Choice Cuts* is a must-have for any serious foodie.

"The most outrageously broad, gregarious food-writing anthology."

—*Saveur*

T385-0814

Gloucester, Massachusetts, America's oldest fishing port, is defined by the culture of commercial fishing.

But the threat of overfishing, combined with climate change and pollution, is endangering a way of life. And yet, according to Kurlansky, it doesn't have to be this way. Engagingly written and filled with rich history, delicious anecdotes, colorful characters, and local recipes, *The Last Fish Tale* is about how fishing has thrived in and defined one particular town for centuries, and what its imperiled future means for the rest of the world.

"In *The Last Fish Tale*, Mark Kurlansky strikes a poignant chord... Beautifully written." —*The Boston Globe*

THE LAST FISH TALE
The Fate of the Atlantic and Survival in Gloucester, America's Oldest Fishing Port and Most Original Town

NEW YORK TIMES BESTSELLING AUTHOR OF *COD* AND *SALT*

MARK KURLANSKY

"An engrossing multilayered portrait."   **—Financial Times**

"Rich, varied, and satisfying, just like a good chowder."
                                                 —Entertainment Weekly

"Mark Kurlansky strikes a poignant chord.... Beautifully written."
                                                 —The Boston Globe

A portrait of American food before the national highway system, before chain restaurants, and before frozen food, when the nation's food was seasonal, regional, and traditional.

In the throes of the Great Depression, a make-work initiative for writers—called "America Eats"—was created to chronicle the eating habits, traditions, and struggles of local Americans. *The Food of a Younger Land* unearths this forgotten literary and historical treasure from a bygone era when Americans had never heard of fast food or grocery superstores. Kurlansky brings together the WPA contributions (including

tiny masterpieces from authors like Zora Neale Hurston and Nelson Algren) and brilliantly showcases them with authentic recipes, anecdotes, and photographs.

In these stories, Mark Kurlansky reveals the bond that can hold people together, tear them apart, or make them become vegan: food.

Through muffins or hot dogs, an indigenous Alaskan soup, a bean curd Thanksgiving turkey, or potentially toxic crème brûlée, a rotating cast of characters learns how to honor the past, how to realize they're not in love with someone anymore, and how to forgive. These women and men meet and eat, love and leave, drink and talk, and, in the end, come together, inextricably linked with each other as they are with the food they eat and the wine they drink.

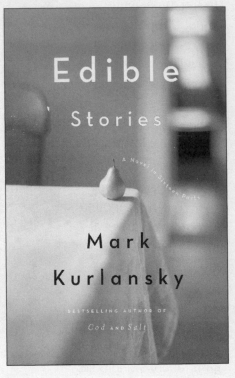

"For those of us who love both stories and food, this book is a delectable feast. Mark Kurlansky's sixteen-part novel is like a long, wonderful meal with friends. It is nurturing, succulent, and, most of all, a lot of fun." —**Edwidge Danticat, author of *Breath, Eyes, Memory***

In San Pedro, baseball is often seen as the only way to a better life.

One in six Dominicans who has played in Major League Baseball has come from one tiny, impoverished region. For those who make it, the million-dollar paychecks mean that not only they, but their entire families as well, have been saved from grinding poverty. The successful few set an example that dazzles the neighbors they have left behind, but for the majority, the dream is illusory. This is a book about poverty and wealth, about tenacity and survival, about colonialism and capitalism, about the Dominican people and their brutal history, about the life of a small Caribbean town—and above all, about baseball and dreams.

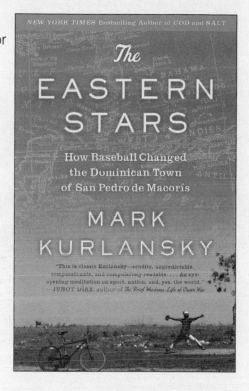

"This is classic Kurlansky—erudite, unpredictable, compassionate, and compulsively readable.... An electrifying read... an eye-opening meditation on sport, nation, and, yes, the world."

—**Junot Díaz**, author of *The Brief Wondrous Life of Oscar Wao*

Can a song change a nation?

The Martha and the Vandellas hit "Dancing in the Street" was supposed to be an upbeat dance recording—a precursor to disco, a song about the joyousness of dance, the song of a summer. But as the United States grew more radicalized in the summer of 1964, "Dancing in the Street" gained currency as an activist anthem. *Ready for a Brand New Beat* recounts that extraordinary time

and showcases the role that a simple song about dancing played in our nation's history.

"Historians and music lovers alike will be grateful for Mr. Kurlansky's thorough appreciation of this iconic song." **—The Wall Street Journal**

"Mr. Kurlansky has come up with a book that will make you hum its theme song." **—The New York Times**